MURDER ON THE GOLDEN ARROW

THE KITTY WORTHINGTON MYSTERIES, BOOK 1

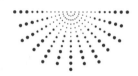

MAGDA ALEXANDER

HEARTS AFIRE PUBLISHING

To my beautiful granddaughter Skylar
May your light ever shine on

SYNOPSIS

What's a bright young thing to do when her brother becomes the main suspect in a murder investigation? Why, solve the case, of course.

England. 1923. After a year away at finishing school where she learned etiquette, deportment, and the difference between a salad fork and a fish one, Kitty Worthington is more than eager to return home. But minutes after she and her brother Ned board the Golden Arrow, the unthinkable happens. A woman with a mysterious connection to Kitty's brother is poisoned, and the murderer can only be someone on the train.

When barely a week after the murder her brother becomes the main suspect, Kitty sets out to investigate. Not an easy thing to do while juggling the demands of a debut season and a mother intent on finding a suitable, aristocratic husband for her.

With the aid of her maid, two noble lords, and a flatulent Basset Hound named Sir Winston, Kitty dives deep into the glamorous world of British High Society and London's dark underbelly to discover the murderer. For if she fails, the insufferable Inspector Crawford will most surely hang a noose around her brother's neck.

A frolicking, historical cozy mystery filled with dodgy suspects, a dastardly villain, and an intrepid heroine sure to win your heart, *Murder on the Golden Arrow* is the first book in **The Kitty Worthington Mysteries.** The second book, *Murder at Westminster,* is set to release in Winter 2022.

PROLOGUE

I need more blunt. If you want me to keep mum about your dirty little secret, bring another 200 quid to Clapham Common next Wednesday at one. Same spot as before. If you don't come, I will tell the coppers, and you will **HANG***.*

𝒩 ote found in victim's possession

CHAPTER ONE

APRIL 1923. ABOARD THE SIMPLON ORIENT
EXPRESS ON THE WAY TO PARIS

*I*T WAS A TRUTH UNIVERSALLY ACKNOWLEDGED
that an unmarried young woman in expectation of a great
dowry had to be in want of a titled husband. Or so Mother believed. I,
however, being of a more modern bent, had no such desire.

But here lay the problem. After failing to secure a successful
marriage for any of my older siblings, Mother had pinned all her
hopes on me. It's not that they refused to marry. They just had more
interesting things to do. Ned, who'd been reading *The Financial Times*
since he emerged from the womb, had followed our father's footsteps
and become a successful business mogul. Next oldest, Richard, took a
quite different route to excellence by decamping to Egypt to become
an archeologist. Or as Mother put it, to play in the sand and rob the
graves of ancient pharaohs. Not my cup of tea, but it made him happy.
And then there was my sister Margaret. Yes, you must absolutely call
her that. No sobriquet like Meg or Maggie for her. Well, she ran off to
Oxford to earn a degree, now that that august university deemed
women worthy enough to get one. So, it had fallen to me to grant
Mother's most fervent wish. That one of her children married into the
aristocracy.

Sadly, I was bound to disappoint her for I truly had no wish to marry. At least not at the present time. The question now became how to navigate my season without dashing all her hopes. I'd devised a plan, but would it work?

I'd been so consumed with that question after boarding the Orient Express past midnight that I'd tossed and turned in bed all night. Anyone with a working intellect would have foreseen how this would end. Unfortunately, mine fell asleep.

∿

THE BED BENEATH ME JOLTED, waking me from a deep slumber. Only then did I hear the frantic pounding.

"Kitty. Are you awake?" My brother Ned. Outside my train compartment.

Heavens! In a panic, I gazed bleary-eyed at the traitorous clock that was supposed to wake me at five. It was now past six.

"Kitty!"

Scrambling to my feet, I dived for the door and thrust it open to find my outraged brother on the other side. He was immaculately attired in a tailored, three-piece business suit, not a hair out of place.

I, on the other hand, was a rumpled mess in disheveled bedclothes and flyaway mane. Of course I was. I'd barely slept.

"We're due in Paris in an hour, and you're not dressed!"

"I'm sorry."

"Did you forget to set your alarm?"

"Of course not. I would never do that." Not when I knew he worshiped the god of punctuality.

"It didn't go off?" He sounded incredulous.

I'd be as well. After all, my Jaeger-LeCoultre travel clock was one of the best in the world, so the fault could not lie with the timepiece, but with me. "I probably slept through it." There was no probably about it. I had. But was it really my fault? On a night when I hadn't dropped on the berth 'til after midnight, there was no hope I'd awaken on time.

"Kitty." Disappointment laced the word.

Only one way out of this sticky wicket. To dress as quickly as I could. "It won't take me but a tick to get ready." Thankfully, I'd set out my traveling clothes last night. "I won't take long. I promise."

All I got in return was a highly disapproving frown. It did *not* display him to advantage.

With no time to waste, I fetched my sage and lavender frock, silk stockings and undergarments—all in the height of fashion, of course —and stumbled past him in nothing but my nightgown and slippers. Praying that the lavatory was unoccupied, I rushed toward it, earning only one disapproving 'harumph' from a passing matron. I had to admit I'd earned that. After all, a lady doesn't dash about in her undergarments in a public setting. Or so *A Lady's Guide to Etiquette and Deportment* declared.

After dressing as quickly as I could, I hurried back to the compartment. Magically, it had been put to rights, and our *petit déjeuner* had been served. Coffee and tea carafes, along with butter, marmalade, and a basket of croissants were set out on the minuscule table that dropped down from the wall. But then one would expect nothing less, for the Orient Express service was par to none. My stomach rumbled, reminding me it needed to be fed. It'd been hours since dinner, after all.

Eager to enjoy the continental breakfast, I made quick work of stashing my nightclothes and clock in the traveling satchel and slipping into my t-strap shoes before attending to our breakfast. "Shall I pour?" I smiled, hoping the peace offering would soothe the savage beast in Ned.

A terse, "Yes. Thank you," said otherwise.

Undaunted, I made a show of preparing his cup of tea the way he liked it and handing it to him, along with two croissants, properly plated of course.

Once he was settled, I helped myself to my own breakfast—coffee and a croissant. Famished, I lathered on the creamy butter and sweet marmalade over the flaky pastry and took a bite. With Ned seemingly being of like mind, conversation lagged while we satiated our hunger.

But once he was done, he returned to his favorite activity of the moment—harping. "Punctuality is vital when traveling, Kitty."

"I agree. It won't happen again." Heaven knew he had cause for his low spirits after traveling from London to Lausanne in the space of two days to retrieve me from a Swiss finishing school. He should have taken a day off to rest, but he'd decided to return to Paris on the next northbound train. He had to be exhausted.

I put on my brightest smile to try and cheer him up. "But everything's right now, isn't it? I'm dressed. We've enjoyed our breakfast." I glanced at my wristwatch. "And we won't arrive in Paris for another half hour."

He took in a breath and released it slowly, allowing the tension to seep slowly from him. "You do have a point."

"Would you like more tea or another croissant?" I asked, happy to see him relaxed. Well, as relaxed as he ever allowed himself to be. He was wound up tighter than a wind-up toy.

"Not just yet. I'd like to discuss your education first. Did you enjoy school?" he asked in a much mellower tone. Food and a hot cup of tea had apparently tamed the wild beast, indeed.

"I did." I hadn't thought I would. After all, I'd perceived my enrollment at a private girls' school as punishment for a transgression, not as something to be enjoyed. But I'd been wrong. "We were taught etiquette and deportment, along with piano, needlework, and drawing. The piano teacher was passable, but they had an excellent drawing master."

"How did you perform in those subjects?"

"I now know the difference between a fish fork and a salad one and how to create a seating chart when both a duke and an earl are present at a dinner table."

For the first time, he grinned. "I trust there was more to it than that."

"There was. Not to worry, Ned. I was a model student."

His arched brow questioned my statement.

"Nothing I can't accomplish when I set my mind to it," I insisted.

"That, I don't doubt."

It was the model student remark he doubted. Fair enough.

"What about recreational activities?" he asked, while helping himself to another croissant.

"Horseback riding, which you know I abhor." I'd been thrown from a pony at an early age and had avoided all equine endeavors ever since. "Archery, tennis, other ladylike pursuits." And a course on self-defense. Being of a progressive bent, the Swiss finishing school firmly believed their young ladies should know how to protect themselves against untoward advances. I'd thoroughly enjoyed the class, but Ned would think it inappropriate to have learned such skills. So, I decided to keep my participation in that course to myself. "And then there was skiing."

"You learned to ski?"

I laughed. "I was in Switzerland, Ned. Of course, I learned to ski. The school sponsored field trips to the nearest slopes. I didn't become proficient, but I did enjoy the thrill of a downhill run."

"What about dancing? I can't imagine that was not taught."

"Of course. The quadrille, the waltz . . . the Charleston."

His brow took another hike. "They taught the Charleston?"

"It wasn't part of the curriculum. We learned it at night, in the privacy of our rooms."

A small grin lifted a corner of his lips. He was absolutely stunning when he smiled. A shame he didn't do it more often. "And what else did you learn at night in the privacy of your rooms?"

I'd learned to mix a mean cocktail. Daiquiris. Bee's Knees. Gin fizzes. Strangely enough it was the American girls who were most knowledgeable about alcohol. But then maybe not so strange. We often want that which is forbidden.

But that was not the only taboo subject we discussed. Some of the young women obtained quite an education from the ski instructors, knowledge which they were happy to share. Although invited to participate, I refused to join their midnight escapades. I was in enough trouble as it was. But I couldn't tell Ned about those conversations, not if I wished for some sort of freedom during my upcoming debut. "My lips are sealed, dear brother. I shall never tell."

To my surprise he didn't pursue the subject but turned to something else. "You've set aside your hoydenish ways, I hope."

"Most of them." I grinned.

"Kitty." A gentle warning tinged his voice. He was a dear, truly, but he could be such a stick-in-the-mud. That's what came from working so hard. He never took time to enjoy life.

I lost the smile. "Yes, I have."

"Excellent."

I had to admit he had good cause to be concerned. A year ago, he'd escorted a hoyden to the finishing school. One who'd been caught in the dark with a man. Having never been kissed, I'd been eager to enjoy that experience and willingly followed Lord Browning into the confines of a garden. But before the deed could be accomplished, we'd been discovered by Ned who'd sent off the noble lord with a flea in his ear.

A fortnight later, I'd been shipped off to Switzerland with the hope I would curtail my wilder impulses. Lord Browning, on the other hand, had suffered no consequences. On the contrary, he continued frolicking about in London. But then he was a man, and they operated under a different set of rules. Unfair, to say the least. At least he'd kept silent about our escapade, no doubt in large part due to my father's management of his family's finances, which meant my reputation had remained intact.

"Do not worry, dear brother. I aim to follow Margaret's example." During her debut, my older sister had complied with Mother's every wish, attended every ball and al fresco picnic, accepted every invitation to the theater and the opera. But at balls, she hid among the chaperones. At the entertainment venues, she refused all conversations, claiming the stage needed her attention. She spent most of her time at picnics reading obscure tomes. If a potential suitor dared approach her, he was rebuffed by a cutting glance that spoke volumes about his lack of worth.

Her brilliant strategy paid off. At the end of her season, not one proposal of marriage was issued, and Mother was forced to admit that

Margaret did not 'take.' So, my cunning sister was granted her fondest wish—to enroll at Oxford and earn a degree.

"Mother will be pleased. She's been planning your debut for a year."

And more than likely planning my wedding as well.

Thing was at soon-to-be one and twenty, I was determined to have a rippin' good time. Dance the Charleston at hot jazz clubs. Drink exotic cocktails. Live life to the fullest! Last thing I wanted was to wed some chinless wonder who spent his days exclaiming 'pip pip and all that' and you hadn't the foggiest what he was talking about.

So, I'd devised a plan which would meet with Mother's approval, but would not end up with wedding bells being rung for me. In short, I would be the perfect debutante. Prim and demure as they came, I would attend every fitting and dull morning call, dance every waltz and staid quadrille at each ball. I would listen spellbound to countless gentlemen expound about their motorcars, their horses, their estates, and their favorite subject—themselves. By the end of the season, I would probably receive several offers of marriage, no doubt in large part to my sizable dowry. Plenty of noble lords out there with pockets to let. Sad to say, I would turn them all down because I was holding out for a love match. Mother wouldn't be able to object. After all, she and Father married for love.

"What would you like to do today?" Ned asked. Seemingly, the inquisition had come to an end.

But his question took me by surprise. He didn't often ask about my preferences. "Wouldn't you rather rest at the hotel? You've been traveling for three straight days."

He shrugged off my comment. "I slept last night."

"Five hours at the most." If that.

"More than enough, dear sister. I'm used to going without much sleep." He brushed an imaginary dust mote from his trousers.

Ever since he was little, he'd been driven to prove himself to Father. He'd succeeded, but at what cost? "Are you sure?"

"Yes, I'm sure."

"Well, in that case, I would love to visit the Louvre." I loved art and everything that went along with it, whether paintings, drawings, or sculptures. After I'd learned to draw at an early age, Mother hired an instructor who nurtured my talent, and an artist had been born.

"We could do that. And after the Louvre, we could stroll through the Tuileries Gardens, visit the Palace," he said.

"And Montmartre?" I asked.

He shook his head. "No."

"But that's where all the artists live. I'd love to absorb that rare atmosphere and be inspired by them." *Heavens!* That bit of fancy sounded excessive even to me.

"There won't be enough time, Kitty." He glanced at his pocket watch. "We'll need to check into the Ritz before we head out to explore Paris. We'll have but a few hours before we must return to dress for dinner."

"But surely dressing won't take long." I'd done it just now in less than fifteen minutes' time.

"I'm also scheduled to meet with a prospective client, and he hasn't confirmed a time. He's a recluse of sorts and difficult to pin down. Hopefully, a message will be waiting for me at the Ritz. But if there isn't, I must remain available."

"I see." There was a business reason for not taking the time to visit Montmartre. I was disappointed, but at least I would get to see the Louvre. "This prospective client would like to invest his funds with Father?"

"He hasn't made up his mind. Thus, the meeting. I have to reassure him his money will be safe and will grow under our management."

Our Father was a very sought-after financier who handled the fortunes of many, nobles and captains of industry alike. He'd been quite successful. But maybe that had changed in the last year?

"Our business isn't suffering, is it?" Some of the families of the students at school had experienced financial setbacks. They'd sent their daughters to Switzerland, hoping the extra polish would help them snag rich husbands. At least, I would not be sold to the highest bidder. My family was wealthy enough on its own.

He shook his head. "Just the contrary. We've had to turn away many a potential investor."

"Then why is Father eager to obtain the business of this particular one?"

"He's rich."

"Disgustingly so, I imagine."

His lips twitched, but he didn't say a word. But then he didn't have to. The prospective client was probably richer than King Midas.

The train lurched and signs of civilization—buildings, houses, people—drifted by outside our window. "We should arrive soon."

"Yes." He leaned forward. "There's one more thing I wished to discuss, Kitty. Your settlement."

"Oh?" Father settled funds on my siblings when they turned one and twenty. Since I would celebrate that august birthday in a matter of weeks, the expectation was not foreign to me. Still, I was half afraid of what Ned would say. I hadn't exactly been a model young woman. Maybe Father thought to withhold the money until he felt I'd matured.

"You'll have access to your funds, at least some of them, on your birthday."

I silently breathed a sigh of relief. "That's good to know."

He cleared his throat. "But Father won't be managing them. I will."

"You?" When Margaret turned one and twenty, it was Father she'd dealt with.

He reclined against the seat. "I asked Father if I could take on that responsibility, and he agreed."

"Why would you want to?"

"The business has grown, especially this last year. We have clients not only from Britain, but France, Germany, the United States. It would be one less thing for him to worry about."

I had a million questions about my settlement, but before I had a chance to ask them, the conductor knocked on our door. "Madame, Monsieur. We're pulling into the gare de Lyon à Paris. Gather your items, s'il vous plaît."

"Thank you," Ned said before turning to me. "I've organized a car and a chauffeur to meet us outside the station. He'll be at our disposal for the next two days."

Clearly, questions about my settlement would have to wait until a more propitious time. "That's brilliant."

He came to his feet. "I'll fetch my bags. Stay here until I return."

Ever the protector. Something for which I was grateful, even if he went a little overboard at times. "I will. Thank you, Ned."

His brow scrunched. "Whatever for?"

"For taking such good care of me. I do appreciate it."

"Anytime, minx. What are brothers for?" he said, before stepping into the corridor.

Once more alone, I gazed out the window at the passing vista. Before long, we entered the station and the compartment grew dark. What would Paris bring? Plenty, as it turned out.

CHAPTER TWO

A GRAND HOTEL

*T*HE SOARING LOBBY OF THE PARIS RITZ greeted Ned and me with its fragrant display of flowers as we entered the grand hotel. True to his word, Ned had escorted me to the Louvre where he'd stood patiently while I'd marveled over its priceless treasures. After a brief lunch at a cafe, we'd gone on to explore the City of Lights.

"Thank you for taking me on an excursion of Paris."

"Glad you enjoyed it," he said off handedly, as he headed toward the front desk to check if the prospective client had finally sent a note. Sadly, none had awaited Ned when we arrived this morning.

As we approached registration, I noticed the back of a woman standing next to one of the tables that dotted the lobby. Dressed in a dark cloth coat, she could have been anyone. But I couldn't mistake the signature Gibson Girl bouffant hair style, nor the fiery red of its shade. "Mrs. Earnshaw?"

She turned toward me, surprise etched on her face. "Miss Worthington. I didn't know you were visiting Paris."

"Not visiting so much as enjoying a respite from our journey. Ned and I traveled from Switzerland."

"Your brother is here with you?" Her lips pursed, as she glanced around searching for him. Ever a stickler for propriety, she believed a gentleman shouldn't leave a lady to fend for herself.

"Yes. He's not far," I reassured her, nodding toward where he stood talking to a registration clerk. "He's checking for messages."

"I see" she said, somewhat mollified. "You must be done with finishing school then."

"I am." Of course, she knew. How could she not? Mother would have shared that information at one of their Ladies Benevolent Society meetings. That group prized etiquette and deportment almost as much as their good works and would have viewed my attendance at a finishing school as vital to my education. Eager to veer the conversation away from me, I asked, "Are you enjoying Paris?"

Her shoulders drooped, and she clenched her hands across her middle. "I'm afraid we did not come for pleasure," she said in a trembling voice.

"We?"

"The Colonel is here with me." She pointed to the gentleman shuffling toward her, the male attendant at his side propping him up. I gasped at his condition. A year ago, he'd appeared hale and hearty at one of the society's fundraising events. But now, his stooped figure, pale skin, and pain-lined face told a different story.

"You remember Colonel Earnshaw?" she asked, once he reached her.

"Yes, of course. Sir." I curtsied. Not only did I owe him the courtesy his rank demanded, but he'd been a hero of the Boer War, single handedly vanquishing an entire guerilla unit for which he'd received the Victoria Cross, an honor awarded for valor in the presence of the enemy.

He mumbled something in a voice so weak I failed to understand.

But Mrs. Earnshaw seemingly did. "Of course, dear. Cedric," she said to the male attendant, "please escort the colonel to our suite. It's been a long day for him."

I watched in sadness as Cedric and the colonel shuffled toward the lifts. He'd always seemed so full of life—tall, robust, a blustering kind of man. Now he was but a shell of himself. I was too polite to ask about his health; but as it turned out, I didn't need to. Mrs. Earnshaw volunteered the information.

"He's quite ill. Cancer."

Her words chilled my blood. Some years ago, one of our retainers had been stricken by the disease. Father had provided as much assistance as he could, paying for specialists and treatments. But in the end, it had come to naught. She'd died within a short period of time. "I'm so sorry."

"Thank you." She bowed her head. "We consulted every physician in London, tried every remedy. Nothing worked. When I heard about a specialist in Paris, I thought maybe he could work a miracle. But the French doctor dashed our hopes. The cancer is too advanced. Nothing can be done."

Wanting to comfort her, I pressed her trembling hands. "I'll hope for the best."

"Thank you, my dear." Tears shimmered in her eyes. "You do your mother proud."

Ned, seemingly finished with his inquiries, joined us. "Kitty?"

"You remember Mrs. Earnshaw? She's a member of the Ladies Benevolent Society."

"Yes, of course," he said with a smile. "Visiting Paris, Mrs. Earnshaw?"

She shook her head. "No. A consult with a doctor."

His brow furrowed. "Nothing serious, I hope."

Her lips trembled with emotion.

Last thing she needed was to discuss her husband's illness once more, so I stepped in, "I'll explain later, Ned."

He nodded. "Very well."

"Well," she said with a sigh. "I better go up to our suite. The colonel becomes restless if I'm not present. He depends on me so much."

"You take such good care of him." I pressed her hands once more.

"I try, dear, although I don't always succeed. This illness has taken a toll." She wiped a tear from the corner of her eye.

"I can imagine," I said. "It was very nice seeing you. If you need

15

anything, anything at all, please let us know." I glanced at my brother. "Right, Ned?"

"Absolutely. The registration desk can relay the message. We'll be glad to be of service."

She breathed a barely audible, "Thank you," before turning and heading toward the lift.

As soon as she was out of hearing distance, Ned asked, "Is the colonel ill?"

"Yes. Cancer. I'm sorry you missed him. He appeared twenty years older than the last time I saw him. His skin was the color of parchment, and his face was wracked with pain. He couldn't even stand upright." I glanced down the corridor where Mrs. Earnshaw was boarding the lift. "And to think, just last spring he was the very image of health."

"Unfortunately, that's the nature of that disease. You saw what it did to Clara." Our faithful servant.

"Yes." I allowed a moment of silence to fill the space before asking, "Did a message await you?"

"No." He glanced at his watch. "Maybe he'll telephone before dinner."

And maybe the prospective client changed his mind. But I would not dash Ned's hopes by voicing that thought.

"Shall we go to our rooms?" he asked. "You must be tired after all the walking."

"Yes." I had to admit I could use the rest.

The stroll down the long corridor allowed me to appreciate the splendor of the Paris Ritz. With its high arched windows, Oriental carpet, blue and gold draperies, gilded chairs, and furnishings in the style of Louis XV, all surrounded by oceans of light, it was a feast for the senses.

I was so enthralled by the magnificence of my surroundings I was slow to notice the couple ahead of us. But once I did, I was riveted. The woman's blond bob swayed as she walked, while her hips swung side to side in an innate, sensual rhythm. People along the perimeter not only saw, but whispered. She took the attention in stride, nodding every now and then as if acknowledging their curiosity.

Tall and slender as I was, I envied her contours. I'd always wished for a more womanly figure, for I'd been gifted with very little in the way of curves. My one advantage was that the current fashions favored me. Still, I would have been grateful for a slightly larger bosom and a more curvaceous shape.

While the woman's stride was all movement, her escort's was rigid and stiff which made me wonder at their relationship. Did he dislike the notoriety? Or was he the jealous type who resented his companion being the cynosure of all eyes?

She may have been an attention-seeker, but her devotion was all for him, given how her arm entwined snake-like around his. Was she claiming possession as if to tell the world he was hers? Or was it pure adoration as if she couldn't bear to be parted from him?

Arriving at the lift before us, the woman pressed the up button with a manicured nail painted bright red. Having done so, she turned to the right. Only then did I see her face. Green shone out of catlike eyes that somehow managed to be seductive and predatory at the same time. This was a woman who would enthrall men, but once you were caught in her spell, you wouldn't emerge unscathed.

When she spotted us—no, not us, Ned, as her gaze was clearly directed toward him—a come hither smile curled her lips. No surprise. Ned often had that effect on women. Heaven knew I'd seen it often enough. Tall and handsome as he was, he often drew the attention of wives from the upper class. Bored with their husbands, they craved some entertainment to while away their time and saw Ned as a way to get it.

Not that he ever took them up on their offers. Oh, he was no monk. He enjoyed discrete liaisons the family never learned about. Well, except for me. Only reason I knew was because every now and then I'd hear a faint whisper from the servants. But the rest of the family remained blissfully ignorant about his *chérie d'amours*. Something he devoutly wished. For if we knew, so would everyone else. Last thing he wanted was for a scandal to touch him or us.

Which explained why I was so astounded when this woman drew a reaction from him. As soon as her gaze arrowed on Ned, he flinched and changed course. "Let's take the stairs," he said in a rush of words.

I was not slow to draw a conclusion. He knew the blonde and wanted to avoid her. Although I had no desire to climb more steps, I did not object. He'd spent the entire day indulging me. The least I could do was acquiesce with his request.

Luckily, our rooms were on the second floor, so we didn't have far to climb. Still, it provided me with sufficient time to wonder about the connection between the woman and Ned. And, specifically, why did he wish to avoid her? A good question indeed. But one that was bound to remain unanswered. Going by his clenched jaw and intense gaze, he'd mentally shut down and did not wish to answer any questions.

Once we reached my room, he handed me the key. "I made our dinner reservation for eight. That should provide you with sufficient time to bathe and dress." His grim face spoke volumes about his state of mind.

"An abundance of it." I grinned, hoping to jolly him up.

Unfortunately, it did not have the desired effect. Dipping his head, he brushed unsteady fingers across his furrowed brow, a clear sign of worry from him. Who was that woman to him? How did she know Ned? But my brother had never been one to share information about his personal life. I doubted he would start now.

There could be another explanation, though, for his perturbed state. Maybe he was worried about the prospective client. "You could telephone him," I suggested.

His gaze bounced up, a question in his eyes.

"The client."

He shook his head as if to clear the thoughts racing through his mind. No. I got it right the first time. His preoccupation was with the woman, not the client. He dismissed my comment with a wave of his hand. "He knows I'm in Paris. It would be rude to contact him."

"He could have gotten the dates wrong. It happens."

"Not this gentleman."

I rested my hand over his. "It wouldn't be the end of the world, Ned, if you can't connect with him."

He shot me a hard glare. "Father expects me to succeed."

Father desired all his children to do well, but Ned's behavior seemed extreme. It had to be the woman who was affecting him. But he would never admit he was worried. Being the oldest, he'd always interpreted his role as the one who suffered silently through life. All I could do was sympathize. "I understand."

He eased his hand from under mine. "No need to be concerned. I should know before dinner."

"I'm sure you're right," I said, before slipping into my room. His life was his own, but I couldn't help but worry about that odd encounter and why that woman had affected him so.

CHAPTER THREE

DINNER AT THE RITZ

$\mathcal{T}$HE RITZ RESTAURANT WAS TRULY A SIGHT TO BEHOLD. Bright chandeliers sparkled over tables draped with snowy white tablecloths and laid with gleaming crystal while waiters weaved through the room. Some with plated dishes, some without. The space teemed with men spruced in black tie tuxedos and women dressed in fashionable evening gowns. With a myriad of diners engaged in conversations, loud music being played, and the constant clink of silverware, the cacophony of it all assaulted the senses. But it was exactly what I ached to experience—life being lived to the fullest by every person in the room.

My mouth watered from the aroma wafting from the waiters' offerings and the food already served. We were fortunate indeed that Ned had made reservations. There was hardly an empty spot to be found.

Thankfully, we only had to entertain a short wait before being led to our table. But as we weaved through the space in the wake of the *maître d'*, someone called out my brother's name. "Ned!"

As we turned in tandem to identify the source, I was not surprised to discover it was the woman from the lift. She and her escort were seated to our right.

After a brief hesitation, long enough for me to notice, Ned approached them. Of course, he did. He was too polite to ignore a summons, no matter how distasteful he may have found it, something that was quite apparent by the tightening of his lips.

Up close she appeared even more stunning. No one could fault her finger-waved coiffure and maquillage. They were flawless, especially the crimson shade she'd applied to her lips. Unfortunately, I couldn't say the same of her red gown. The deep plunging neckline, although certain to attract the attention she craved, was now *passé*. And the patterned sequins belonged to gowns worn two years ago. If that were all, it would not be sufficient to brand her as unfashionable, but the faux silk used for the dress possessed an inferior shine, and the workmanship with its not-quite-straight seams screamed ready-made. At best, it was an imitation that sought to impress.

Distaste was evident on Ned's face as he whispered her name, "Rose." Who was this woman? And who was she to him?

"Hello, Ned." Her voice held a seductive tone. Seconds rolled by while he stood not saying a word. She finally broke the ice. "Well, aren't you going to introduce me?"

His pinched lips and rigid stance told me that was the last thing he wished to do, but politeness demanded it. "My apologies. My sister, Catherine."

She stuck out her hand, leaving me with no choice but to shake it.

"How do you do?" I asked. If Ned could be polite, so could I.

"Fine. More than fine, actually." She pointed to the man seated across from her. "This is Jack Trevvyan. My husband." The smile that rolled over her face was that of a cat that had drunk all the cream and gone back for seconds.

My brother appeared beyond surprised, shocked even.

Aware of the undercurrents, I said in my brightest voice. "Congratulations."

Ignoring me, Rose reached out to cover her husband's hand. "This is Ned Worthington, darling. I told you about him." She waved a dismissive hand toward me. "And his sister, Catherine."

The husband's face reddened. He appeared beyond embarrassed.

But somewhere along the way someone must have taught him good manners because he came to his feet and nodded. "Mr. Worthington. Miss Worthington." Curiously, he didn't offer his hand.

Following suit, Ned nodded back. "Mr. Trevvyan."

His color still high, Jack Trevvyan retook his seat.

"We just got married," Rose Trevvyan said, flashing the gold ring on her finger. "Two weeks ago. A sudden, whirlwind romance. Jack surprised me with a honeymoon in Nice. He's the sweetest."

Neither confirming nor denying that statement, Jack pursued his fascination with the tablecloth. I got the feeling that if he could disappear, he would.

"But sadly, Jack can't leave his business for too long," Rose continued, totally ignoring her husband's discomfiture. "We'll be returning home tomorrow on the Golden Arrow."

The same train we would be on. Hopefully, we would not run into them.

The *maître d'* cleared his throat, recalling us to his presence. "Monsieur, your table." As busy as the restaurant was, he didn't have time to dilly dally.

"Yes, of course," Ned noted the reminder. "Sorry. We must go," he said to Rose.

"Great seeing you, ducks."

Ned didn't acknowledge the nickname. He rather looked like he'd swallowed the aforementioned duck, feathers and all.

Once we were seated at our table, he whispered sotto voce, "Please don't ask any questions."

"I wouldn't dream of doing so." Whatever had taken place between Rose and Ned, it was his private affair. And I suspected it had been just that. An affair. Therefore, he would neither appreciate nor welcome any intrusion on my part.

After we spent a few minutes reviewing the menu selections, our waiter approached to take our order. Ned requested the Beef Bourguignon and I asked for the Cognac shrimp with beurre blanc. We both opted for salade Nicoise and potages Parmentier for our first and second course. Noting our dinner choices, the sommelier recom-

22

mended a pinot noir and a pinot sauvignon blanc to accompany our meal. After the wine was duly approved by us, Ned and I discussed the splendidness of the room, the effervescence of the guests, the perfect spring weather. Anything but what was foremost in our minds. Or at least in mine.

But a few minutes later, much to my surprise, he broached the subject. Without looking at me, he said, "I know her socially."

"Oh?"

"I had no idea she'd married. To tell you the truth, it took me by surprise."

I'd noticed. But not wanting to interrupt the flow of conversation when he'd finally opened up, I only ventured, "Did it?"

"Yes. I didn't expect her to be. Married, that is." He gazed off into the distance as if something captured his attention.

Glancing in the same direction, I spotted the Trevvyans sauntering toward the restaurant's exit. Good thing they were leaving. Wouldn't want to run into them again.

Ned heaved out a sigh. Of relief? Or something else? Who knew? "It's been a while since I last saw her. Her husband seems a nice enough chap."

"Yes, he does." When he wasn't memorizing the tablecloth and turning red-faced, that was.

Our salads Nicoise arrived ending his confession, such as it was. I had many questions, but he now appeared reluctant to continue the discussion. My curiosity would need to remain unsatisfied.

We'd just been served our entrees when the *maître d'* arrived with a note. "For you, Monsieur Worthington."

"Thank you." Ned opened it, and a smile lit up his face. "It's the client. He wants to meet at ten."

It was almost nine. "Will you have time to finish your meal?"

He shook his head. "Afraid not. He lives in a chateau outside of Paris. It will take most of an hour to get there. I should just about make it."

I frowned at the rudeness of a person who'd waited until the last second to set up a meeting. But Ned, of course, wouldn't think of it as such. He'd see it as an opportunity to acquire a very rich client. One he was not about to turn down.

"The driver I hired should be in front of the hotel waiting for me. You don't mind if I desert you, old bean? Father is rather eager to get this client's business."

"Of course not." I smiled, even though I did mind. For him. "Do what you must. Don't worry about me." I meant it. I knew how important this meeting was to Ned.

"I'll sign the check for our meal. You'll be fine walking back to your room by yourself?"

"Of course. I'll go straight there after dinner. I promise."

"Very well." Coming to his feet, he glanced at his pocket watch. "The train departs at noon tomorrow. I'll come fetch you at half past nine. Don't oversleep."

"I'll set the alarm and request a wake-up call from the front desk."

"Splendid. Order breakfast from room service." After squeezing my shoulder, he rushed out, weaving his way through the throng of diners and tables alike.

Alone with my thoughts, I pondered everything that had happened in the last hour. Obviously, Rose and Ned knew each other, but her husband was uncomfortable with the relationship they'd enjoyed. Everything pointed to one undeniable fact. Rose and Ned had been lovers. She'd moved on, which should have settled things. And yet, I got the feeling they were not in fact settled. There was something there. Something I was ignorant of and, more than likely, would never know. I shrugged as I could do nothing about it.

When I finished my excellent dinner, I headed out, only to find someone in a Ritz uniform at the front of the restaurant waiting for me. It appeared Ned had requested someone accompany me to my room. Rather than rail against my brother's arrangement, I thanked the staff member. It was not his fault Ned was the managing sort.

When we arrived at my room, I tried to tip him, but he waved the money away. "Already taken care of, *Mademoiselle*."

"*Merci* then."

He tipped his cap. "*Bon Nuit.*"

"*Bon Nuit*," I whispered and closed the door.

The correct thing to do would be to bed down for the night, but it was only ten, and I was not in the least bit sleepy after taking an earlier nap. I could read a book recommended to me by one of the school students—a murder mystery by Agatha Christie. But the thought did not appeal to me. I did not want to spend my one night in Paris hiding in a hotel room.

Wandering outside the confines of the hotel would not be wise. But what if I remained within? Surely that would not offend Ned. Before I could give it another thought, I grabbed my clutch and room key and took the lift to the ground floor where Temptation Walk and its wonderful array of exclusive shopping boutiques were located. To my great disappointment, not only were the stores closed, but their wares were not on display. They had been stored for the night.

Rather than return to my room, I decided to stroll around the floor, for there was much to appreciate at the Ritz. After meandering for a few minutes, I discovered the Ritz bar, loud with men's voices. To my surprise, not one woman was within. Rather than breach what was so obviously a male dominion, I sat on a wingback chair directly opposite the establishment where I could observe the patrons inside.

A dark-haired gentleman threw his head back with a boisterous laugh drawing my attention. His companion seemingly agreed with the man since he patted him on the shoulder in a 'Hail fellow well met' kind of way. From their postures, they didn't seem so much drunk as bosky. It would probably take half the night for them to get well and truly sloshed. Inspired by the convivial scene, I retrieved my sketchbook from my clutch. With so much happening in the last two days, I hadn't had time to draw. But the two men inspired me to do just that.

With quick resolve, I penciled an outline of the dark-haired, square-jawed man facing me. He was young, close to me in age, and had a wild, careless air about him. Within a few minutes, I'd fairly captured his larger-than-life persona and soon was absolved in perfecting the lines.

"*Qu'est-ce que vous faites?*"

What was I doing? I jerked my gaze up to find the man from the bar in front of me. I already knew he had dark-hair, but now I was able to appreciate his tall height and blue eyes. His atrocious French accent reminded me of an American student from my finishing school.

Caught red-handed, I did not back down. After all, there was no law against drawing someone in a public place. "I am sketching you. See?" I turned the sketchbook toward him.

He bent down and peered at my work before coming upright again. "Well, aren't you clever?" He raised his glass in salute.

The compliment pleased me no end. "Thank you."

Turning around, he yelled, "James, come here, will ya?" I'd been right. He was definitely an American.

The gentleman he'd shared a drink with approached, a glass also in his hand. He was older than the dark-haired gentleman, in his early forties would be my guess, and of similar height. A pair of thick, pince-nez glasses perched on his nose, while a felt hat rested on his head.

The American pointed to me. "This girl here is an artiste."

"Are you, lassie?" James said. Irish by the musical lilt to his voice. "Maybe we should invite her to Gertrude's salon tomorrow."

The American slapped James on the back. "What a splendid idea. How about it, umm, what should we call you?"

"Catherine." I was not about to provide my last name to a pair of strangers.

"I'm Hem." He patted his chest, before pointing to the older man, "And this is James."

"Nice to meet you." The whiff of alcohol wrinkled my nose. They both smelled like a brewery.

James must have seen my reaction because he said, "You have nothing to worry about, Catherine. We're both married men."

Hem took affront with that. "You're not married."

"Might as well be," James said and sipped from his glass.

"You're frightening her," Hem exclaimed.

I had to laugh at their antics. They were drunk, but harmless. "No, he's not. Is there really a salon tomorrow?" I'd heard about them. It was the place where artists congregated to discuss topics of interest to them.

"Yes, there is. Can you come?"

"Unfortunately, no." I couldn't help but be disappointed. "I have a train to catch."

"That's a shame. You have talent," Hem said.

"Do you paint or draw?" I asked him.

He snorted. "Not even a straight line. I'm a journalist for *The Toronto Star*, but I've penned short stories. James here has written a whopper of a novel. Had it published too."

"Oh, splendid. What's the title?"

"*Ulysses.*"

"Like the mythical hero?"

"Not quite," James said while Hem chortled.

I made a note of it on my sketchbook. "I'll buy it as soon as I get home."

"No, you won't, lassie. The English philistines banned it."

Heavens! "Why?"

"They claimed it was obscene. Ruddy bastards." He swayed on his feet.

I'd underestimated their level of intoxication. Clearly, it was time for me to leave, but not before saying a proper goodbye. Coming to my feet, I said, "Gentlemen, it was very nice meeting you. I thank you for enlightening me."

James duffed his hat and bowed. "Our pleasure, Catherine."

Turning to the other, I asked, "Hem is not your entire name, is it?"

He belched. "Excuse me. No, it's not."

"Would you mind writing it in my sketchbook? If it's not too much of an imposition, that is. I like to include the names of the persons I sketch written in their own hand."

"Of course not." He took my drawing pencil and wrote out a large H, small e and m, along with the rest of his name.

"Hold on to that," James said, dropping a hand on Hem's shoulder. "This lad will be famous one day. He's a hell of a writer."

"I'll be on the lookout then." I meant it. "Good night, gentlemen."

"Good night," they both said.

I headed down the long corridor, only turning around to look back after I reached the lift. The two were no longer where I left them. They'd probably gone back to the bar. I glanced at the sketch I'd drawn of Hem and noted his full name. Ernest Hemingway. It had a nice ring to it.

It was now close to eleven, a good time to tuck into bed. But I was too enervated by the encounter with the two writers to sleep. That mystery novel would help me unwind, though.

After I'd stepped off the lift, a conversation drifted toward me from the hallway on the right, one I would have to pass on the way to my room. A woman and a man, arguing. The woman's tone reminded me of Rose Trevvyan.

In the next moment, my guess was confirmed. "Rose. Why are you doing this?"

"Money, darling, why else?" Her voice came across peevish, as if she resented his question.

"We have enough," he said.

"You fool," she barked out. "It's never enough. I'm not going back to being poor again."

"But why are you demanding money from him? Why Ned Worthington?"

I gasped. Was she blackmailing Ned? No wonder he was so perturbed when we ran into her.

"Because he's rich, and he'll pay," Rose answered.

"But he's not the father of our child. I am."

She was pregnant and claiming Ned was the father of her baby? What a horrible woman. I'd heard enough. All I wanted was to reach my room, but there was no way I could do so without them seeing me. So I was stuck where I was until they were done.

"You have to understand how toffs think, Jack. He's got a business to run. A business that depends on his good reputation. And that sister of his? Catherine." She spit out my name like it tasted foul on her tongue. "She'll be making her debut soon. The last thing he wants is a scandal. He'll do anything, pay any amount of money, to stop me from making a stink. Which I will do if he doesn't pay."

"But that's not fair to him."

"Life's not fair, Jack," she lashed out. "You should know that by now."

"I hate being part of this scheme. I wish I'd never married you."

"Do you, ducks?" she scoffed. "Well, it's too damn late to regret it. You're well and truly caught. And don't even think about leaving me. Ned Worthington is not the only one with a career to worry about. What would your employers think if you left me high and dry with a full belly? You think you'd keep your job after that?"

"You're evil."

"No. I'm not. I'm an opportunist." In her next breath, the wind seemed to be taken out of her sails. "Now I'm going to bed. I'm tired. You can come or not. It's up to you."

The clickety click of high-heeled shoes moved away at a fast clip. Seconds later, slower steps followed. And then I heard the snick of a door being opened and closed.

Finally free to do so, I rushed to my room and bolted the door. Outraged by what I'd just heard, I tossed my purse on the bed and madly paced the room. I wanted to do something, anything that would make the blackmail go away. But what could I do? I couldn't tell Ned I'd overheard the conversation. He would not appreciate me knowing about Rose's attempt to extort money from him. He'd rather think me ignorant of what was going on in his life. For a long time, I wracked my brain trying to come up with a solution. But I finally reached the indisputable conclusion. There was absolutely nothing I could do.

CHAPTER FOUR

THE FLECHE D'OR

TROUBLED AS I WAS BY THE TREVVYANS' REVELATIONS, I got little sleep that night. But dawn did not care about my troubles. Morning came too soon with the strident alarm of my travel clock.

Exhausted, I crawled out of bed, bathed, and dressed, determined to be cheerful next time I saw Ned. If I turned into a grump, he was bound to notice and would want to know the reason behind my sour mood. Of course, that was something I couldn't reveal. So it'd be best to put on an act.

Knowing food would lighten my spirits, I forced myself to eat every breakfast morsel, even if everything tasted like chalk. It helped, but not as much as I wished.

Promptly at half past nine, there was a knock on the door. Ned, of course. Slapping on a smile, I rushed to open it and twirled to show off my frock. "What do you think?"

His gaze crinkled in appreciation. "You look smashing, old bean."

The comment almost broke my heart. How could he be so pleasant in the face of such adversity? But I couldn't allow my agitation to show. He had enough to deal with. Playing the role I'd set on, I curtsied. "Why thank you, sir."

He shook his head at my antic but smiled nonetheless as he stepped into the room. "Have you had breakfast?"

I nodded. "An hour ago."

With his usual attention to detail, he scrutinized the space. "And you're packed?"

"Nothing much to pack. Only my night clothes and yesterday's gowns."

"Splendid."

"How did your meeting with the client go?"

He retrieved something from inside his jacket. "He gave me a bank draft. 'An initial outlay,' he called it. If he's satisfied with the return, he'll invest more."

"How wonderful." I clapped. At least one thing had gone right. "So, a celebration is in order?"

"Yes. But it will have to wait until we board the train." He tucked the draft back in his inner pocket. "Should I call for the porter?"

"Absolutely."

In no time at all, the hotel employee showed up to take our bags. Soon, our luggage was tucked into the boot of the motorcar Ned reserved for our time in Paris. And then we were off to the Gare du Nord station from where the Fleche d'Or would depart.

"How long is the journey to Calais?" I asked on the way.

"Three and a half hours. We should reach the Gare du Maritime by half past three. I recommend we eat a light luncheon on the train. Nothing too heavy."

"Of course." At Calais, we would board the Canterbury steamer which would deliver us to Dover. But one never knew how the crossing would go. It could be choppy or smooth sailing so the best strategy would be to avoid anything heavy in the way of food.

Upon our arrival at the Gare du Nord station, porters swarmed our motorcar and loaded our luggage on their carts. The weather had turned blustery, so I was glad I'd chosen my fur-trimmed coat. I snuggled into it as we headed toward the departure gate.

The hall teemed with humanity, some smiling, some frowning as they made their way toward their destinations. Ambling alongside the porter, I heard the notes of an old French song. To my surprise, someone was playing the tune on a grand piano in the concourse. Enthralled as I was by the serenade, I failed to see a gentleman ahead of us until I bumped into him.

"Kitty!" Ned's warning came a moment too late.

The gentleman turned around.

Heavens! He was handsome. Dark hair, dark eyes. Even taller than Ned and of athletic build, he had an air of authority about him. This man was no one's fool. Going by the arch of his brow, he was peeved with me.

"I beg your pardon," I said, feeling my face flush. "I wasn't paying attention. The music." I waved toward the piano as if that would excuse my *faux pas.*

He took his time scrutinizing Ned and me before tipping his Homburg hat. "No harm done, Madam." And then he faced forward, dismissing me, and continued on his way.

Determined to forget the embarrassing incident, I held my head high while Ned led the way to our train. Thankfully, it was waiting for its passengers on the tracks. Once we settled into our compartment, I stared out the window wishing things could have been different. I could be at Mr. Hemingway's salon right now, hobnobbing with artists and writers. But such was not to be. I sighed with a strange kind of longing.

"What's wrong?" Ned asked.

"I wish we could have stayed longer. I would have loved an additional day to explore Paris."

"And visit Montmartre?" he asked with a quirk to his lips. He knew me so well.

"Among other places." I grinned.

"You'll have other opportunities to visit Paris. Maybe your husband will indulge you after you marry."

That wouldn't happen for a long time. But, of course, I didn't share my intention to remain unwed with Ned. He was of the mindset that women should marry young and start a family. If it'd been up to him, Margaret would never have attended Oxford.

"Should we head to the dining car?" he asked an hour after the train departed the station. "I made a reservation for one and it's almost that time now."

Breakfast had been hours ago. Needless to say, I was famished. "Of course."

We arrived to find the dining car crowded, but a table had been held for us. No sooner were we seated than I spotted familiar faces at the entrance—Lady Ainsley and her companion, Ivy Burton, with similar forlorn expressions on their faces.

"There are no seats available?" Lady Ainsley's usual hauteur boomed across the space. She was of the belief that the world revolved around her and her wishes.

"Sorry, madame," the bow-tied *maître d'* explained. "We're full up as you can see. I could provide a reservation at two. Would that suit?"

"That won't do, young man," she huffed, stamping her cane. "We're hungry now."

"Ned." I nodded toward the entrance. "Lady Ainsley and her companion. It appears they can't get a seating. Do you mind if I ask her to join us?" We'd been seated at a table for four.

"Of course not."

I came to my feet and headed toward them. "Lady Ainsley, Miss Burton."

"Miss Worthington," Lady Ainsley said. "How pleasant to see you," she said, all sweetness and lightness. Quite differently from the way she'd addressed the head waiter.

"Thank you. Ned and I have two empty seats at our table." I pointed in his direction. "Would you like to join us?"

"Splendid." Lady Ainsley said and turned to Miss Burton. "Come, Ivy."

"Yes, Lady Ainsley," Ivy whispered.

I'd always felt sorry for her. Being constantly at Lady Ainsley's beck and call had to be a trial. But I reminded myself she had it better than many others. She had a roof over her head and was well fed. Many others did not.

When we arrived at our table, Ned came to his feet. "Lady Ainsley."

"Thank you for allowing us to join you," Lady Ainsley said.

"Our pleasure," responded Ned. He was always courteous to a fault. "Would you like to sit by Kitty's side or your companion?"

"Neither. I'll take a seat next to you, if you please. It's not often I get to enjoy a meal next to a handsome gentleman," she simpered.

Ned tussled with a smile. He often had that effect on women, especially the older ones who looked upon him as a way to recapture their lost youth.

As soon as we were situated, the waiter rushed over to take our orders. Ned and I ordered *salades de chèvre* and *croque mesdames*. While light in tone, they were sure to be a feast for the tongue. Lady Ainsley opted for heavier fare, while Ivy chose a lighter dish.

"Were you visiting Paris, dear?" Lady Ainsley asked while we waited for our first course to be served.

"Briefly. Ned was kind enough to fetch me from my Swiss finishing school. We only had time for a one-night stay before continuing our journey home."

"Ahh, yes. Your mother mentioned it. But my memory is not what it was. How unfortunate you were unable to remain longer. Paris is quite beautiful this time of year."

Before I could say anything, Ned interjected, "Duty calls, Lady Ainsley. I must return to London. Business must be attended to."

"Yes, of course."

Conversation came to a stop while the *garçon* delivered our food. Unlike us, Lady Ainsley had asked for French onion soup.

"Delicious," she said, once she was done. "But I really shouldn't have ordered it. Too rich for my constitution. But I can't seem to resist. Isn't that right, Ivy?"

"Yes, Lady Ainsley," Ivy Burton said in a soft voice, barely glancing up.

Seated as I was next to Miss Burton, I had the rare opportunity to study her. Something I'd rarely done. Although she accompanied Lady Ainsley to the meetings of the Ladies Benevolent Society, I was only present when invited to attend, which was almost never. I hadn't observed her at length. She'd remained silent while eating her quiche.

Only spoke when spoken to and not once had she volunteered her opinion until asked to do so by Lady Ainsley. She had no distinguishable features to speak of—light brown hair, unremarkable brown eyes —and was dressed in a nondescript brown suit that had never been fashionable. A casual passerby would have a hard time describing her. And yet, I sensed there was more to her than met the eye.

We'd just been served our entrees when the Trevvyans entered the car. With her now familiar swagger, Rose strode in our direction, flashing that seductive smile of hers. Her husband's expression was quite the opposite. As soon as he noticed us, his face flamed up.

As they passed, Ivy's complexion grew deadly pale. Her fork clattered to her plate.

Rose did not share in her discomfiture. As she walked past, she murmured, "Lady Ainsley, Ivy."

Small mercies she didn't greet Ned. That would have truly set the cat among the pigeons. But how did she know our luncheon companions? I didn't have to wait long to find out.

As soon as the Trevvyans were seated, Lady Ainsley snapped out, "The cheek of that girl."

"Oh?" What on earth had prompted that remark?

Before I could find out, she turned to her companion. "Ivy dear, would you mind fetching my dyspepsia medicine? The onion soup is having an effect on me."

"Of course, Lady Ainsley." Ivy jumped to her feet and rushed out.

As long as I'd known Lady Ainsley, she'd complained about one ailment or another, most of which turned out to be imaginary. But in this case, I was wont to give her the benefit of the doubt. It was entirely possible she could be suffering from stomach upset after eating the rich soup. But then again, she may have used it as an excuse to get rid of Ivy.

As soon as her companion was out of hearing distance, Lady Ainsley whispered. "I didn't want to say anything in front of Miss Burton. But I feel it's my duty to let you know about that couple that walked by us. Mr. and Mrs. Trevvyan."

Lady Ainsley loved to gossip, something she'd mastered to an art.

She always couched the revelations in terms of doing it for the greater good, a warning, if you would, against a perceived evil. I usually disapproved of it. But I wasn't about to ignore it in this case. Not when Rose Trevvyan was involved. Pressing forward, I prompted, "Yes?"

"Jack Trevvyan is a cad of the worst kind."

"Is he?" He didn't appear that way, at least from the conversation I'd overheard. After all, he'd urged Rose to stop blackmailing Ned.

"He was practically engaged to Ivy," she continued. "A promise of a promise, if you will. And then along came Rose Miles, common as dirt." She glared toward where Rose was sitting. "I suppose there is a certain animal attractiveness to her that men can't help but be drawn to."

Ned turned away from us as his face grew red.

Thankfully, Lady Ainsley didn't notice. "Well, before Ivy even suspected something shifty was going on, that trollop had stolen Jack from her and married him."

"No." That explained how Ned knew nothing about Rose's marriage. It must have happened rather quickly.

"Yes. Ivy was beside herself. Inconsolable. The poor girl."

"How very sad."

"If you ask me, she's well off of him. A man who abandons a decent girl for a floozy. He'll come to regret it, mark my words."

I could have told her he already did.

"As soon as I heard about it, I suggested a trip to Paris to cheer her up."

"That was very kind of you."

"Well, yes. Not that it was the sole purpose, mind you. I also needed to refresh my wardrobe. Nowhere better to do it than the House of Worth."

"Of course." The House of Worth was Paris's leading couturier. It only accepted clients who could afford their fashions. Lady Ainsley certainly qualified. Although she'd acquired her title from her second husband, it was the first one, a railroad mogul and industrialist, who'd left her pots of money. After his death, she'd been smart enough to hand over the management of the funds to Father who'd easily trebled her fortune.

She glared at the Trevvyans who were busy ordering their food. "And where do they get the money to travel first class, I'd like to know. He's nothing but a law clerk and she's a ... well, I don't know where she works but I'm sure it's nowhere decent."

"How do you know so much about them?"

"Through Ivy. That's how that floozy met Jack."

"Really?" I wanted to ask more questions, but before I could do so, Ivy returned.

"Your medicine, Lady Ainsley," she said handing the bottle to her employer.

"Thank you, dear," Lady Ainsley said.

Ivy's presence barred any further discussion about the Trevvyans. So I spent the remainder of the meal talking with Lady Ainsley about Paris and my stint at the finishing school while Ivy and Ned remained silent. Obviously distraught, Ivy kept pushing her food around her plate. Ned remained stone-faced. I knew him well enough to know he was upset.

At the end of our meal, Ned paid the tab for the entire party. Blushing like a schoolgirl, Lady Ainsley thanked him before saying goodbye. And then Ned and I returned to our compartment where we passed the time talking about the weather and sundry other topics, anything but Rose Trevvyan.

CHAPTER FIVE

ABOARD THE GOLDEN ARROW

*T*HE CHANNEL CROSSING WAS RATHER CHOPPY. But neither Ned nor I suffered any consequences. We could thank our light luncheon for that.

In a bare ninety minutes the Golden Arrow would deliver us to London's Victoria Station, where Neville, our family chauffeur, would be waiting to drive us home. I was very much looking forward to the end of our journey and the sure welcome that awaited us.

Unlike the French train, the Golden Arrow was not partitioned into compartments. Rather, it was comprised of parlor cars where wingback chairs faced each other and were separated by tables illuminated with tulip lamps.

Since we were the first to arrive, we had our choice of seats. Wanting to be neither too close to the lavatory for fear of noxious odors, nor the noisy entrance to the train, we decided on a central location. As soon as we were seated, Ned buried himself in *The Financial Times*, a copy of which he'd obtained at Dover station. His absorption with the newspaper allowed me to observe the other passengers as they arrived.

The Trevvyans were the first to join us. To my surprise, Rose chose the chairs opposite us. I expected another one of her special smiles, but it'd gone missing as she appeared rather wan. Maybe the crossing had not been kind to her.

Next to board were the Earnshaws, with the Colonel's attendant taking special care he was settled comfortably in the seating behind us. As before, the colonel's face was lined with pain.

Lady Ainsley and Ivy Burton came next. The matron complaining about the state of her health while Ivy commiserated with her. That poor girl must have heard those diatribes a thousand times. For some reason, Lady Ainsley opted for the seats beyond the Trevvyans. Probably because those were closest to the loo. In case an emergency trip was needed, of course.

The last to arrive was a couple I hadn't seen before who took possession of the chairs behind Ned. They were a study in contrast. While the gentlewoman, dressed in burgundy wool and matching cloche hat, seemed quiet in nature as she barely spoke a word, the man who accompanied her was a livelier sort whose Fedora could not hide a head of leonine, dark hair and easily monopolized their conversation. But then, as was often said, opposites attract.

As soon as the train departed Dover, the waiter made the rounds. He was young—no older than five and twenty would be my guess—and dressed in a pristine, white jacket, with the name Dickie Collins sewn into the front pocket. A pair of dark trousers completed the uniform. While he took Mrs. Earnshaw's order, I debated what to order. Mother would hold back supper until after our arrival so we could enjoy it as a family. But that would be at least two hours away, maybe longer, so it would be best to ask for a light meal, a hot one. The crossing aboard the Canterbury had been downright chilly, and it had only grown colder after we'd reached Dover. After a quick consultation with Ned, I requested hot soups, sandwiches, and tea and coffee.

Once the waiter moved on, I burrowed into my warm fur coat, thankful I'd chosen it for the journey home. With Ned immersed in his newspaper, conversation was not to be found. So I retrieved my sketchbook and drawing pencils from my purse and started drawing the passengers. The herky-jerky movements of the train meant they would not be my best work, but I was not looking for precision only a way to pass the time.

Ivy Burton was directly in my line of sight, so she was the easiest to draw. I penciled in a quick sketch of her in the brown cloche hat and coat she wore. A dragonfly brooch pinned to her lapel was the only bright spot in her outfit. I hadn't seen it on the French train, but then she hadn't worn her coat in the dining car. Her expression was harder to draw as her face laid half in shadow as she stared out into the night, but the half I could see told me she was suffering. Well, it was no wonder with the man that got away and his wife on the train mere feet from her. I'd barely finished her sketch when she excused herself to visit the lavatory.

All I saw of Lady Ainsley were her shoulders and the top of her head. Much like Ned, she'd decided to read, a gothic novel by the cover. So her sketch took no time at all.

Rose Trevvyan, who was seated across from me, made a much more interesting study. Her face, which had been so animated and colorful every time I'd seen her before, was downright pale. As I watched, a moue of pain crossed her lips. Obviously, she was not feeling well.

"How are you doing?" her husband asked, concern etched on his face.

"I have such a head." She brushed trembling fingers across her brow. "And my stomach's pitching something awful."

"The channel crossing was rather rough. Would your medicine help?" He pointed toward her purse.

"A cup of tea would be better, I think." She pressed trembling fingers against her stomach.

The waiter returned with our orders prompting me to stash my drawing supplies in my bag. After he served the couple in front of us, Jack Trevvyan demanded his attention.

"Excuse me, would you mind bringing my wife some chamomile tea? She's not feeling well."

"Of course, sir." The waiter turned toward the car entrance, presumably to get the tea. But before he could take two steps, Lady Ainsley stopped him.

"Young man, I'd like some service too." Her tone brooked no opposition.

The waiter rushed back to her. "Yes, of course, madam. What would you like?"

For several minutes, Lady Ainsley hemmed and hawed until she finally decided on tea and dry toast. All the while Rose was growing sicker and sicker. "Jack, please. I need the tea now."

"Of course, darling. I'll get it myself." He came to his feet and rushed toward the front of the car.

Noticing, the waiter hurried after him. "No, sir. I'll do it."

The man with the leonine head of hair came to his feet. To my surprise, he stepped toward Rose. "Sometimes something stronger than tea helps. Would you like some?" He held up a silver flask.

"What's that?" Rose asked, holding a handkerchief to her lips.

"Whiskey."

Rose took a sip and then groaned. "Oh, Bertie, my head."

Bertie? She knew the man. No wonder he'd offered relief. Although, honestly, whiskey would not help her. If anything, it would make her sicker.

"I have a ginger biscuit," Bertie's companion said. "It helps calm stomach upsets."

Rose glanced bleary-eyed at the woman. "I don't know if my stomach could take any food."

Ned, who up to now had ignored the commotion, plunked down the newspaper and joined the fray. "For heaven's sake, Rose, take your medicine. It's the only thing that helps. Do you have it with you?"

She started to nod but then thought better of it. "My clutch."

The black purse was on top of the table closer to the edge than her. Ned grabbed it and retrieved a small dark bottle.

"Here you go." He tried handing it to her, but she pushed his hand away. "I can't. You do it."

I could see why she asked for his help. Her hands were trembling.

She probably could not hold a spoon long enough to pour the medicine. But apparently there wasn't one on the table.

"We need a spoon," Ned said turning to me. Before I could hand one to him, Jack came rushing back, holding a cup, followed closely by the waiter. "Sir, that's my job. Please allow me."

Ignoring the waiter's plea, Jack plunked down the teacup and saucer in front of Rose hard enough that a bit of liquid sloshed over. "Here you go, Rose. Chamomile tea."

"Sugar. It needs sugar," she croaked out.

"Oh, for the love of—"

Mrs. Earnshaw, who was seated behind us, handed over her table's sugar bowl. "Here's some."

"Thank you." Jack plucked two sugar cubes into the cup and stirred the tea before turning to Rose. "Now, drink it," he barked at Rose. I didn't have to wonder why he'd suddenly turned nasty. Ned's presence had caused him to act out.

"Stop yelling at me," Rose whimpered.

Lady Ainsley, whose back was to Rose, seemingly had had enough. "Go help that girl, Ivy. Otherwise, we'll get no peace."

"Yes, Lady Ainsley." Ivy tucked away the book she'd been reading in her purse and made her way through the men standing around Rose.

Ned put down the bottle, probably believing his role was done.

Bending down, Ivy looked Rose straight in the eye. "You must take your medicine. You know it's for the best. I promise it will be over soon."

Rose shot a bleary-eyed glance at the woman she'd betrayed and huffed out a breath. "Oh, very well." Flashing a weak imitation of her seductive smile, she glanced toward Ned. "But I want him to give it to me."

Jack made some sort of strangled sound.

With a heavy sigh, Ivy turned to Ned. "If you would, sir."

Ned picked up the spoon Jack had just used to stir the sugar and the medicine bottle he'd put down. He opened he stopper, poured a small amount into the spoon and administered the potion to Rose.

Rose's lips curled up in distaste. "Ugh, that's so bitter."

"Chase it down with the tea, girl," Bertie ordered.

Rose did as she was told. The aftermath was immediate. Her color totally fled. Holding a hand to her mouth, she stumbled to her feet. "I'm going to be sick."

Ned and Bertie jumped back while Jack grabbed her. Together they dashed toward the loo.

No sooner was the door thrown open than the retching started.

"Oh, my," Bertie's companion exclaimed, "She's really ill, isn't she?"

"Yes, she is, love," Bertie said, a worried look on his face.

The horrible sound of sick went on forever and then, just like that, it stopped, as if somebody had turned off a faucet.

Jack Trevvyan stepped into the bathroom. "Rose? Rose? Are you all right?"

An ominous silence answered him.

Within seconds, he stumbled back out, a stricken look on his face. "Oh, God. Oh, God." And then he darted an anguished gaze toward us. "She's dead."

CHAPTER SIX

SCOTLAND YARD INVESTIGATES

*W*E SAT FROZEN LISTENING TO JACK TREVVYAN'S GRIEF. While he sniffled and wailed, his gaze kept darting toward the bathroom where Rose laid. She no longer had a care in the world, but, going by his anguish, his troubles were just beginning. He'd loved her, that much was clear, even if he no longer wished to be married to her.

The waiter, who'd rushed out after Jack's shocking statement, returned with a man who wore the uniform of a train line conductor. He warily approached the bathroom. After glancing inside, he recoiled from the sight or stench or, more likely, both. For a few seconds, he shook his head while staring in horror at the sight inside. Finally, he muttered a few words, which sounded like a prayer, before turning back to the transfixed passengers.

"Ladies and gentlemen, my name is Warren Jenkins." He brushed a trembling hand across his brow. "I'm the senior conductor on the train. I would like you to remain in your seats while I obtain assistance to sort out this tragedy." He whispered something to the waiter before hurrying out.

"Heavens, that stench," Lady Ainsley said, her voice filled with disgust. "Go close that door, Ivy."

Ivy looked up from the book she'd resumed reading when the waiter ran out, glanced to the bathroom and back. "I don't think I can," she said in a voice filled with regret. It was probably the first time she'd denied one of her employer's demands. "The conductor told us to remain in our seats."

"Then open a window and let in some fresh air, girl."

"Yes, Lady Ainsley." She tucked the book away, jumped to her feet and wrestled with the window. For a few seconds, it proved stubborn. Finally, it gave way, slamming down with a bang. Retaking her seat, she resumed her reading. I doubted she took in so much as a word. More than likely, the book was a way to keep from unraveling.

In less time than one would think, the conductor rejoined us, a tall, dark-haired man by his side. I recognized him right away. He was the same man I'd bumped into at the Gare du Nord, the one with the furrowed brow and the disapproving glance. His forbidding demeanor was once more in full evidence as he scrutinized the passengers and the scene.

"Ladies and gentlemen," the conductor said. "This is Detective Inspector Robert Crawford from Scotland Yard. He's kindly agreed to examine the facts surrounding this untimely death. Inspector Crawford, sir."

No wonder I thought he had an air of authority about him. He was the law. But what on earth was a Scotland Yard inspector doing on this train? Was he traveling for pleasure or a more official purpose?

"Thank you, Mr. Jenkins," Inspector Crawford said before turning to us. "I will be conducting a preliminary investigation into what happened here. While I do, please remain in your seats." Addressing the train employee once more, he whispered, "Now, if you could lead the way to the body."

The body. A few minutes ago, Rose Trevvyan had been alive. But now she was nothing more than human remains to be poked and prodded by those who investigated crimes. In life, I'd had no sympathy for her, but I certainly hadn't wished her such a horrible death.

The inspector followed the official toward the back of the carriage where the bathroom was located. To his credit, Inspector Crawford didn't recoil from the sight or stench that greeted him. But then, he worked for Scotland Yard. He must have seen and smelled worse things. While he carried out his preliminary investigation, he held a low conversation with the conductor who provided brief answers.

Done, he addressed the passengers. "I've been informed this is Rose Trevvyan. Is that correct?"

"Yes, sir." Jack Trevvyan said, wobbly voiced.

"And you are?"

"Her husband, Jack Trevvyan."

"Very well. I will talk to you first." He turned to Mr. Jenkins. "What's the next station?"

"Ashford, sir. We should arrive in the next ten minutes or so."

"I need a telegram sent to Scotland Yard. Is that something they could do?"

"Of course. They have a fully equipped telegraph setup."

"Very well." Inspector Crawford retrieved a paper pad and a pencil from his jacket, scribbled something, and handed it to the train official. "Can you read the message?"

"Suspicious death on the Golden Arrow," the conductor read out loud. "Request an investigative team and police officers meet the train at Victoria Station. Include a woman on the team. Detective Inspector Robert Crawford."

He was requesting a female police officer? For what purpose?

"Very well. I'll also need the bar car vacated. I'll interview these passengers there."

"No problem, sir."

The conductor bustled out of our car, leaving Inspector Crawford in command. We all stared at him with bated breath, waiting to hear what he had to say.

"As you've probably heard, Mr. Jenkins will be emptying the bar car. Once it's been cleared, I will request you walk there so I can interview each of you individually. You will leave your belongings here."

"Why?" I couldn't help but ask.

"What part of my statement are you curious about?"

46

"The part about our belongings. Why do we have to leave them behind? We might have need of something."

"Your possessions will need to be searched. And so will each of you. If you need something, Mr. Jenkins will fetch it for you."

"Searched? As in my person?" Lady Ainsley barked out, all indignant ruffled feathers.

"Yes, ma'am. We will need to search each and every one of you. That's why I requested a female police officer."

"Well, I never," Lady Ainsley huffed.

"Now if I could continue without any more interruptions?" He cast a disapproving glance at us. My, he had that glare down to a science. "In the bar car, you will be seated separate from each other. You will remain where I assign you. You will not discuss anything that occurred after the train left Dover with anyone but me."

"We can't talk to each other? That's outrageous," Bertie exclaimed.

"What is your name?" Inspector Crawford asked.

"Bertie Jackson."

The Inspector made a note in his pad before spearing Bertie Jackson with another forbidding stare. "If you find it so, Mr. Jackson, I'll be more than glad to conduct your interview at Scotland Yard."

Bertie Jackson blustered around a bit, but he didn't say one more word that was intelligible.

Given such a dire warning, we all sat silently while we waited for the conductor to return. Clearly, Inspector Crawford suspected Rose Trevvyan had not died a natural death. More than likely, she had been murdered, and one of us was the killer.

When the conductor returned, we were transferred to the bar car where Inspector Crawford told us where to sit. After a short conversation with Mrs. Earnshaw in which she'd asked for a special dispensation given her husband's illness, the inspector allowed the colonel's attendant to remain with him. The rest of us were isolated from each other.

After commandeering a semi-private space at the far end which was partitioned by glass from the rest of the car, Inspector Crawford interviewed Jack Trevvyan first. The conversation lasted over twenty

minutes which made sense since he was Rose's husband. But its dura-
tion was balanced by Col. Earnshaw's which he conducted seated next
to him and took no time at all. Apparently, as soon as Colonel Earnshaw boarded the train he'd been dosed with laudanum for his pain.
He'd faded in and out and hadn't noticed a thing. I believed it since he
was barely conscious now.

Mrs. Earnshaw's interview was next, and it was conducted in the
secluded space. Between his request to keep their voices low and the
rattle of the train, I didn't hear one single word.

Seemingly, the inspector did not trust us to keep mum because
he'd asked the conductor to keep his eye on us. He need not have
worried. Knowing we would be dragged to Scotland Yard if we went
against his wishes made for a powerful motive to maintain our
silence.

Restless as I was, I itched to do something, anything, to pass the
time. Noticing a paper pad on the bar counter, I asked for permission
to doodle on it. After consulting with the inspector, the conductor
nodded his approval. As there was a pencil next to the pad, I put it to
good use.

Lady Ainsley made her displeasure known with a lot of mutterings
beneath her breath. The words 'insufferable', 'upstart', and 'who does
he think he is' reached me. The conductor did not shush her. After all,
she was only talking to herself.

After what seemed like forever, we reached Victoria Station only
slightly behind time. It'd been decided that the train would remain
where it was until the police were done processing the evidence. The
station would reroute later arriving trains to alternate tracks.

The passengers on the other Golden Arrow cars were allowed to
disembark before the Scotland Yard Investigative Team came aboard.
After a short discussion, Inspector Crawford walked them to the car
where Rose Trevvyan's lifeless body lay. He returned with two police
officers who took over for Mr. Jenkins in keeping their eyes on us.

In most instances the interviews had been quite lengthy, so the
inspector still had several of us to interrogate when we arrived at
Victoria Station. After everyone else had been questioned and

released, Ned and I were the only ones left. I expected I would be next, but to my surprise he chose Ned.

I strained to hear his answers, but I barely discerned a word here or there. The train yard was almost as noisy as the journey had been.

Once his interview was finished, Ned squeezed my shoulder on the way back to his seat. I took comfort from his gesture. After all, he could do no more.

Determined I would not allow Inspector Crawford to get the better of me, I walked toward the interview area with my head held high. But as soon as I sat across from him the nerves got the better of me. I had to clench my hands to keep them from shaking.

"Your name?"

"Catherine Worthington. Kitty to my friends."

"Miss Worthington. Show me on this chart where you were seated in relation to Rose Trevvyan."

"Directly to her right." I pointed out my seat and he wrote my name in an elegant hand. Somebody had taught him well.

"Did you know the deceased?"

Knowing that question was sure to be asked, I'd thought long and hard about my answer. "My brother and I met her at the Paris Ritz Hotel. The restaurant to be exact."

"Come, Miss Worthington." He flicked a challenging gaze at me. "Your brother didn't meet her there. He knew her previously. Isn't that correct?"

"Did Ned tell you that?"

With a tight line to his lips, he demanded, "Please answer the question, Miss Worthington."

Knowing Ned, he'd spoken the truth, so I answered truthfully. "Yes, they knew each other. I, however, had never met her."

"What about her husband, Jack Trevvyan?"

"My brother didn't know him. He was sur—" I bit my tongue before finishing.

"Surprised?"

"Yes. That she was married."

"Ahh." He scribbled something on his notebook.

I needed to stop volunteering information since it was hard not knowing what Ned had said.

"What did you discuss at the hotel?"

"Not much. She introduced Jack as her husband. Said they were returning from their honeymoon. That was the extent of our discussion. The restaurant was very crowded, and the *maître d'* was eager to seat us."

"And you didn't see them again?"

"Not until we boarded the train." I'm not telling him about the blackmailing conversation I overheard.

"The Golden Arrow?"

"No. The *Fleche d'Or*. They entered the dining car while we were having lunch."

"Your brother Ned and you?"

"As well as Lady Ainsley and her companion, Ivy Burton. They hadn't secured a reservation, and we had space at our table. So we invited them to join us."

"Did you discuss anything with the Trevvyans?"

"No. She greeted Lady Ainsley and Ivy Burton when she passed us on her way to her table."

"But not your brother?"

"No."

He scribbled something else on his notebook before he glanced up again. "Didn't that strike you as odd?"

"No. She might not have seen him. He was seated next to the window, away from the aisle. And it was very busy in the dining car with tight quarters."

He raised another questioning brow but didn't pursue it. Instead, he asked, "What did you have for lunch?"

"Really, Inspector."

He waited patiently while I got my temper under control.

"*Salade de chevre* and *croque mesdames*."

"And what did you have to drink?"

I blew out a breath. "A glass of Chardonnay."

"And dessert?"

"Nothing. We did not care for anything heavy before the channel crossing."

"How did your brother know Rose Trevvyan?" he asked, suddenly changing tack.

"He didn't say."

"And you didn't wonder?"

"My brother is a businessman, Inspector. He knows people, many of whom I have never met. I assumed he knew her through his business circles."

He curled a disbelieving brow. He didn't believe me.

"Walk me through your time on the Golden Arrow."

"We had reserved seats on the last car."

"Was anyone there before you?"

"No. We were the first. After we settled ourselves, others began arriving. First the Trevvyans. They sat directly across from us."

"How did your brother react?"

"He didn't. He was reading *The Financial Times*."

"He didn't acknowledge their presence?"

"No. As I said, he was busy with the newspaper."

"Who came next?"

"Mrs. Earnshaw, the colonel and his attendant. The colonel is quite ill."

"How do you know?"

"We ran into the Earnshaws at the Paris Ritz. Mrs. Earnshaw shared the state of his health."

"Who was next?"

"Lady Ainsley and her companion, Ivy Burton, came directly after them. The last to board was a couple I'd never met."

"The Jacksons."

I nodded.

"What happened next?"

"The train started rolling. Since Ned was deep into the financial news, I decided to sketch the other passengers."

A small smile curled around his lips. "You're an artist?"

"Not a professional one. I do it for enjoyment."

He made another note. "Go on."

"I retrieved my pad and pencils and proceeded to draw."

"Who did you sketch first?"

"Ivy Burton. She was in my direct line of vision."

"What about the Earnshaws?"

"They were behind me. I couldn't see them unless I turned around.

"What happened next?"

"The waiter came by to take our orders—the Earnshaws first and then us." Since the inspector seemed to be interested in our menu, I gave him the exact details. "I ordered soup, sandwiches, tea for Ned, coffee for me. It's rather chilly in the train, and we wanted something hot."

"Who did you sketch after Ivy Burton?"

"Lady Ainsley, but I could only see her shoulders and the top of her head. Oh, and the novel she was reading. A gothic one."

Resting his hand on the table, he studied me for a few seconds. "You are very observant."

"I try, Inspector."

"Who was next?"

"No one."

"You stopped with Lady Ainsley?"

"Yes. Rose Trevvyan would have been next. But she was quite ill, so I chose not to draw her."

"How did she appear?"

"She complained of an upset stomach, and an aching head. At first, I thought it was nothing more than the effects from the channel crossing. But as time passed, she got sicker. Her husband suggested tea. The waiter was busy with Lady Ainsley's order, so he came to his feet and headed toward the car entrance, presumably to get it. The waiter rushed after him, saying something like that was his job or that he'd get it."

"And then?"

"Bertie Jackson stepped in. He offered his flask to Mrs. Trevvyan. Apparently, it contained whisky. She must have known him because she called him Bertie. She took a sip."

"What came next?"

When I kept quiet, he chided, "Oh, come Miss Worthington. Several witnesses mentioned it. That's when your brother attended to her, didn't he?"

"Yes, I suppose."

"What did he say?"

"Take your medicine, Rose."

"Didn't that statement surprise you?"

"I didn't know what to think. Everything was happening so fast. He asked where it was, and she pointed to her clutch. He opened it and took out a brown bottle."

"Is that when she took the medicine?"

"No. Her husband returned with the tea, the waiter right on his heels, still claiming it was his job. Mr. Trevvyan placed the cup in front of her, but she wanted sugar. There was none on the table. Mrs. Earnshaw offered the bowl on hers."

"Did she drink the tea then?"

I shook my head. "She refused it. Her husband said something, and she said, 'Stop yelling at me.' Lady Ainsley asked Ivy to take care of it, that otherwise she'd get no peace."

"What did Miss Burton do?"

"She encouraged Rose to drink the medicine. She said something along the lines of 'Stop being so stubborn' and 'drink the medicine. You'll be well soon.'"

"Did Mrs. Trevvyan take the medicine then?"

"Not right then. Rose wanted Ned to give it to her."

"Not her husband?"

"No. I guess she was mad at him for yelling at her."

"What did your brother do?"

"He grabbed the spoon from the saucer, poured the medicine, and gave it to her. She made a face and said, 'That's so bitter.' That's when her husband pushed the tea at her. She took one sip and, well, that's when things went from bad to worse."

"What happened?"

"She said 'I'm going to be sick.' When she stumbled to her feet, her husband helped her to the bathroom. He wrenched the door open just in time for her to lose her stomach contents. At that moment, I felt sorry for her."

"Go on."

"The retching seemed to go on forever and then it just . . . stopped. Her husband entered the bathroom saying 'Rose, are you alright? Rose? Rose?' And then 'Oh, God. Oh, God.' He stepped out and stared at us, a horrified look on his face and said, "She's dead."

CHAPTER SEVEN

AN ADMISSION IS MADE

*A*FTER INSPECTOR CRAWFORD FINISHED HIS INQUISITION, Ned and I had to submit to a search. We'd been escorted to a private area in the train station where we'd been ordered to strip down to our unmentionables. Separately, of course. The experience had been humiliating, to say the least.

By the time we were finally allowed to go home, it was after ten. Thankfully, our chauffeur Neville had held fast throughout our ordeal and was waiting outside Victoria Station with our luggage secured in the Bentley. I wanted nothing more than to crawl into my nice warm bed, pull the covers over my head, and forget about this horrible day. But first, there was something I needed to do—get Ned to open up about his relationship with Rose, and it had to be done now before we arrived home. Afterward, there would be no opportunity to discuss it as he would decamp for his own home after I'd been welcomed back. So it was now or never.

In the past, I wouldn't have dreamed about inquiring into his private life. But, as they say, needs must. So, taking the bit between my teeth as it were, I raised the glass partition between our chauffeur and us so he couldn't overhear the delicate conversation I was about to hold with my brother.

Clamping my hands together, I said, "Ned."

He glanced at me a question in his eyes.

"I have an admission to make." I hated that my voice shook.

"Yes?" That self-assured air he'd carried in Paris had vanished.

I wished I didn't need to delve into his pain, but it had to be done. "At the Ritz, I overheard a conversation between Rose and her husband."

He startled. "When?"

"After dinner, I wandered around the hotel."

His brow knitted. "By yourself?"

"Yes." I knew he wouldn't approve, but that was not important now.

"I asked the concierge to have someone accompany you to your room. Did he not follow through on my instructions?" That master-of-all-he-surveyed attitude was back.

But that was not about to stop me. It was too important to get to the truth. "Someone did, but I wanted to visit the boutique shops." I fiddled with my gloves. "Unfortunately, the stores were closed. It was much too late for them to be open. So I returned to my room." No sense telling him about my meeting the two writers outside the Ritz bar. I had no wish to suffer any more lectures.

I thought he'd say something, comment about my wild ways, but he remained silent.

"After I stepped off the lift on our floor, I headed down the corridor. That's when I overheard a conversation—an argument, really—between Jack and Rose Trevvyan."

"What were they arguing about?"

I took a deep breath. "They were discussing Rose blackmailing you."

He jerked as if he'd suffered a physical blow.

"Is it true?" I asked, hoping for the best, but fearing the worst.

He gazed off into the distance before he answered. "Yes. It's true."

"Why was she blackmailing you?" Even though I already knew, I wanted him to confirm it.

"She claimed the baby she was carrying was mine."

"She was your *chere amie*." A polite word for mistress.

The visible part of his face flushed red. Still facing away, he nodded.

"I . . . see. And was it?" I had to know the truth.

"No!" he said, turning back to me. "I broke off the relationship six months ago. Obviously, she was not that far along. Her pregnancy had to be of a more recent nature."

"But you still paid? Why?"

"Because I don't want a scandal attached to our name, Kitty. She threatened to send a letter to that gossip newspaper Mother loves so much."

"The *Tell-All*."

"Yes. She'd claim I'd abandoned her after getting her pregnant."

"But you didn't!" I was outraged for him. If such a situation arose, he would never shirk such responsibility. He'd make sure the infant would be well taken care of.

His lip curled with disdain. "The truth does not matter, Kitty. Once the story appeared in the paper, the rumors would spread like wildfire to every upper-class household. We would be talked about, shunned. All of us would suffer, Mother, Father, the business, you. Most especially you. And your season would become an unmitigated disaster. You might not find a suitable husband."

I had no wish for a suitable husband, or any husband at all for that matter. But now was not the time to tell him. "For what it's worth, Jack Trevvyan objected to the blackmailing."

"He seems a nice enough chap." Suddenly, the reality of the situation seemed to crash down on him, as he dropped his head on his hands. "What am I going to do? If the police discover the blackmail . . ." He left the rest of the sentence hanging in the air. But then he didn't have to finish it. I knew what would happen. He would become the prime suspect.

"But how would they find out?"

His tortured gaze bounced to me. "I gave her bank drafts."

Drafts. As in more than one. "Not cash then. Why?"

"They were rather large sums."

"How much?"

"Five hundred pounds each."

"How many were there?"

"The first demand came four months ago. At that time, I believed her. It was within the realm of possibility." His face turned a ruddy color once more. He was ashamed to discuss this with me.

But I needed to learn all the details. It was the only way I could help him. "And the second?"

"Two months later. I balked at first. Clearly, she was not expecting a baby. But she reminded me of everything I had to lose." He gritted his teeth. "She promised it would be the last time."

"Was it?"

He shook his head. "Another letter came last month. I burned it and refused to pay."

"Was that the end of it?"

"No. She came to the office, threatened to march into Father's office and tell him. She showed me the letter she'd written to the newspaper. If I didn't pay her right then and there, she would post it immediately."

"And so you paid."

He gazed at me out of stricken eyes. "What choice did I have, Kitty?"

"You wrote out another draft."

"Yes. I did not have 500 pounds on me. Or ever really. It'd be foolish to carry so much cash."

"I know." A ten-pound note was the most he ever carried. "Bottom line is there's proof."

"I'm afraid so." He sat up, scrubbed his face. Couldn't scrub the misery out, though. "Inspector Crawford is bound to find out. He appears quite good at his job."

Yes, he certainly did. Inspector Crawford wouldn't leave a rock unturned. It won't take him long to discover that Ned and Rose had been in a relationship. From there, it would be a short journey to the blackmail. All he needed to do was obtain a copy of Rose's bank records.

"How did you meet Rose?"

"She was a hostess at Jackson's Gambling Saloon."

"The same Jackson who was on the train?"

"Yes."

"She must have been on friendly terms with him because she called him Bertie."

He shook his head. "That doesn't mean anything. He encourages all the girls to do so. He thinks it's good for business to see them being friendly toward him."

Well, that dog wouldn't hunt, but maybe another one would. "He offered her his whiskey flask. That seems like a rather personal thing to do."

"Maybe."

Glancing up, I realized the streets were growing familiar. In minutes, we'd be arriving home. I needed to wrap this up.

"Was she still working for him?"

"I don't know. I haven't visited the club for months."

If Rose had been poisoned, any of the four men--Bertie Jackson, Jack Trevvyan, the waiter, or Ned—could have done the deed. She'd drunk from Bertie's flask, taken the tea, and accepted the medicine from Ned. For all I knew, the waiter could have poured the tea into the cup and dosed it with poison.

And then there was Ivy who'd encouraged Rose to take her medicine. She hadn't given it to her, though. But Mrs. Earnshaw certainly came into the frame, as well. She'd handed the sugar bowl to Jack and that could have very well been laced with poison.

The only ones who'd had no contact with Rose or anything she'd ingested were Colonel Earnshaw, his attendant, Lady Ainsley, and Mrs. Jackson. Colonel Earnshaw had barely been awake. Neither he nor his attendant had risen from their seats. Lady Ainsley had never left her chair, not even to visit the lavatory. She abhorred public bathrooms, called them menaces to public health and visited them only when she must. Mrs. Jackson had remained seated, as well. Although she had offered Rose a ginger biscuit, Rose had not taken it. So no blame could be laid on her.

So much of what happened on that train revolved around Rose. But I knew next to nothing about her. Somebody had killed her. Someone who had a powerful motive to do away with her life. Ned would never do such a thing. But he would become a suspect, and a prime one at that. The circumstances surrounding Rose's death, never mind the blackmail, almost guaranteed it.

I couldn't leave the investigation solely in the hands of Scotland Yard. Not when Ned was such an easy target. I had to get involved and investigate Rose's past. For the secret to her murder could only be found there. More than anything else, I needed to find the murderer before Inspector Crawford could hang a noose around my brother's neck.

CHAPTER EIGHT

A WELCOME HOME

A KNOCK ON MY BEDROOM DOOR woke me from the deepest sleep I'd had in days. "Come in."

Cummings, my mother's maid, crisped and starched as they came, not a hair out of place. Not that she would ever allow it. "Mrs. Worthington's compliments, Miss. She wanted me to remind you of your appointment with the modiste."

Remind me? Mother had said nothing last night. But then again, maybe she had. My mind had been such a jumble, I may not have heard. "At what time?" I grumbled.

"Eleven, Miss."

I glanced bleary-eyed at the clock on my nightstand. "It's barely eight now, Cummings. Plenty of time to rise and shine."

"You'll need to breakfast and bathe first, Miss."

"Ugh." I dived under my pillows, hoping she would banish into thin air.

But Cummings was made of sterner stuff. "Your Mother's been looking forward to your debut these last six months. I'm sure you would not want to disappoint her," she said in a disappointing tone.

She cut to the quick, this woman. "I heard it was an entire year," I mumbled from my self-imposed cocoon.

"If you say so, Miss." Clearly, she wasn't leaving, no matter what I said.

Mother and Cummings were strong believers of the rise-and-shine-school of thought, where I subscribed to the laze-away-the-morning-while-eating-breakfast-in-bed doctrine. Heavens knew I'd earned it after the two restless nights I'd endured on the train and Paris. Although I had to admit, I'd slept very well last night indeed. Giving up the hope of a leisurely coze, I emerged from my down-filled cave and propped my pillows behind me. "May I at least partake of some food before I have to dash about the day?"

A smug smile rolled across Cummings's thin lips. "It should arrive any moment."

She may have won the battle, but the war had still to be fought. One I intended to win. Another rap on the door got my attention. "Enter."

A sprite in a maid's uniform with loud coppery hair and bright blue eyes stepped lightly into the room, carrying a tray laden with all sorts of foodstuff. "Good morning, Miss."

"Betsy! You're a sight for sore eyes."

Her fair skin pinked up. "Thank you, Miss."

"I'll leave it to you then, Betsy," Cummings interjected. "Mind you, Mrs. Worthington expects the young miss to be dressed and ready by ten of the o'clock."

Ten? What happened to eleven? Knowing my extremely organized Mother, I expected she'd set aside time to inform me about a long list of events she'd arranged for my debut.

Betsy curtsied. "Yes, Miss Cummings."

Head held high; Cummings sailed out in full knowledge of her position in the pecking order of servants. Along with Father's valet, she stood almost all the way at the top. Only the butler, housekeeper, and Cook ranked higher. Betsy, being the upstairs maid, was rather lower in the servant rung. But she had one thing going for her Cummings did not. She was very dear to me.

Resting the tray on the round table in the middle of the room, Betsy said, "I brought your favorites. One of Cook's blueberry muffins

baked especially for you. Eggs, sausage, toast, butter, and marmalade."
She pointed them out in turn.

My stomach rumbled at the sight and aroma of such delicious foods. "You're an angel descended from heaven." It seemed like forever since I'd last eaten. True, Ned and I had enjoyed a cold collation last night after our arrival, but I'd been so consumed by my thoughts, I'd barely eaten. "If you have any love for me, tell me you brought coffee."

She grinned. "Yes, Miss. Freshly made." She poured the steaming beverage into a cup, added milk and sugar, and handed it to me.

I took a sip and breathed out a contented sigh. "How did you even know I drink coffee now?"

"From Cummings, Miss. Apparently, you wrote to Mrs. Worthington about the wonders of it. Cook's been perfecting a recipe with a continental flair. She hopes she got it right. If not, she charged me to let her know. She's that happy to have you home. But then, we all are." She grinned. "The place was not the same without you, Miss, if you don't mind me saying so."

She was easily one of my favorite members of our staff. Bright, cheerful, always with a ready smile. If I had my druthers, and I did, I'd make sure she'd be more than the upstairs maid. "And I'm happy to be home." Even with the dark cloud hanging over my head.

A scritch-scritch at the door got all of my interest. Could it be?

Betsy thrust it open and a droopy-eyed, loose-jowled Basset Hound waddled in on short legs. "Woof."

It was! "Sir Winston!" I flew off the bed to rain kisses on my beloved friend.

"Oh, Miss. He's missed you so. He's been downright miserable all this time. Moping about the kitchen, refusing treats."

"Well, it looks like it hasn't done him any harm. You're still a chunk. Aren't you, boy? I've missed your doggie kisses and your long ears and . . ." Suddenly, a malevolent stench assaulted my nostrils. "What is that smell?"

"He has a bad tummy. The dog doctor put him on a special diet of chicken and rice. It has helped. But there are times when—"

"He clears out a room." I waved a hand in front of my face as my eyes watered from the putrid smell.

Betsy chuckled. "Yes, Miss."

"Let in some fresh air, please."

She pulled back the damask curtains, thrust open the window and the outside rushed in—the tweets of birds, a fragrant breeze, the patter of soft falling rain. Of course, it wouldn't be an English spring without it. From farther off in the distance, civilization made itself known as the honks of cars and the whinny of horses joined in. It was good to be home.

Once the fresh air cleared out eau-de-Sir Winston's special fragrance, I was eager to learn the lay of the land. "Tell me all the gossip."

"Well, Miss." She'd started to rattle off the comings and goings of the staff, when there was another knock on the door. Honestly, Victoria Station had less foot traffic.

"Come in," I yelled.

"Good morning, dear." Mother said, sailing into the room. She would want to make sure I was truly awake. More than once, I'd risen only to crawl back in bed the second her back was turned.

"Sleep well?"

"Yes, I did." Even with all the worries roiling my mind, I'd nodded off the second my head hit the pillow.

"Thought I would stop by to discuss . . ." Glancing over to the side, she realized Betsy was still in the room. "That's all for now, Betsy. Miss Worthington will ring you when she needs you." With a moue of distaste, she pointed to Sir Winston. "And take that creature with you."

"Yes, ma'am." After fetching Sir Winston, Betsy curtsied and made her exit.

Father and I adored the hapless hound, but Mother had never taken a liking to him. Now that he was experiencing stomach issues, he had apparently become even more of a doggie non grata to her.

"You know about the modiste appointment." A statement, not a question.

"Cummings informed me."

"I'm sorry to rush you. I'm fully aware after your long journey, you would have preferred to rest for the day. Unfortunately, it cannot be helped. With your court presentation set for next week, your gown must be finished. Angelique was kind enough to agree to my schedule. But only if you attended a fitting today."

"I understand." Mother was a force of nature. She made plans, and you went along with them. Disregard them at your peril.

"As you know, Lady Kingsley has very kindly volunteered to sponsor you. She will be at Angelique's as well to make suggestions. Her input is invaluable. She's presented several debutantes."

"Yes, Mother." According to court rules, every debutante had to be sponsored by a member of the nobility which meant my own mother could not present me. Never mind she was more refined and better educated than many a so-called aristocrat. But such were the rules of the court.

"Lady Kingsley will join us tomorrow morning as well to coach you through your presentation."

"I look forward to her instruction." Lady Kingsley was a long-standing friend of our family, ever since she'd become a widow a decade ago. When her husband had passed on to his glory, he'd left her with a widow's jointure to live out the rest of her days. She'd been canny enough to seek Father's aid. He'd grown the income generated from the inheritance into a modest fortune.

"Another issue we must discuss is that of your maid." I felt like she was ticking things off a list in her mind. Modiste, Lady Kingsley, Kitty's maid. "As you know, Simmons left us. Her sister is quite ill and needed help with her children."

Simmons was my former maid. She'd served me, along with Margaret, since I turned ten. Once Margaret decamped for Oxford, I became her only charge. "Yes. You wrote me. I'm sorry about her sister's poor health." I was, however, not sorry to see Simmons go. She had an unfortunate tendency to tattle to Cummings about my comings and goings which meant Mother had been informed as well.

"As you can understand, that placed us at a disadvantage. And so close to your debut, too." She tsked. "You'll need a new lady's maid. An experienced one. I've posted the position at a top domestic agency. They assured me it won't be a problem finding one for you. We are, after all, known for our generous remuneration and excellent working conditions."

She was right. Not only was Father generous with servant salaries, but we employed sufficient staff no one was overworked. And Father, being the innovative thinker he was, had set up a pension fund for everyone who served twenty years. Once they retired, they would enjoy comfortable lives. All this meant that we normally did not have any trouble filling positions, from the teeny maid who cleaned and swept the fireplaces to the footmen who answered the door and served at the table.

But no matter how much Mother wanted me to have an experienced lady's maid, I had no wish for one I had never met. Chances were she would know which side her bread was buttered on and would most surely inform Cummings of my slightest transgressions. Now when I would be ferreting out a murderer, I needed someone I could count on to be loyal to me. "I would like to take Betsy on."

She startled. "Betsy? But she's the upstairs girl. She knows nothing about being a lady's maid."

"Actually, Mother, she's quite knowledgeable. Simmons depended on her to mend and iron my clothes, take care of my footwear. And she even learned how to style my hair." That last part was a bit of a stretch. I usually styled my bob myself.

"But she's just a common girl," Mother objected. "We hired her straight from the farm, as it were." Cook had recommended Betsy, her niece, to Mother when the upstairs maid position had become vacant. Mother had agreed to take her on sight unseen, mainly because she didn't want to upset Cook. "Granted her work is above reproach, but a lady's maid requires experience, knowledge."

"She's a quick learner, Mother, and she's already familiar with my wardrobe and, of course, myself." An idea struck me. "And she does beautiful needlepoint." Mother set great store by needlework, a talent I sadly lacked.

For a moment, she remained silent while she pondered the situation. Mother could be stubborn, but then, so could I. On this issue, I was willing to dig in my heels.

"Well, I suppose we could take her on a trial basis. Say, thirty days?"

Thirty days would not be long enough, but I'd make it work. "Thank you, Mother."

"You're welcome, dear." She kissed me and brushed a soft hand across my cheek. "It is good to have you home."

My eyes misted. She was the sun in our lives. The one who provided unending love. The one we ran to when things went wrong. And things were possibly going as wrong as they could for Ned. I knew without question; she'd fight tooth and nail for him. But I couldn't tell her. It was not my secret to tell.

I kissed her back. "It's good to be home."

"Well—harumph—better finish your breakfast before it gets cold. I'll send Betsy back to help you with your bath."

Betsy reappeared just as I'd demolished the food. "Should I run your bath, Miss?" Like every other member of the family, I enjoyed a private bathroom. Something Father had insisted upon when the house had been built. That decision prevented many arguments when we were growing up.

"Yes, please. And lay out the dark blue wool gown with the long sleeves. There's a chill in the air. It should keep me warm enough."

"Yes, Miss."

But before she could head toward the bathroom to fill the tub, I stopped her. "Betsy. How would you like to be my lady's maid?"

Her eyes grew wide. "Permanently, Miss?"

It would give her false hope to lie to her, so I had to tell her the truth. "Mother has agreed to give you a thirty-day trial period. If you do well, then it will become permanent."

"Oh, Miss." She clamped her hands together as tears filled her eyes. "It would be an honor. I will do my best."

"I'm sure you will. How is your needlepoint?"

"Needlepoint, Miss?"

"Yes, I told Mother you were a whiz with the needle."

"Repairing hems and such, yes, Miss. But needlepoint? When would I have the time?"

"Well, we'll just have to buy a fine needlework piece at one of the shops—a cushion or something you could hang on your bedroom wall. We wouldn't want to disappoint Mother."

She nodded as her eyes rounded with wonder.

CHAPTER NINE

FASHION AND GOSSIP

"Stand still, dear," Mother said. "Angelique is likely to stab you with a pin if you squirm."

"Yes, Mother." We'd been at this for what seemed like hours. After our prompt arrival at eleven, Angelique had proudly displayed my court presentation gown. White as it needed to be and made entirely out of satin silk, the floor length creation was truly lovely. My only objections were the two ostrich feathers perched on my head, and the three-yard train that flowed from my shoulders. They were ludicrous, to say the least. But needs, as they say, must.

"You look lovely, Kitty," said Lady Kingsley. "As tall and slender as you are, you have the perfect figure for this gown. You'll be the envy of every debutante."

"Thank you." Her effusive praise, well intended as it was, made me uncomfortable. I had no wish to shine at my court presentation since I considered it to be a relic of the past. A necessary rite of passage to kick off a debut season with the goal of snaring a husband. Unlike debutantes of old, I had no desire to marry, nor did I have to. The fortune Father would settle on me, as he had done with my older siblings, would be sufficient to set me up for life.

My plan had been to stick to Mother's plans during my debut

season. After all, it would be only a few months of my life. And then I could cut loose and have a rollicking good time. But now a different priority demanded my attention—the investigation into Rose's death. Unfortunately, as much as I desired to get on with it, I could not do so, at least not at the moment, for Mother had seen to it that every minute of my time would be taken up with preparations for the court presentation and my first ball.

"Kitty!"

Was I fidgeting again? "Yes, Mother?"

"Angelique asked you to curtsy. You'll need to do it before the King and Queen."

"Yes, of course." Well, that was one thing I'd mastered in finishing school. How to curtsy before royalty.

Stepping off the dais, I sank to the floor, eyes cast down, the very picture of obeisance.

A sigh issued from all three women. "Lovely." "Pure grace." "My beautiful girl."

As I rose, a bell rang somewhere in the distance. A few minutes later, one of the modiste's assistants walked into the private fitting space. "Begging your pardon, Miss Angelique. It's Mrs. Jackson. She has . . . concerns about her wardrobe."

Angelique sighed before turning to us. "If you would excuse me, I shall only be a moment."

While the modiste was attending to her other customer, Mother circled me admiring the handiwork. "You really do look lovely, Kitty. You will shine at your presentation."

Her pleased smile warmed my heart. I could not help but feel, though, it should have been Emily who stood here instead of me. Sadly, that could never be. Several years ago, my beloved sister had been taken from us by the Spanish Flu before she could make her debut. Emily would have excelled at it, too, for she truly wished to marry and have children.

After her death, Margaret and I made a secret pact to be the perfect debutantes, even though neither of us wished to enter the 'marriage mart.' We knew how much pleasure Mother would gain from showing off her daughters. If it took me standing here for hours on end to make Mother happy, I would do so.

Lady Kingsley came to her feet and slid on her kid fawn gloves. "I'm afraid I have to dash, Mildred. I have another appointment, an unavoidable one I'm afraid. But I shall see you tomorrow?"

"Yes. Thank you for helping with Kitty's presentation," Mother replied. "She couldn't do it without you."

"My pleasure, dear. It's not often I have such a beautiful debutante to present at court." She kissed Mother's cheek before sailing out of the room.

As I was wondering how much longer it would take, Angelique returned. "My apologies. A nervous client. She's ordered a new wardrobe and wanted to make sure I had the measurements right." Turning once more to me, she smiled. "We're done, Miss Worthington. Clarisse will help you remove your gown."

"Thank you." I was relieved to step off the dais as the train was quite heavy.

"I'll make the final alterations and personally deliver the gown. That way, if it needs any minor adjustments, I can make them right there and then. But I don't expect there will be."

"When do you think that would be?" Mother asked.

"No later than Thursday." Angelique said. "After your court presentation, Miss Worthington, we'll need to discuss the rest of your wardrobe, n'est-ce pas?

"Mais oui," I replied. Although the court presentation gown fitting had been dreary, I looked forward to getting new clothes, especially from Angelique who was seen as one of the best London modistes. She not only had a flair for fashion but could be quite avant-garde with her designs.

"She'll need ball gowns, at least four," Mother said, "as well as walking dresses, afternoon and tea gowns and whatever else you think best. We put ourselves entirely in your hands."

"We will do our humble best, Mrs. Worthington, to design the most fashionable gowns for your beautiful daughter." Angelique's smile was that of a contented cat. No wonder. She'd be able to live off the profits from my wardrobe for at least the next year. Mother paid all her bills promptly, unlike many members of the aristocracy who ordered gowns and never paid. "We have your measurements and an entire staff at your disposal, so you'll only have to visit the shop on occasion."

Well, that was great news, as my investigation into Rose's murder was bound to take up a great deal of my time. "*Merci.*"

After Mother and the modiste withdrew to Angelique's private office to discuss my future wardrobe, Clarisse stepped into the fitting room to help me change.

"Thank you, Clarisse," I said, stepping out of the gown.

"You're welcome, Miss Worthington." She carefully laid out the presentation gown on one of the tables in the room. Because of its weight, it had to be laid flat, rather than hanged.

Having recognized the name of the woman who'd entered the shop, I asked, "Was the lady you attended Mrs. Bertie Jackson?"

"Yes, do you know her?"

"Only in passing. We were aboard the same train."

Her eyes grew wide. "Was it the Golden Arrow?"

The remark took me aback. "Yes. How on earth do you know?"

"Oh, Miss. It was in The *Tell-All* this morning."

That horrid newspaper was London's most notorious tabloid. "What did it say?" I asked.

"It said someone had died aboard the train, and Scotland Yard thought the death suspicious."

How did that gossip rag find out? More importantly, had Mother read it? She had it delivered every morning to our home, mainly so she could keep up with high society news. But she had not mentioned it. Maybe she'd been so preoccupied with me she hadn't gotten around to it.

"Is that all it said?"

"Yes, Miss."

"Any names mentioned?"

"Only that of the dead woman."

I needed to get my hands on that sorry excuse of a newspaper as soon as I returned home.

"And to think we knew her," Clarisse said.

"Who? Rose Trevvyan?"

The assistant nodded. "About a year ago she came into the shop wanting to order a few gowns." She lowered her voice. "But Miss Angelique sent her off with a flea in her ear."

"Why?"

"Bertie Jackson had sent her."

"And that was a problem?" I did not understand what she was suggesting.

"Angelique thought she was his *chere amie*."

"Bertie Jackson's mistress?" You could have knocked me over with a feather, not an ostrich one of course. They were way too dear. But a year ago would have been before Ned, maybe. He said he'd ended his affair six months past, but not when it started. Had Rose moved on from Bertie Jackson to Ned, a younger, well-heeled man?

"Yes, Miss. With Mrs. Jackson being a regular customer, can you imagine if she and Mr. Jackson's *chere amie* had visited the shop at the same time? It would have been a disaster. Angelique could not take that chance."

"Of course not." Ned had claimed Jackson's relationship with Rose had been that of a gambling saloon owner and his hostess. But I'd sensed a familiarity that went beyond that. And Angelique seemingly had felt the same way. It was something I would need to investigate, starting with the purpose behind Mrs. Jackson's visit. "Why is Mrs. Jackson ordering a new wardrobe?"

"Well," she glanced around, probably to make sure Angelique was still tied up with Mother. "She's expecting a little one."

"Really?"

"Yes. We're so pleased for her. Hopefully, this time nothing will go wrong."

"What do you mean?"

"Two years ago, she lost a babe when she'd been but a few months along. And she'd been so happy too."

"What a tragedy."

"Yes. She didn't return to the shop for a long time afterward. But then a little while back she came in, bright as a penny, wanting to order a new wardrobe. We're all bustling to get it done, too."

"You like her."

"She's one of the good ones, Miss Worthington, just like yourself and your mother. Always treats us right. Never looks down upon us. And her husband always pays his bills on time." No wonder they wanted to keep in Mrs. Jackson's good graces. After all, mistresses come and go, but a wife is forever. The gain of a few bob was not worth the loss of hundreds of pounds. Angelique was not only a clever designer, but an astute businesswoman as well.

"Are you ready, dear?" Mother said, stepping back into the room with Angelique by her side.

"Yes," I said. "Thank you, Angelique, Clarisse. I'm sure the presentation gown will be a triumph and a credit to you and your shop."

"How could it not be with you as its model?" Angelique said.

As I left the shop, I decided my first step into my investigation of Rose's death would be to talk with Bertie Jackson. I needed to find out if he'd in fact cheated on his wife with Rose. And if he had, might Rose not have taken advantage of such an opportunity and blackmailed her lover? After all, she had a penchant for it. She could have threatened to go to his wife and tell her about the affair. With Mrs. Jackson being in a delicate condition, Bertie might fear the shock of such a revelation could cause his wife to lose the baby as she had done before. If such was the case, he might have very well determined to put a stop to Rose. Permanently.

CHAPTER TEN

KITTY'S FIRST BALL

*M*OTHER DECLARED MY COURT PRESENTATION A TRIUMPH after my photo appeared on the front page of The *Tell-All*. If one were judged by the fact I'd been graciously received by her royal majesties without tripping over my gown or losing the ostrich feathers firmly stuck to my head, I had to agree.

Shortly after that august event, invitations to breakfasts, al fresco picnics, theater outings, and balls flooded in, with the first one being Lady Kingsley's who was eager to show off her newest protegee. The first of many ball gowns arrived on time, and as Angelique predicted, it had needed no alterations. She'd designed a quite stunning creation made from the finest silk satin in a glorious shade of sky blue. As I descended our mansion's stairway to my family's, and half the staff's, oohs and aahs, I couldn't help but feel like Cinderella on her way to the dance.

That feeling dissipated after Ned informed me during dinner the inquest into Rose's death would be held in two days' time, and we'd been called to testify. But since I had a ball to attend and a mother to make happy, I determined to put on a happy face, no matter the news.

Soon after my arrival at Lady Kingsley's, my dancing card was filled with the names of lords, captains of industry, and no doubt, rakes, rogues, and scoundrels, all eager for a turn about the room with the newest debutante. Apparently, the word was out that Miss Kitty Worthington was this season's 'diamond'. The idea would have turned my head if not for my firm belief that most of my attraction came not from my supposed beauty, but from the generous dowry that came with my hand. But I took it all in stride, as I'd promised myself I'd do, mainly because it brought Mother such a great deal of joy.

The going was not easy, however. Just as I'd expected, many a dancing partner spent his time extolling his prowess at different sports, bragging about his property, title, wealth. If they lacked these attributes, they went overboard with praise, believing if they dumped a figurative butter boat over me, I would look favorably on them. They were wrong.

Halfway through the festivities, I was beyond exhausted and wanted nothing more than to get off my feet. After a dance with a clodhopper whose heavy tread crushed every one of my toes, I searched for a spot to take a breather and found the perfect place among the wallflowers.

"Hello," the spectacled, young lady next to me said extending her hand. "I'm Lady Emma Carlyle."

I shook it. "Catherine Worthington."

"I know. You're this season's incomparable."

"Oh, please, don't brand me with that moniker."

"Why not?"

"Because that will lead to more dancing, more invitations, and more boring conversations."

She snickered behind a gloved hand. "I heard they tend to go on and on."

Heard, not experienced. "They most certainly do." She was lovely, truly lovely with abundant, brown hair. Her eyes were also brown, although I could not detect their exact shade behind the thick glasses she wore. Her bright personality shown through, however, which would go a long way to attracting a beau. But whoever had dressed and styled Lady Emma had done her no favors. Her gown was a size too large and her coiffure with its corkscrew curls reflected a fashion from several years ago.

I thought to inquire about her circumstances. Unfortunately, I did not get a chance as Lord Marlowe came forward to claim his dance.

"Miss Worthington," he said, executing an elegant bow.

"Milord." As I curtsied, Lady Emma shrank into her seat. How unfair. He should be asking her to dance. After all, both came from a titled world. Besides, Lord Marlowe and I had already danced, and in my opinion, it would be impolite to take another turn about the room when no one had come forward to claim Lady Emma.

As I caught sight of Lord Newcastle, one of Ned's friends, an idea came to me. "I am so sorry, but I seemed to have made a mistake, Milord. I allowed you to reserve this waltz when I'd already promised it to Lord Newcastle. And here he is to claim his dance." My arm shot out to grab Lord Newcastle as he walked by.

"Miss Worthington." Although Newcastle appeared confused, he politely bowed. Ned occasionally invited him to dine at our house, so he knew who I was.

Hoping Newcastle wouldn't give me away, I turned to Lord Marlowe. "I feel bad about leaving you without a partner." I turned to my newest acquaintance. "Have you been introduced to Lady Emma Carlyle?"

"Yes, I have," Lord Marlowe said, bowing his head. "A pleasure to see you again, Lady Emma."

"You know each other. How wonderful. As it happens, she doesn't have a partner for this set. Do you think you could spin her around a bit?"

"It would be my pleasure," Lord Marlowe said, before leading a smiling Emma away. He was nothing if not polite.

Having nicely settled the other couple, I allowed Newcastle to lead me to the dance floor where the refrains of a waltz were already playing. "Thank you, Milord, for following my lead."

His brow scrunched. "You did not wish to dance with Marlowe?"

"Oh, No. It's not that so much as—"

"—Lady Emma did not have a dance partner."

"Yes," I said, feeling my face heat up. "I apologize for waylaying you. You didn't have plans to dance with someone else, did you?"

"No, I didn't." He glanced off into the distance where a beautiful woman was carrying on a heated conversation with a much older man. She seemed downright miserable.

"Someone you know?" I nodded toward her.

Unsmiling, he nodded. "Lady Sybil Wakefield."

"And the gentleman?"

He bared his teeth. "Her husband, Lord Wakefield."

Heavens. I would not want that much animosity directed toward me. "You do not like him."

His gaze snapped back to me. "I despise him." Hate dripped out of every word before he came to his senses. "I apologize. I should not have said such a thing."

"Don't apologize. I'd rather have honesty. Why do you hate him?"

"He doesn't treat her the way he should."

"Oh?" Whatever did he mean?

He pinned a direct gaze on me. "I would appreciate it if you kept my remark to yourself."

"Of course. I would never betray a confidence."

Seemingly satisfied with my response, he whirled me around the floor for several seconds before an idea struck me. Gambling saloons catered to fine gentlemen like him. Maybe he knew Jackson's?

"Are you familiar with Jackson's Gambling Saloon, Milord?"

"Yes, of course. It's one of the better ones."

"How well do you know its owner?"

"Bertie Jackson?" He shrugged. "As well as anyone who patronizes his establishment."

"Well enough to get me an interview with him?" I asked.

He scrutinized me closely. "Now why would you want to do such a thing?"

"Have you heard about the death on the Golden Arrow?"

"Of course. It's all over the papers."

He was right. Barely a week after our arrival in London, Rose Trevvyan's death had captured the imagination of every gossip rag in town. They wrote countless stories about her death, each more outrageous than the next. Every passenger on that train car had been named, including Ned and me, but not one of the newspapers had dared do more than that. I had a feeling that would change after the inquest.

"Ned and I were on that train. We were seated across from the woman who died."

"Were you?" I had all his attention now.

"Mr. Jackson was aboard the train as well. I wish to question him."

"Why?"

I lowered my voice even though the chances of anyone overhearing me were slim. "An inspector from Scotland Yard was also aboard the train. He investigated the scene right after it happened. He suspected poison."

"By Jove."

"Unfortunately, Ned had a connection to the victim." I paused to drive in my meaning. "A strong connection."

"Did he really?" Newcastle was a man of the world. He had to know what I meant.

"Yes. I wish to question Mr. Jackson and his relation to the victim. Apparently, she worked for him at his gambling saloon."

"I . . . see."

"Could you arrange a meeting?"

"I can but try my best, Miss Worthington."

"Thank you, Lord Newcastle."

When the waltz ended, I asked him to escort me to Mother's side who was engaged in a conversation with Lady Kingsley. Hopefully, I would get a respite before the next gentleman came forward to claim the next dance.

After he'd agreed to do so, a strange expression rolled over his face. One I did not recognize. "Don't take this the wrong way, Miss Worthington. You're not the featherbrain you appear to be."

"How very astute of you to recognize that, Milord," I deadpanned.

He grinned. "Minx."

I was that and more.

After taking me to Mother, he bowed. "I'll be in touch."

"I'll be waiting." I curtsied.

Amazingly enough, the ball was still going strong when Mother and I departed at midnight. But having danced every set, I desired nothing more than my bed.

~

As we had nothing scheduled the next morning, I'd looked forward to sleeping late. But to my surprise, Betsy woke me with the news Ned was waiting for me in the drawing room. While I dressed, I wondered what he needed to discuss to warrant such an early start for me.

"Kitty," he stood when I strolled into the room. "My apologies for waking you, but I needed to see you before heading to the office. I asked for coffee. I know how much you like it." He pointed to the service set out on the table in front of him.

"Thank you, dear brother." I helped myself to a cup before sitting on the couch across from him. "What prompted such an early visit?"

"I made a list." He reached across the table to hand it to me.

"A list?" I asked, confused.

"Yes, of those gentlemen I consider suitable for your hand."

I put down the cup and saucer and stared at him. "My . . . hand. As in marriage?"

"Yes, of course. What else would it be? I've ranked Marlowe at the top."

"You've ranked them?" I glared at the offending paper. The 'list' consisted of ten names, some with titles, some mere misters. All apparently looking for a wife.

"Yes. He's definitely a first-class choice."

"I see," I said, trying hard to control my temper. "Do I have any say in this matter?"

"Of course. That's why I made the list. So you can determine which one suits you best." A superior male smile rolled across his face.

"How fun!" I said, biting down on my tongue. "It's like shopping for a pair of shoes—stylish, do not pinch, made of the finest materials."

Putting down his cup, he frowned. "I would hope you'd give the choice of a suitor more thought than a pair of shoes."

"Do you, Ned? Do you, really? How about I give the matter no thought at all?"

"Something wrong, Kitty?"

No longer able to contain my ire, I jumped to my feet. "Yes, Ned, something is bloody wrong."

"Kitty, language!" His eyes widened, apparently taken aback by my outrage.

I stabbed the air with the sheet of paper he'd handed me. "How dare you make a blasted list?"

His startled gaze bounced to the closed door and back to me. "Lower your voice before the servants hear you. And sit back down."

"Fine." I spit out, before retaking my seat.

"Now, if you could explain to me—in a calm tone, if you please— what exactly is wrong with the list?"

"Everything."

"Well, that clears it all up then." He slouched against the back of the couch, obviously frustrated with me.

Taking a deep breath, I forced myself to calm down. Ned would respond better to a quiet approach, rather than an emotional outburst. "Did it ever occur to you I have no wish for a list? Or a husband, for that matter."

He leaned forward. "But that's what the season is about, finding a husband for you."

"Not for me, it isn't."

"I don't understand."

Unable to sit still, I took to pacing the floor once more. "I've led such a sheltered life, Ned. A privileged one, I know. But all I've known is my family, this house, and everyone in it."

"You attended finishing school in Switzerland."

"Where my activities were severely curtailed. I've barely lived, Ned. The thought of being trapped in a marriage when I haven't tasted life"—I shuddered—"is a thought not to be endured. I want to visit jazz clubs, dance the Charleston, drink fizzy cocktails. Drive a motorcar."

"But you could do all that after you marry."

I propped my hands on my hips and faced him. "How would I manage that, Ned? I'd be too busy having babies."

"Not necessarily." He paused before carefully measuring his next words. "If you discussed your concerns with Marlowe, or anyone else you married, he should be amenable to waiting until you were ready. There are ways to prevent conception, you know."

"Any of them foolproof?"

"Well, no."

"One slip, one miscalculation, and Bob's your uncle, I'd have a baby on the way. That's if I survived. Do you know how many women die from childbirth?"

"Err, no."

"Forty in 1,000."

"That seems . . . high."

"It is high. It's a horrible statistic."

"How do you know this?"

"Margaret. She sent me a pamphlet entitled 'The Yoke of Womanhood,' with information about childbirth and birth control, including condoms."

His jaw dropped. "She knows about condoms?"

"Yes, and, thanks to her, now so do I."

"You haven't? She hasn't?" The horrified look on his face was priceless.

"I don't know about her, but no. I have not. I'm still pure as the driven snow." I said with a snark to my tone.

Which he totally missed. "Thank goodness for that. I'll have to visit her at Oxford, though, and—"

"Don't you dare! She's a smart woman capable of making her own decisions. It's her body, after all."

"But she shouldn't engage in . . . What does that mean for her marriage chances?"

I laughed. "Oh, Ned. If she'd wanted to marry, she would have done so at the end of her season, don't you think?"

"Yes, well, I thought, after she got that Oxford degree out of the way, she'd settle down."

"In all the time you've known her, has Margaret ever shown the slightest interest in marriage?"

"Well . . . No."

"There you go."

"She's not . . . She can't be . . . Interested in women?"

I bit back a smile. It would not do to laugh at him. "Darling, you are priceless. She likes men, in an intellectual sort of way. She is Margaret, after all. What she is passionate about are women's issues."

"What does that mean?"

"Voting, equality, employment, women's health. You'd know if you talked to her."

His voice dropped. "I've been busy with the business." And then his tone rose in his own defense. "There are only so many hours in the day, you know."

My brother was such a darling. Clueless, but a darling, nonetheless. "You're right. I'm sorry. I should not have yelled at you. It's just you can be so . . ."

"Idiotic." The twist to his smile told me all was forgiven.

"Old fashioned." I crossed the divide to sit next to him. "You are so very dear to me, Ned, and I do appreciate everything you've done and are doing for me. But this list?" I tapped the sheet. "No. When I marry, and I do plan to eventually do so, it'll be a man of my choosing. One I will love with all my heart. It won't matter how much money he has or whether he has a title or not. What will matter is that he's a decent chap who loves me. Not my money, me."

His gaze softened. "You will have money, you know. Pots of it. Father has been very generous with all of our portions."

"I'm very grateful. Truly. And am glad you're handling my settlement. But please allow me to direct my own life. I promise if I need help, I will ask for it."

"You don't mind if I step in if the occasion calls for it."

"Like if I took a walk down a dark garden path with a gentleman?"

"Yes."

"No, I don't mind." I poked him on the chest. "Just don't make a habit out of it."

Mother suddenly burst into the room, out of breath, her chignon coming loose. "Is anything wrong?"

"No, Mother. Just the opposite. Everything is right. Ned dropped by to say hello."

"Oh? I heard . . . There was . . ." Her gaze bounced from Ned to me and back again. "Well, if everything's fine I'll leave you to it then." She started to walk out but then turned back to Ned. "You are coming to dinner tomorrow night?"

"Wouldn't miss it for the world, Mother."

"Invite Lord Newcastle. He showed an interest in Kitty last night." She blessed me with a smile which I returned.

"I will ask if he's available."

"Do," she said before marching out of the room.

"Am I allowed to comment about Newcastle?" Ned asked, a worried look on his face.

"You don't have to. I know his interest lies elsewhere."

"Then why allow Mother to hope?"

"It makes her happy, Ned. Don't worry. I will temper her expectations when the time comes."

"Very well." He checked his pocket watch. "I better go. Father will wonder where I am."

"Wait." I put my hand on his arm. "Don't you want to discuss the inquest?"

He shrugged it off. "There's nothing to discuss. The coroner is only interested in the facts to determine the cause of death."

"The Scotland Yard Inspector thought Rose had been poisoned."

"But that was not an official ruling. It's up to the coroner to decide."

"What happens after the inquest?"

"If the coroner believes a crime has been committed, he will order Scotland Yard to investigate."

"That's what I'm worried about."

He covered my folded hands with his own. "Don't."

"How can be you be so calm?"

"I've had time to think it over. No matter what the police discover, I'm innocent of Rose's death. There's no way they can pin the murder on me." He came to his feet. "Now, I really do have to run. I'll see you tomorrow night." And then he was gone.

I wished I had his confidence that no blame would attach to him. But too many innocent persons had been jailed for crimes they did not commit. He wouldn't be one of them if I had anything to do about it. And I did.

CHAPTER ELEVEN

INQUEST AND JACKSON'S GAMBLING
SALOON

$\mathcal{T}$HE INQUEST WREAKED HAVOC ON MY NERVES.
Except for Colonel Earnshaw who could not attend due to
his poor health, and his attendant, we were all there—from Jack
Trevvyan to Lady Ainsley and Ivy Burton, the Jacksons, Mrs. Earn-
shaw, the waiter Dickie Collins, Ned and me—as well as Inspector
Crawford who represented the Metropolitan Police.

Each of us testified as to what happened that night on the train. As
more witnesses spoke, a somewhat confusing narrative emerged, for
hardly two persons seemed to have seen the same thing or heard
identical words. I sat with clenched hands as Ned spoke. The coroner
asked a couple of follow-up questions, but other than that, he seemed
to be satisfied. When my turn came, I approached the witness stand
on shaky legs. The coroner must have realized how nervous I was
because he did his utmost to put me at ease. I related the truth as I'd
seen it, which contradicted some of the earlier testimony. And then,
thankfully, it was over, and I was allowed to return to my seat.
Inspector Crawford's time came next, and his account was very
straightforward. After being approached by the conductor, he'd exam-
ined the body and determined a suspicious death had occurred. He'd
then secured the scene and interviewed the witnesses.

But it was the pathologist who'd conducted the postmortem who provided the most explosive evidence. He testified Rose Trevvyan had died from cyanide poisoning which had been administered no more than a few minutes before her death. In other words, the murderer could only be someone aboard the Golden Arrow. When it was over, the coroner issued the foregone conclusion—death by an unlawful killing—and referred the matter to Scotland Yard to investigate.

As horrible as the inquest was, our departure proved even more harrowing. For the last week, the lurid details of Rose's death had been splashed across the pages of every London gossip rag, each of which seemed to have assigned staff to cover the inquest. Not only that, but a mob, eager for news, had gathered outside the courthouse, as well.

The police kept the crowd at bay while the other witnesses exited the courthouse. But when Ned and I emerged, the frenzy rose to a fever pitch, and the officers lost control. Questions were yelled out, flashbulbs blinded us. At first, Ned tried to be polite, but when the crowd did not give way, he grabbed my arm and pushed through the horde to our waiting Bentley. Neville, our chauffeur, must have seen what was happening because he'd driven the motorcar right onto the kerb. A bare second after Ned closed the door, Neville sped away.

"You alright, Miss?" Neville asked, a worried tinge to his voice.

"Yes, thank you." I straightened the cloche hat I'd almost lost in the madness before facing Ned. "That was unnerving."

"It sells newspapers, Kitty." He righted his crooked tie before turning around to look through the rearview window. "Good lord, they're still snapping away. What could they possibly have to gain from photos of our motorcar?"

Plenty, I thought. I'd grown increasingly more alarmed as the newspapers focused on Ned and me. At first, I couldn't determine the reason, but then I realized we were the youngest and most glamorous of the Golden Arrow passengers who'd witnessed the murder. Unfortunately, today, we'd fed that illusion by dressing the way we had. Ned, in his gray, three-piece suit and Homburg hat, was the perfect image of a successful businessman, and I, in my stylish navy-blue gown and fur-collar wrap coat, could have stepped from the pages of a fashion magazine. We should have worn something less conspicuous. But it was much too late to reach that conclusion. The damage was done.

~

I ARRIVED home to find a note from Newcastle waiting for me. He'd arranged for me to talk with Bertie Jackson for the very next day.

Since there were precious few places I was allowed to visit with only a maid for company, I had to come up with a proper reason. A trip to the modiste would provide the perfect excuse. Without batting an eye, I told Mother I needed a tennis outfit to wear at Wimbledon, and I wanted to discuss the design with Angelique. Mother unfortunately could not accompany me since she was meeting with Cook about this week's menus, a discussion they both enjoyed.

After Mother bestowed her blessing, I dug out the mourning gown I'd worn to Emily's funeral, for I could not visit a gambling establishment dressed as I usually did. Emily would feel it was the right thing to do since she'd been especially close to Ned. A black veil completed my transformation. No one would know the woman in deep mourning was me.

Once Mother was ensconced with Cook in the morning room, Neville drove Betsy and me away. Our first stop was at Angelique's. After all, I couldn't lie to Mother, and I really did need a new dress for the tennis match, as well as a special gown I requested from her. Having accomplished that task, I directed Neville to Jackson's Gambling Saloon. He didn't balk at my request. Betsy had already gained his compliance by arguing we'd be safer if he drove us rather than if we took a taxi. I suspected it was not only her argument that won the day, but the fact he was rather sweet on her.

Ten minutes before the appointed time, I arrived at Jackson's, as I discovered it was called. After I asked if my maid could wait somewhere private, Betsy was whisked to a small room where I was assured no one would disturb her. Only then was I shown to its owner's office. The stylish room surprised me. Paneled with dark mahogany and furnished with supple leather chairs and a striking desk, it was the height of elegance. Although the scent of expensive tobacco lingered in the air, it was neither pungent nor unpleasant.

I only had to wait a few minutes before Bertie Jackson walked in and closed the door behind him. "Miss Worthington." His greeting was polite, but I couldn't tell how he felt about my presence. A surprise, for I could usually read people.

I pulled back the veil. "Thank you for seeing me, Mr. Jackson."

"Would you like something to drink? Tea, coffee? Sherry?" He was polite. I had to give him that. He was neither tall nor short and had a brawny build to him. If anything, he resembled a prize fighter, although a well-dressed one. Gray streaked a full head of hair which he probably fought to tame. His business suit was elegant, yet understated, same as his office. The message was clear. He spent money on the finer things in life but didn't flash his wealth about.

"Coffee, if you have it."

"Of course." He picked up the candlestick telephone on his desk, dialed a single number, and spoke into it. While we waited, I asked him about the apparatus. Turned out it connected to different places in his establishment—the kitchen staff, the majordomo at the reception desk, his chief assistant. He could reach anyone by dialing a single number. The contraption seemed a wonder to me, one I would suggest to Mother. At the very least, it would be a more efficient way to communicate with the staff.

A white-liveried servant soon walked into the room carrying a silver tray laden with not only coffee but sandwiches, as well.

"I get peckish if I go too long without food," Mr. Jackson explained.

"I understand. Shall I serve?" It's usually the woman's duty to pour even when she's not in her own home.

He waved toward the service. "Please."

To my surprise, the coffee was quite excellent. Certainly nothing I'd expected from a gambling saloon. But then, so was everything else. I'd expected a cheap gambling business, but I'd encountered an establishment that competed with the finest places in Mayfair. We exchanged more pleasantries while he enjoyed his meal and I the coffee. But finally, he leaned back into his burgundy leather chair. "Well, Miss Worthington. What can I do for you?"

"I wanted to discuss Rose Trevvyan."

"Thought as much."

"I understand she worked for you."

He lowered his gaze before he spoke. After taking time to gather his thoughts, he gazed at me. "Yes, she did."

"How did you come to know her?"

His heavy sigh spoke volumes, whether it pertained to his relationship with Rose or a reluctance to discuss the subject, I had no idea. But clearly, she had been more than an employee to him. "I found her wandering the streets. Gaunt faced, emaciated. She had a haunted look about her. I believed she was one step away from, well, I can't really say in front of a lady."

"I can imagine, Mr. Jackson," I said, trying to put him at ease. "No need to spell it out."

"As thin as she was," he continued, "she reminded me of someone I knew long ago. Figuring she could use a meal, I brought her back here."

"And she came?"

"When you're starving, food is a powerful incentive, Miss Worthington."

"I understand."

"She ate like someone who hadn't eaten for a long time, sandwiches, pasties, anything that I put in front of her. Once she had her fill, she drifted off. Right there where you're sitting."

"You brought her here? To your office?" That was a surprise.

"Yes. She had suffered enough. I didn't want my employees to get the wrong idea about her."

Was he referring to her physical state, or the likelihood they'd think her a doxy? And why would he even care what his staff thought of Rose?

"Once she woke, we talked. That's when I found out what had

happened to her. She'd gone into service right out of an orphanage. After working there for three years, she was accused of stealing some silver. She swore it wasn't true."

"You believed her." It was clear he had.

"Yes. I'm very good at reading people, a useful skill in my business."

"You need to know who's lying and who's telling the truth."

"And who I can trust. Her story rang true. I asked her if she would like to work for me as a hostess, set out the wage I would pay her, and the duties."

"And she agreed?" Why wouldn't she? It was either a paying job or selling herself on the streets. No choice at all.

"Yes. But she needed to regain her health before she could do that. I own properties throughout London, some commercial, some residential, including a few flats. They've come in handy when a patron of Jackson's is in need of one."

Had Ned set up Rose in one of Jackson's properties? It made sense. After all, he couldn't have brought her home. "I could see how convenient that would be." I bet Mr. Jackson charged a pretty penny for those flats too.

He flicked his fingers, dismissing the subject. "I told Rose she could stay in one of them until she was fit enough to work for me."

Thinking the worst, I raised a doubting brow.

He laughed. "She glared at me the same way you're doing now."

"She didn't believe it was an honest transaction. That you wanted something else from her."

"Yes. I explained I wasn't interested in any kind of liaison. That I was married to a woman I loved very much, and my only interest was to hire her as a hostess for the saloon. But she was too thin for the job. The men who come here like women with more meat on their bones. She had to gain some weight before she could work for me."

"What if it wasn't merely lack of food that kept her so thin? Maybe she was truly ill."

"I wondered the same thing. To tell you the truth, I half suspected consumption. So, along with the flat, I asked her to see a doctor I have on retainer, one who takes care of the girls."

I took umbrage at the word. After all, these were fully grown women. Or at least I hoped they were. "You mean your hostesses?"

"Yes. Part of the requirements of the job is that they see him every three months, more often if a problem arises."

I could just imagine one particular problem that might arise. "Are they expected to . . .?" How could I possibly phrase this?

"No. Miss Worthington. I'm not a whoremonger."

I gasped.

"That's where you were going, wasn't it?"

"Yes." I could feel my face flush.

"The hostesses' duties entail greeting the patrons, jollying them up, encouraging them to spend more money at the tables, bringing them drinks and food. That is all. If in the course of business they set up different arrangements with the patrons, it's always their decision, not mine."

"I see. Did Rose go to see the doctor?"

"Yes, she did. She was not ill. All she needed was some food in her. I supplied her with enough money to buy as much as she wanted, as well as new clothes. A month later, she returned. I hardly recognized her. She had changed that much."

"She came to work for you then?"

"Yes. She was a great success. Lively, charming. The patrons loved her."

"Including my brother?"

Now it was his turn to be surprised. "You know about him and Rose?"

"Yes. He didn't kill her, but somebody else certainly did. And I need to find out who it was."

"I can assure you it wasn't me. I looked upon her as a daughter."

Somehow, I didn't believe that. Or maybe that was wishful thinking on my part. Someone had killed Rose. It could very well have been him. "How long did she work for you?"

"Three years. In all that time, I didn't have one complaint about her. On the contrary. Everyone praised her, including my other employees. She was a good sort."

"When did she resign?"

"About two months ago. She left to marry Jack Trevvyan. He was knocked on his pins, he was. Totally smitten with her. As you can imagine, he didn't want a wife who worked as a hostess at a gambling saloon." He cleared his throat. "She intended to be a good wife to him."

Maybe at the beginning, but it had gone very wrong. Jack Trevvyan had ended up hating his marriage.

"On the train, you suggested Rose drink some whiskey. Why?"

"She suffered from headaches. While employed here, she discovered a small amount helped with the pain."

"I see." Well, that certainly explained his offer. "One last question, Mr. Jackson. Do you know who she worked for before she was let go?"

"Yes. Mary Earnshaw. She hired her straight out of the orphanage as her downstairs maid."

That's where I needed to go next. If Rose had worked for the Earnshaws and she'd been let go, there had to be some bad blood there. One I clearly needed to investigate.

CHAPTER TWELVE

A CALL ON MARY EARNSHAW

*T*WO DAYS LATER, Mother decided to visit Mary Earnshaw to inquire about the Colonel's health. As I was eager to learn more about Rose, I accompanied her, grateful I wouldn't have to concoct a reason for talking to Mary Earnshaw. Since etiquette demanded morning calls last no more than twenty minutes, I needed to make the most of my time.

As in the past, Mrs. Earnshaw welcomed us in the most gracious of ways offering the ubiquitous tea along with her cook's very excellent shortbread. As always, she was immaculately dressed in a gown that had a Parisian flair to it. I'd seen a woman wearing a similar one at the Louvre. Maybe Mrs. Earnshaw had taken the time while in Paris to shop for new clothes. Odd, when you thought about it. After all, she'd been distraught over her husband's health.

While we enjoyed the refreshments, Mother broached the subject that prompted her visit. "How is the colonel faring?"

Mrs. Earnshaw's pleasant mood vanished as she took a deep breath. "I'm afraid he's not getting any better."

"How very sad," Mother said. "The specialist was not able to help?" Of course, she would have known about the Earnshaws' trip to the City of Lights. As co-chair of the Ladies Benevolent Society, Mrs.

Earnshaw was duty bound to inform the other members in case a pressing matter needed to be resolved in her absence.

"He prescribed a medicine to help with the colonel's pain but beyond that did not offer any false hope."

"Oh, dear," Mother commiserated. "Wouldn't a surgical procedure help?"

Mrs. Earnshaw shook her head. "Unfortunately, no. The cancer has spread to the point it would not be a solution."

"I'm so sorry, my dear. If there's anything we can do, please let us know."

"Thank you for offering, but I'm afraid there's nothing much that can be done." She must have been eager to change the subject because she directed her next statement at me. "Let's talk about happier things. How was your court presentation, dear?"

"It went well." Last thing I wanted was to blow my own trumpet when she was obviously in such distress.

"Don't be so modest, Miss Worthington," she chided. "I heard it went better than that. You're being touted as a success. I may not be able to get out and about much these days due to the Colonel's illness, but I do have visitors."

Did I detect a note of pique in her voice? As a member of the Ladies Benevolent Society, she attended many social events, but since the Colonel's health began to deteriorate, she'd had to curtail her attendance. Or so, Mother informed me. After all, she couldn't be seen gadding about when her husband was so ill. Maybe she resented the confinement.

"Oh, I see I've embarrassed you, my dear. Forgive me." While her words signaled contriteness, her eyes shined with another emotion. Was she eager to see me squirm?

I was beginning to think there was another side to Mrs. Earnshaw. But I had to remain polite. For Mother's sake if nothing else. "You haven't. There's nothing to forgive."

"Of course, your debut is not the only subject getting coverage in the newspapers. All of London is abuzz with the news about the Golden Arrow murder. It's all anyone can talk about."

"I find it extremely distasteful of the papers to encourage such lurid gossip," Mother exclaimed. Although she subscribed to several newspapers, including the *Tell-All* gossip rag, it was the society news she followed with avid interest. But the newspapers also dedicated plenty of ink to the latest scandals, 'The Golden Arrow Murder,' as they called it, being the latest example.

"It's their bread and butter. Crime sells." Mrs. Earnshaw dropped her voice. "The *Tell-All* hints of blackmail."

I choked on a sip of tea.

Mother grew instantly concerned. "Are you all right, dear?"

"Yes." I whispered with the mere iota of oxygen I was able to take in.

"I, for one," Mrs. Earnshaw spit out "wouldn't put it past that girl. She was always trouble."

"You knew her?" I asked when I got my voice back. Of course, I already knew but it was good to have it confirmed. It meant that Bertie Jackson had not lied, at least not about this.

"Yes. She came to work for me straight from the Children's Home." The orphanage the Ladies Benevolent Society sponsored. "She was sixteen at the time and a hard worker. But even from the start, something about her bothered me." She sniffed.

Mother tsked her disappointment with the turn the conversation had taken. She'd never approved of gossip. But since it was important to obtain as much information as I could from Mrs. Earnshaw, I ignored it and pushed on.

"How long was she employed by you?" I asked.

"Three years. She started as a tweeny, then cook's assistant, and finally downstairs maid. That's when the silver started to disappear. A fork here, a knife there, many more pieces than could be dismissed as carelessness. The butler started locking it up. But even so, items went missing. I knew it had to be one of the servants. But which one?"

"How did you find out it was her?" I inquired.

"We set a trap. I asked the butler to leave an expensive silver piece on the dining room sideboard. Next morning it was gone. It was her half day off, so I had someone follow her. She'd gone straight to a pawnbroker. When she returned to the house, I confronted her with the theft. The brazen hussy denied it, claimed she had done no such thing. Needless to say, I didn't believe her."

"What did you do?" I asked.

"I told her to pack her bag and leave. She got no reference from me." A servant who left an employment without a letter of recommendation would be seen as damaged goods. No wonder Rose had ended up in the streets.

"But why did it take her three years to take the silver? You'd think she would have done it sooner." Mother's tone was that of pity, not condemnation. But then she always thought the better of people and could not envision the same thing happening in our home. She had good cause to believe in the honesty of our staff. Not one of them had ever betrayed her trust.

"As she grew older, Rose started getting ideas above her station. She wanted pretty things. When she took to wearing a gold chain, I knew something was up."

"Where did she go after she left?" Mother asked.

Mrs. Earnshaw turned up her nose. "No idea. Once I dismissed her, she was not my problem anymore."

Mother's silence spoke volumes. I could tell she was shocked. She probably could not envision throwing a young woman unto the violent streets of the city for thugs to prey on her. I had to agree. No matter what Rose had done, she hadn't deserved such a fate.

After that uncomfortable exchange, we said our goodbyes. Our visiting time was up.

Once we were seated in the Bentley with Neville at the wheel, I brought back the subject in a roundabout way. "Mrs. Earnshaw's revelations about Rose Trevvyan were a trifle overwrought, don't you think?"

"She's upset about her husband's illness, Kitty. If she seemed emotional, no doubt it can be traced to that cause."

I didn't know what I'd hoped to gain from my question. Maybe a recognition that Mrs. Earnshaw was not the person she appeared to be. But Mother would never criticize another member of the Ladies

Benevolent Society, especially its co-chair, when she'd fought so hard to be admitted to that group.

Her membership had opened doors to high society, something she'd craved since she'd been a young woman. As the daughter of a church minister who owed his living to a noble lord, she and her father had been often invited to the nobleman's home to make up numbers for dinner. Although Lord Castleberry and his family had always treated Mother and her father with the greatest respect, that had not been the case with his guests. Some derided Mother for her low social status, while a few of the so-called gentlemen made improper advances toward her. It was something she'd never forgotten and was particularly painful to her.

It had taken my father, Lord Castleberry's man of business, to see her true worth. He'd asked for her hand in marriage after he'd fallen in love with her. Since she reciprocated his feelings, she'd happily accepted. She'd never regretted her choice. As Father's business grew and he took on the management of those less wise in the handling of funds, our family's social standing improved. But she'd never been able to gain entrance into the highest of circles until her admittance to the Ladies Benevolent Society. It had opened doors she'd sought to walk through all her life.

It wasn't her modest background that had gained her admittance, though. Father's connections to wealthy men had done the trick. All she had to do was ask them to sponsor the charitable organization's endeavors, and they gladly complied. But having gained admittance, she remained ever vigilant. She knew well enough if she committed the smallest *faux pas*, her membership could be withdrawn.

Caught up in my thoughts, I kept silent during the ride home. I disagreed with Mother about Mrs. Earnshaw. She'd been upset about her husband's illness in Paris but hadn't lashed out in a particularly nasty way. I doubted that was the reason for her vehement dislike of Rose. Certainly, a theft of silver did not provide enough impetus either. Especially one that occurred years ago. There had to be another reason. One I intended to discover.

And heaven knew, time was of the essence. If rumors were

swirling about blackmail in the newspapers, most certainly Scotland Yard knew about it. But maybe there was more than one victim. Would Rose Trevvyan have been satisfied to sink her hooks into only Ned? Or would she have targeted more victims? Bertie Jackson made a likely candidate. After all, Angelique believed he had been having an affair with Rose. As much as he insisted he thought of Rose as a daughter, that could be true. I needed to discuss things with Detective Inspector Crawford to find out what he'd discovered, but first I had to talk to Ivy Burton. That was one story I was missing. And the sooner the better.

CHAPTER THIRTEEN

KITTY VISITS IVY BURTON

$\mathcal{A}$S IT TURNED OUT, a discussion with Ivy Burton had been frightfully easy to arrange after Mother and I spied Lady Ainsley at the opera—a three-hour performance of Rigoletto. Knowing how much the matron loved her sleep, I expected she wouldn't rise until noon the next day which would leave Ivy free to enjoy a coze.

I planned my escape for the following morning when Mother would be busy with the housekeeper going over household matters. If Mother were to inquire about me, I instructed the footman to tell her I was visiting the lending library so she would not worry. And then Betsy and I climbed into the Bentley and let Neville whisk us away.

Lady Ainsley's home, a large three-bay, four-story house on Eaton Square, was happily situated in one of the better neighborhoods in Belgravia. She'd inherited it, along with a sizable fortune, from her first husband, a wealthy industrialist who'd passed away a couple of decades ago. She'd then married Lord Ainsley, who'd seen the benefit of marrying a wealthy widow who could keep him in the style he was accustomed to. A few years ago, he'd succumbed to some disease, leaving her widowed once more. After his demise, both men of means and of the nobility had pursued her, but she'd chosen not to marry again. But then, why would she? She had the prestige awarded by the title and the wealth to enjoy a well-appointed life.

Upon my arrival at her home, I handed my card to the footman. Barely a few minutes passed before Miss Burton arrived in the drawing room. As always, she was dressed in a nondescript manner, a beige dress which was designed not to call attention to her. She profusely apologized for Lady Ainsley's absence, but I set her anxiety at ease, explaining it was her I'd come to see.

Her brow wrinkled with surprise. "Me?"

"Yes."

Her gaze bounced around the room, maybe in search for a reason for my visit, before returning to me. "Shall I ring for tea?"

She'd settled on the polite thing to do. But it was not needed. As our time was bound to be limited, I needed to make the most of it. "No, thank you."

"Very well." She clasped her hands on her lap. "What can I help you with, Miss Worthington?"

"I wanted to discuss Rose Trevvyan."

"Oh." Tears suddenly glimmered in her eyes before she hid them by lowering her gaze.

What a very strange reaction to someone who had betrayed her trust. "Were you close to her?"

She nodded. "Yes. We grew up in the same orphanage, you see."

Well, this was news to me. But maybe it shouldn't have been. The Ladies Benevolent Society practiced what they preached by hiring from that institution. "The Children's Home?"

"Yes. Some thought it odd since she was three years older. But we enjoyed a special bond. We were orphaned at an early age, you see."

"Ah, I understand. She took you under her wing." It seemed out of character for Rose who appeared to be concerned only with herself. But maybe she'd been different at an early age.

"You might say that. An orphanage can be a lonely place. Friends are hard to come by. After Rose took a special interest in me, I felt less alone."

"I understand. You were treated well, though?" From all accounts, the Children's Place was an exemplary orphanage, something Mother took great pride in promoting during fund raising events. The Ladies Benevolent Society did not just take the staff's word for it, as they made regular visits to ensure the place was being run as it should. Still, it helped to verify the truth from someone who'd lived there.

"Oh, yes. We were housed, fed, educated. As we grew older, we were taught a trade, mostly domestic service."

"How long did you live there?"

"Ten years. I was six when my mother died from consumption."

What a horrible age to lose a mother. But then was there ever a good time? "I'm so sorry. I can't imagine what it must have been like for you."

She swallowed hard. "The pain of it never goes away. Not really. But the orphanage did the best they could."

"Did you come directly here from The Children's Home?"

"Yes. Lady Ainsley needed a tweeny."

"How did you come to be her companion?" It was such a huge promotion. Going from a dogsbody to a lady's companion would require somebody who could speak the King's English, know etiquette, and possess the ability to be seen but not heard.

"After I'd served as tweeny for a year, I was promoted to downstairs maid. And then Lady Ainsley's companion suddenly quit to marry a widowed shopkeeper, leaving her in the lurch. She was at sixes and sevens as to what to do. It was the season, you see. I'd been doing a fair amount of fetching and carrying for her, and she liked my work. So she asked me to step in on a temporary basis. But we got along so well, she offered me the position permanently."

"When did Lady Ainsley first take you on?"

"Five years ago."

Which meant she was one and twenty. Rose had to have been four and twenty when she died.

"Did you continue your friendship with Rose after you left the Children's Place?"

"Not immediately. Being three years older, she left before I did. She was taken on by—"

"The Earnshaws."

"Yes."

"When did you see Rose again?"

"About two years ago. I was picking up one of Lady Ainsley's medications from the chemist, and Rose was there fetching one of her own." A small smile blossomed across her lips. "It was grand seeing her. I hadn't realized how much I'd missed her. I couldn't tarry long, though, since I had to get Lady Ainsley's remedy to her. So we made an appointment to meet again at a tea shoppe on my half day off. After that, it became a regular occurrence."

"You enjoyed your conversations?"

"Oh, yes. Very much so. I loved hearing about her work as a hostess at Jackson's Gambling Saloon."

"Did you?"

"It was so different from what I do, you see." She tangled her hands on her lap. "My life tends to be very subscribed."

"I can see that." The position of a lady's companion required her to always be on duty. Except for her half day off, her time would not be her own. To Ivy, Rose's life would have seemed to provide more freedom to come and go. But that was not what Rose had been taught to do. "Didn't you think it odd she was working at such a place? After all, she'd been trained as a domestic."

"I wasn't. I know others who'd been hired to work at grand houses only to be let go when the family's finances became strained. They had to scramble for any position that paid. A member of the lower class does not have the luxury of waiting for the right opportunity to come along. She must keep body and soul together any way she can."

And so did Ivy. "Was she content with her change of fate?"

"She was happy and healthy. Her work was not onerous. She didn't have to fetch and carry or spend the entire day at her mistress's beck and call. All she needed to do was greet guests and make sure they enjoyed their time at the gambling establishment." Ivy became absorbed by the tip of her fingers. "Rose certainly enjoyed more freedom than I did."

That was the second time she'd mentioned it. Did I detect a note of envy? One would think Ivy had the better position, for she would not be looked down upon or condemned by society. But regardless of what I thought, I couldn't afford to be derailed from my purpose. I needed to get on with my information gathering. "How did Mr. Trevvyan come to meet her?"

Her face tightened up. She'd been willing enough to share details about her life, but she was not happy to do the same about Mr. Trevvyan. To her credit, she did answer my question.

"Lady Ainsley wanted to revise her will, so she contacted her solicitors. Jack works for them, and he accompanied the partner when it was time to sign it. That's when he asked me if I'd like to have an ice at Gunter's."

"And you said yes?"

She nodded. "I was thrilled. I'd never had a gentleman pay the slightest attention to me. I tend to blend in with the wallpaper." A small, self-deprecating smile flitted across her lips. "We kept seeing each other on my half day off, sometimes at Gunter's, other times at the tea shoppe. Not every week, mind you. Only when he could get away from work. On those days we couldn't meet, I arranged to see Rose. But one week I forgot to tell her I was otherwise occupied, and she showed up." She gazed off into the distance as a sad look rolled over her face. "It was like a thunderbolt had struck him. He was instantly smitten with her." Same words that Bertie Jackson had used.

Ivy was a pretty woman, but Rose had been another thing altogether. An uncommon beauty with a certain allure who drew men like moths to flames. No wonder Jack Trevvyan had reacted the way he had.

"I'm so sorry that happened, Miss Burton." I could only imagine how shattered she must have been.

"Mr. Trevvyan and I tended to meet every other week. But after he spotted Rose, he started making excuses." She preoccupied herself with her fingers again. "He was busy at work, had to travel out of town, had become ill. As time went on, our meetings became fewer and fewer. One day, after he told me he was visiting friends, I stopped at the tea shoppe, and there they were, holding hands, gazing deep into each other's eyes. I was instantly sickened by it."

"How awful for you."

"I must have made some sort of sound, because he glanced toward me. I'll never forget the expression on his face. Surprise, shame, horror. He called out my name, but I would not, could not, remain there another second. I fled. Next day, he came here to apologize and explain. He had fallen in love with Rose, and they were getting married."

Heavens. A personal apology? It would have been kinder to have sent Ivy a note. At least she would have been allowed to suffer in private when she learned he was marrying another woman. "You must have been devastated."

"I was. You see, he'd hinted we would be getting married. He'd even given me a promise ring." She pulled out a chain from around her neck and showed me the small ring dangling from its end.

How could she still be wearing such a thing after he'd broken faith with her?

"When Lady Ainsley discovered what he'd done, she wanted to end all her business with her solicitors and demand they fire him. I didn't wish that for him, so I talked her out of it."

I squeezed her clenched hands. "You have such a good heart. I don't know if I would have done the same." Frankly, I would have wanted him hanged, drawn, and quartered. And his entrails burned.

She glanced down as she issued a soft sigh. "The heart wants what the heart wants, Miss Worthington. I couldn't punish them for loving each other."

"Is that when Lady Ainsley decided to travel to Paris?"

"Yes. She thought the change of scenery would do me good. It did." A brave smile flitted across her mouth. "I've accepted my fate."

I itched to ask more questions, but just then, a maid entered the room. "Pardon, Miss Burton, but Lady Ainsley is asking for you. She's feeling rather poorly."

Of course, she was. Lady Ainsley tended to suffer from many ailments, most of them imaginary. It was her way of getting attention.

"Yes, of course. I'll be right up." Standing up, Ivy gazed at me, a tight smile across her lips. "Lady Ainsley ate too rich a meal last night. Unfortunately, this morning she's paying the price."

"I understand." I came to my feet. "Thank you for your time."

"You're welcome. I'll escort you out."

As I climbed back into the Bentley, there was much to think about. Jack Trevvyan was certainly the villain of the piece. He'd fallen for Rose's beauty, tossing aside the less spectacular Miss Burton, who, in my opinion, would have made him a better wife. If the conversation I'd overheard at the Ritz was anything to go by, he'd come to regret his marriage. His outrage over Rose's blackmailing schemes had certainly seemed true enough, whether it stemmed from an innate sense of right and wrong or that the fear of discovery would ruin his career. He couldn't divorce her, even if his thoughts had trended in that direction. Not only was she expecting their child, but a divorce would not be looked upon favorably by his employer. He would have had to remain married to Rose until death. Maybe, just maybe, he'd chosen that way out.

CHAPTER FOURTEEN

KITTY VISITS INSPECTOR CRAWFORD

*A*S MUCH AS I WANTED TO TALK TO JACK TREVVYAN, I couldn't figure out a way to arrange it. After all, I had no personal connection to him, and my family did not do business with his firm. I would have to devise another way to arrange a meeting.

But that was not the only avenue of investigation I needed to pursue. I also needed to discover what Scotland Yard knew. And that required a discussion with Inspector Crawford. Telephoning him was out of the question. First of all, I had no idea if he had one in his office. Second, although we had two in our home, one was for Father's business use, and the other one was in the hallway, which meant anyone could listen in on a conversation. And third, if he were to reject my request, which I fully expected he would do, I would just as soon be spared the embarrassment of anyone overhearing it.

After sending a carefully worded note asking for a few minutes of his time, I waited the rest of the morning and most of the afternoon for his reply. It wasn't until just before we were due to leave for supper at Lady Dalrymple's that the missive arrived. Betsy, knowing how eagerly I'd been awaiting the letter, rushed up the stairs with it. But it was too late. Mother was in my room, wanting to give me last minute instructions before we set out, so the reading of the note would have to wait.

"Lord Marlowe will be at Lady Dalrymple's."

"Yes, Mother." She'd only mentioned it half a dozen times in the last day or so.

"He is eminently suitable. Not only is he an earl, but he possesses a large fortune and extensive property." She paused for effect. "And he is quite handsome, don't you think?"

I nodded. Everything she said was true. And yet, my heart did not beat any faster when my eyes lit on him.

"I would like you to consider him, Kitty."

"Yes, Mother."

I couldn't complain about the quality of that evening's outing. The company was convivial. Conversation never lagged. And Lord Marlowe was everything that was amiable. Still, the time crawled by. It wasn't until midnight that we finally returned home.

"You did well, Kitty." Mother's eyes shone with high hopes.

"Thank you," was all I could think to say. After kissing her cheek, I forced myself to walk, rather than run, to my room where Betsy waited, note in hand. I tore open the envelope and breathlessly read the few lines.

"Dear Miss Worthington,

Per your request, I will make myself available to meet with you at eleven of the o'clock on Thursday. If this meets with your approval, please kindly reply,

I remain your humble servant,

Robert Crawford

London Metropolitan Police"

Having expected a rejection, I was overcome with relief.

"It's good news, Miss?" Betsy asked.

"Yes. He wants to meet on Thursday at eleven."

"Tomorrow then."

I glanced at the clock. It was past midnight Wednesday, so indeed the meeting was to be held the next day. "Yes, tomorrow." Happily, the time coincided with one of Mother's charity endeavors when she would be away from home, so there would be no impediment to leaving the house. However, since she would take Neville with her, Betsy and I would have to resort to another mode of transportation.

As I didn't want to be recognized at Scotland Yard, I chose my outfit with care. I opted not to wear the mourning clothes. After all, I wanted to make a favorable impression on Inspector Crawford. I needed something to obscure my face, so I decided on a fascinator pillbox hat with a dark veil which came to just above my lips. The black sleeveless gown had a dropped waist and tiered skirt which fell to just below my knees. A pair of lace gloves, t-strap shoes, and black pearls completed the look with the fur collar wrap coat over it all.

When the time came to leave, I asked one of the footmen to hail Betsy and me a cab. He would not tell on my escapade, but neither would he lie, if asked. It was more than his job was worth. So I had to hope no one would.

As we set forth in one of London's finest taxis, I was a nervous wreck; Betsy, on the other hand, was grinning for all she was worth.

"Oh, Miss. This is so exciting. I've never been to Scotland Yard before." Anyone could see she loved the adventure of it all.

I, however, couldn't share in her joy, not with my stomach in knots. "And let's hope you never have to again."

When we arrived at Scotland Yard, I gave my name to the beefy constable stationed at the front desk. After checking my name off a list, he asked a uniformed officer to escort me to Inspector Crawford's office. Clasping my hands to keep them from shaking, I asked Betsy to wait for me.

"Yes, Miss." Her eyes danced with excitement as she gazed around the reception area.

The lift took us to the third floor where Inspector Crawford's office was located. It was neither large nor small. Not elegant by any means, more utilitarian than anything else. A wood desk commanded a large part of the space with an oak and leather revolving chair, somewhat worse for the wear, perched behind it. A many-drawered tall cabinet which had seen better days butted against a wall. Papers and folders were piled up on the desk. Some in a wire basket, others on the surface. He certainly seemed a busy man.

He stood when I walked into the room. "Miss Worthington."

Goodness, I'd forgotten how very handsome he was. In an age when men sported beards or mustaches, his chin held not the smallest hint of fuzz. But then men often wore facial hair to hide weak features. Inspector Crawford had no need to disguise his chiseled good looks.

"Inspector Crawford. Thank you for seeing me."

"Please take a seat." He waved to the one wooden chair in front of his desk. "I'm afraid I can't offer the niceties—tea and such."

"No worries," I said to put him at ease while availing myself of the wooden seat. Comfortable it was not. "This is not a social call." I pinned up the veil so I could see him clearly. And just as importantly, so he could see me. I'd been vain enough this morning to slap a bit of rouge on my cheeks and color on my lips.

"You didn't say why you wanted to meet. Did you remember something else?"

He thought I'd come to offer more information. No wonder he'd agreed to the meeting. He was bound to be disappointed, though. "No. I came to inquire about the investigation."

Where before he'd leaned forward, he now dropped back into his chair. "You've wasted a trip then. Scotland Yard does not comment on ongoing cases."

"I was wondering—"

"No."

I huffed out a breath. "You don't even know what I meant to ask."

"It doesn't matter. If it has to do with Rose Trevvyan, I can't answer any of your questions."

I ground my teeth. "You are being awfully stubborn."

He arched his left brow. "Personal remarks won't help."

I decided to take another tack, one that hopefully would convince him to share what information he had. "Rose Trevvyan's murder concerns me. After all, I was there."

"You are a witness, Miss Worthington. Nothing more. As such, you are not entitled to access privileged information."

Impossible man.

Some emotion flitted across his face, one of concern. Leaning forward once more, he threaded his hands. "If you are . . . worried about being implicated, let me put your mind at ease. You are not under suspicion of murder."

As if that was what kept me up at night. "How do you know?"

"You never went anywhere near Rose Trevvyan." He tapped a folder on his desk, one filled to the brim. "Everyone I interviewed confirmed it."

So he'd talked to several people. How very curious. Other than that initial interrogation, he'd never questioned me again. But I was not about to give up on my quest. Taking another tack, I decided to challenge his proficiency. "It's been three weeks since the murder. You should have arrested someone by now."

"Scotland Yard does not rush an investigation, Miss Worthington. I must have irrefutable evidence before taking action. Right now, I don't have enough to charge anyone." A rueful smile rolled across his lips. "That is more than I should tell you."

Well, thank heaven for small mercies. At least he didn't have sufficient evidence to take Ned into custody. But it was not nearly enough information. I needed more. A lot more. While I mulled over my strategy as to the best way to proceed, I studied him.

"Are you memorizing my face so you can sketch me later, Miss Worthington?"

Exactly what I was doing, insufferable man. "You missed a spot."

"What?" Well, that threw him off kilter.

"When you shaved. Right there." I pointed to the right side of his face. "Not only that, but your collar is starched and ironed, but you didn't tuck it down. All of which suggests you were in a rush this morning."

His gaze narrowed to a sliver. "Observant little thing, aren't you?"

"Yes, Inspector Crawford. I draw. I sketch. I notice things. Right now, you're exasperated with me. Your breathing accelerated since I entered the room. A small line of perspiration dots the skin above your lips."

"Christ."

"Oh, and you blaspheme as well. Tsk. Tsk."

A knock sounded on the door, and the inspector yelled, "Enter."

A fresh-faced young officer stepped in. "Begging your pardon, Sir. But Inspector Brown has a question about one of your cases."

"I'll be right there." He turned back to me. "As you can see, I'm quite busy. If that will be all?"

Wishful thinking on his part because I was not about to leave. "No. It's not. I'll wait upon your return."

He harshed in a breath. "Excuse me," he said, before dashing out the door.

Having long ago acquired the ability of reading upside down, I'd noticed the file folder on his desk was clearly labeled 'Rose Trevvyan'. Without even one iota of regret, I flipped it open. A photograph of Rose spilled out. Covered with a sheet, she was still as death. Of course, she was. Clearly, it had been taken during the postmortem. I swallowed hard. But with no time to indulge my sensibilities, I flipped to the medical examiner's report and skimmed through it as quickly as could. 'Cause of death cyanide. Death probably occurred within minutes of ingesting the poison.' Nothing new. I already knew that from the inquest. I continued scanning the report and found something I didn't expect. 'No evidence of pregnancy.' The pathologist had not mentioned that at the inquest.

She'd blackmailed Ned by telling him the child she was carrying was his and yet she had not been pregnant. I flipped to another section labeled evidence and found a note on a torn, crumbled piece of paper. "I need more blunt. If you want me to keep mum about your dirty little secret, bring another 200 quid to Clapham Common next Wednesday at one. Same place as before. If you don't come, I will tell the coppers, and you will hang."

"Miss Worthington!"

Startled, I lost hold of the file.

Inspector Crawford slammed shut the door and marched toward me. "How dare you?" Angry did not begin to describe him.

"I'm—"

"Save your breath. The last thing you are is sorry." He leaned down to recover the folder and the contents which had spilled all over the floor.

I thought to offer assistance but thought better of it. He would neither appreciate nor accept my help. "She wasn't pregnant."

Having secured the file and all the papers, he stood and pinned me with a hard stare. "Saw that, did you?"

"Which means she lied." And probably about more than one thing.

He slammed the folder on his desk and yelled, "Constable."

The same officer who'd accompanied me to his quarters rushed in. "Sir?"

"Please escort Miss Worthington back to the lobby."

"Yes, Sir."

Knowing I would get no more from him, I reluctantly came to my feet. "Thank you for seeing me, Inspector."

He grunted. "I warn you, Miss Worthington. Whatever you think you're doing, don't."

Heavens! He was miffed with me. "Very well, Inspector. I shall do as you wish." I wasn't about to stop, but it wouldn't do to make him even more upset with me by telling him so.

A strange kind of light shone in his eyes. He knew exactly what I was doing. "Just go."

"This way, Miss," the constable said in a rush. He must have noticed the tension in the room.

I walked a silent path back to the building's entrance mulling over what I'd learned. Although it hadn't been much, the implications were tremendous. She'd lied about the pregnancy not only to Ned, but her husband. Could she have used that to force him to the altar? According to Mr. Jackson and Ivy, he'd been supposedly smitten with Rose, but would he have married her if he'd known the pregnancy was a lie? What if he'd found out she'd played him false? Would he have poisoned her to get rid of her once and for all? And that blackmail note. Who was the intended victim? Not Ned. She'd demanded 500 pounds from him which he'd paid. This note asked for a lesser amount. So it had to be someone else. And I was willing to bet it had been someone aboard the train. But who?

Our arrival back at the lobby forced me to stop my mental cogitations. Betsy was still enthralled with the comings and goings as her eyes had grown wide with all the joy of a child at Christmas. As I walked toward her, a miscreant in handcuffs broke free. It took three police officers to take him down while he screamed obscenities.

"Shut your trap, Skeeter. There are ladies present," one of the officers said.

The prisoner responded with a growl.

Time to leave. Last thing I wanted was to get caught up in a commotion. Lowering my veil, I said, "Come Betsy. Let us depart."

"Yes, Miss." She appeared reluctant to vacate the premises but then the whole thing had been a bit of a lark to her.

We did not make a clean exit. Several reporters were loitering outside. As we emerged, they pelted us with questions, which I did not answer. Ignoring them, I grabbed Betsy's arm and hurried down Victoria Street toward Westminster where we managed to flag down a cab.

Only when we were ensconced in the safety of the taxi did I look back. No one appeared to be chasing us. I prayed those news hounds hadn't known who I was. At least, no photographers had been present. But heaven help me if they'd figured it out. In the weeks that followed the inquest, the gossip rags had been relentless. They'd dug up facts about Ned and me, going back to his Oxford days and my Swiss finishing school. Mother, who'd previously enjoyed reading the society columns, now abhorred the arrival of the tabloids. Still, she read every word, which meant she'd grown more and more alarmed with each passing day.

"Those reporters. They didn't come into the building?" I asked Betsy.

"Oh, no, Miss. They're not allowed."

"How do you know?"

"The desk sergeant told me. He was ever so nice. Offered me a cuppa."

Which was a whole lot more than I had been.

"How did it go, Miss?"

"Better than I expected." Not only had I discovered new information about Rose Trevvyan, but I'd found a chink in Inspector Crawford's armor. Somehow, I'd managed to crack his composure. I didn't know how. I didn't know when. But when we met again, I intended to take full advantage of it.

CHAPTER FIFTEEN

A DINNER PARTY

*T*HAT NIGHT, we were holding a dinner party, one made up of friends and clients alike as Father believed such a mix created more interesting social gatherings. Mother, of course, always obliged.

Wanting to make a good impression on our guests, I'd dressed with care, choosing a floor-length midnight blue, short-sleeved beaded gown with a modest v-neckline and matching evening shoes. I entered the drawing room, expecting to see my parents. But to my surprise, I found only Mother, gorgeously attired in a crimson gown. Before these gatherings, she was usually an ocean of calm, but today restless fingers fiddled with her ruby necklace while she paced up and down the drawing room.

I rarely saw her this unsettled. "Is everything all right?"

She looked at me, worry evident in her eyes. "Your father hasn't arrived."

"Maybe something came up at the office." Wouldn't be the first time he'd been delayed.

She offered a tight smile. "He would have called, Kitty, if that was the case."

Just as I was about to suggest we telephone him, the door burst open, and Father rushed in. As his gaze sought Mother's, he had a rather frantic air about him which Mother immediately picked up on.

"Edward. What's wrong?"

It took him a beat before he answered, "Ned was taken to Scotland Yard for questioning."

I hitched a breath. Mother's face lost all color.

"What does that mean?" I asked.

His lips twisted. "They're seriously looking at him as a suspect for Rose Trevvyan's murder."

"But he's not . . . They can't." Mother collapsed on the couch as her hand went to her throat.

Kneeling next to her, Father captured her clenched hands. "Mildred. Ned would never commit such a heinous crime. He just doesn't have it in him."

"But they wouldn't be interrogating him unless they knew something." Her voice wavered. Tears shimmered in her eyes. "What if they charge him?"

"It won't come to that, dearest. They have the wrong end of the stick, that's all." He was trying to soften the blow, but I could tell he was just as worried as Mother.

"If they find him guilty, he'll hang. I can't lose him, Edward. I can't lose another child," she cried. Normally, she was the very rock of our foundation, the person we could rely on the most. But after Emily's death, she'd become more anxious about my siblings and me. The newspaper articles she read incessantly had not helped. And now Scotland Yard's action seemed to make real what she'd feared the most. Action needed to be taken before her anxiety became full blown.

Stepping to the side of the room, I rang for our butler, Carlton. Within seconds, he stepped into the room.

"Mother is indisposed. Can you please alert Cummings?" Having nursed Mother through the aftermath of Emily's death, she knew how to soothe Mother when she became overwrought.

In no time at all, Cummings arrived. It took her but an instant to take in Mother's distress. "Now Mrs. Worthington here you've gone and gotten yourself into a state. That won't do. That won't do at all." It always amazed me how kind she always was with Mother when she was such a martinet to me.

"Thank you, Cummings," I said. "If you could escort Mother to her room and make her as comfortable as you can. She'll need tea, her powders. You know the ones I mean."

She glanced at me, understanding and worry in her gaze. "Yes, Miss. I do."

Father and I silently watched as Cummings tenderly helped Mother out of the room, with her sniffling all the while.

Dropping into the seat Mother had just vacated, Father scrubbed his face. "I hope she . . ." The rest remained unsaid. But then he didn't have to finish. I knew how much he suffered along with Mother. He was just better at hiding his pain.

"Don't worry. Cummings knows how to settle her."

He gazed at the door Mother had just passed through. "Yes, she does."

That had to be enough for now. There were other things to worry about. "She's in no state to deal with our guests, Father," I said, recalling him to the here and now.

"No, she's not." He brushed strong, lean fingers across his brow. Tonight's supper had to be the last thing on his mind.

"It's too late to cancel. The first guests should arrive within the hour."

His confused gaze found me. "But we can't. Not without Mildred."

"I can take her place," I offered.

"You?" His questioning brow told me what he thought about my proposal.

"Yes. Me," I said, as kindly as I could. "Finishing school taught me how to host a dinner party."

"But." His gaze bounced between me and the door before finally settling on me. And then he showered me with a warm smile as if he was seeing me in a new light. "Very well, my dear."

"You'll need to change into your formal attire," I reminded him. Supper was a black-tie affair.

"Yes, of course."

"Don't worry. I'll handle everything." At least, this was one thing I could do for him. He would not need to worry about supper, for I would be the perfect hostess. For once, I was thankful of the instruction I'd received at the finishing school.

After he walked out, I consulted with Carlton about the change of plans. I wasn't familiar with the guest list, but he was. The plan had been twelve for dinner—Father, Mother, Ned, and I. Plus eight guests, which included one client and his wife and a few friends, including Lord Newcastle, whom Mother invited hoping to encourage our courtship. It would never happen. He was in love with someone else. The eighth guest was Father's old friend, Lord Rutledge who often dined with us. With Ned and Mother out, at least the numbers would be even.

"Reset the table for ten, Carlton, please. Mother and Ned won't be joining us."

"Yes, Miss."

It wasn't long before the first of our guests arrived. Thankfully, it was Lord Rutledge. Since he was a close friend of Father, I didn't stand on ceremony with him. After I explained the situation, he agreed to play host along with me until Father joined us.

"It was Robert who caught the case, you know," he said.

Yes, I was exquisitely aware of that fact. But how did Lord Rutledge find out and why did he refer to the Scotland Yard Inspector in such familiar terms? "You know Inspector Crawford?"

"He's the one who saved my life."

"I didn't know it'd been him." Over a decade ago, Lord Rutledge had been set upon by thieves. A brave police officer had interceded, saving him from certain death. The officer had been injured much more seriously than Lord Rutledge. Once he'd healed, Lord Rutledge had been so grateful he'd sent him to Oxford University to earn a degree. Although I'd known about the assault, the identity of his savior was news to me.

"He's meticulous, honorable, as true as they come," Lord Rutledge said.

"He arrested Ned," I bit back.

"No, he hasn't, my dear. He brought him in for questioning. There is a difference."

"How do you know he's interrogating Ned?"

"Robert knows I'm a friend of your family," he continued in a calm tone. "He sent a message so I wouldn't be alarmed by the news."

"What did the note say?"

"What I told you, nothing more. Hopefully, it will be of some comfort to you."

I waved my hand about. "That my brother was dragged down to Scotland Yard?"

"Kitty, it's a murder investigation. Robert wouldn't be doing his job if he didn't get all the facts."

Unfortunately, the 'facts' might very well put Ned's head in a noose. "What if he arrests him?"

"He won't unless he's sure the evidence inexorably points to Ned."

"My brother did not kill Mrs. Trevvyan, Lord Rutledge."

"Then he won't be charged."

"But sometimes"—I swallowed hard—"sometimes the evidence points the wrong way."

"Robert is not easily fooled. He'll get to the crux of the murder. You'll see."

I continued to prod him, but he had nothing more to share. Reluctantly, I allowed the matter to drop.

The next guests to arrive were Lord and Lady Clinton who were quickly followed by Lord Newcastle and our other guests. While we waited for Father, Carlton served drinks all around. As we were winding up the cocktail hour, Father appeared. Deeply apologizing for his delay, he explained Mother was suffering from one of her megrims and wouldn't be joining us. Neither would Ned. He was dealing with something that had come up at the firm. It was so smoothly done, I would have believed him if I hadn't known the truth.

During dinner, conversation flowed freely. But it was not until the ladies retired to the drawing room that the claws came out.

"Isn't it horrible about that murder on the Golden Arrow?" Lady Clinton asked.

It didn't surprise me she'd brought it up. She was a gossip of the worst sort.

"Yes."

"I read the account of the inquest," the wife of Father's business guest said. "Weren't you on the train, Miss Worthington?"

"Unfortunately." Maybe by limiting my responses to one-word answers, they would stop asking questions.

"Did you see anything?"

I'd seen it all, for the murder happened in front of me. But I was not about to talk about it, especially since I had no idea who'd killed Rose Trevvyan. "I prefer not to discuss the subject. It was rather unpleasant."

"It was poison, wasn't it?" Clearly, Lady Clinton was not ready to let the matter drop.

"That's what the papers say." The papers and the pathologist. But I was not about to feed that particular fire.

"Mary Earnshaw was on board as well. If you ask me, the police should be seriously looking at her," Lady Wembley said.

Well, that piqued my curiosity. "Why do you think that?"

"She used to work at a hospital. That's where she and Colonel Earnshaw met. She nursed him back to health, after he was injured during the Boer War."

"Really?"

"Yes. If anybody would know a thing or two about poisons, it would be her." Having spread her own poison, she sat back to enjoy her coffee.

The note I'd found in Rose's file suddenly took on a new meaning. What if it had been intended for Mrs. Earnshaw? What if Rose was blackmailing her as well? After all, Mrs. Earnshaw had fired Rose. Maybe there was some bad blood there. And if she was blackmailing two people, why couldn't she blackmail a third? Like Bertie Jackson.

After the gentlemen finished with their cigars and port, they joined the ladies in the drawing room. I ordered coffee and tea for all.

Once I'd taken care of the other guests, I guided Lord Rutledge to a private corner where we would not be overheard.

"Now what would you want with an old relic like me when Lord Newcastle is present?"

"He's a friend, nothing more."

"Ahh." He gazed expectantly at me.

"About Inspector Crawford."

"He's piqued your curiosity." He slowly sipped his tea, probably determining the best way to proceed. I'd seen him employ that delaying tactic before. "What would you like to know?"

"What is his background?"

"Modest. His father taught school. His mother kept their house. He was an only child, so they doted on him. At age twenty he decided to become a police officer, much to his father's disappointment I must say. He'd hoped Robert would follow in his footsteps."

I noted his empty cup. "More tea?"

"No. Thank you." He rested the cup and saucer on the low coffee table in front of the settee.

"Our . . . encounter happened barely a year after he joined the force. I was set upon by thieves. My fault entirely. I shouldn't have been in that part of London so late at night. I barely suffered a scratch. He, on the other hand, was severely injured."

"How terrible."

"Yes, it was. I got him the best medical care my money could buy. Even so, it took him months to recuperate. But he was young and had a strong constitution, and in time he did. I came to know him very well during that long period of recuperation. Saw great intelligence and ambition in him. The upshot of it was that I offered to pay for an Oxford education. He turned me down. But in the end, I prevailed." He leaned toward me and whispered. "I talked to his parents you see."

I grinned. "You played dirty."

"For his own good, my dear. I couldn't allow such a wonderful intellect to go to waste."

I laughed much as he intended me to do.

"After his graduation, I exerted my influence to get him a position at Scotland Yard. But the Great War intervened." He grew serious. "He felt it his duty to volunteer. I argued against it, but there was no gainsaying him."

"He made it through, though."

"After he was injured. Again. Once he healed, he was eager to return to the battlefield. I vehemently argued against it. With so many men fighting the Huns, the Metropolitan Police ranks had been depleted. He could just as well fulfill his patriotic duty at Scotland Yard as the front. But he still balked. So I played my ace. I reminded him his father was all alone. His mother had passed, you see."

I gasped. "You guilted him into it."

"Yes, my dear. I did. And I'd do it again, should the need arise."

"And now he's a detective inspector at Scotland Yard."

"I arranged the initial opportunity. The rest was up to him. It's his own industry and intelligence that has gotten him this far."

"He never married?"

"No." He gazed off into the distance. "There was a flutter when he was off at school. Nothing serious as it turned out. And now, of course, his total devotion is to Scotland Yard and the law."

"I . . . see."

"Kitty, my dear." He availed himself of both my hands. "I know your curiosity about Robert stems from your worry about Ned. But do I also sense a more personal interest in him?"

I freed myself from his hold. "Whatever gave you that idea?"

A small smile rolled across his lips. "Call it an old man's intuition."

"You are not old." He was barely a decade older than Father, and he was in his fifties.

"As always, polite to the core."

I came to my feet. It was time to draw this discussion to a close. "If you'll excuse me, Lord Rutledge. I must attend to the other guests."

"Of course, my dear." I didn't fool him for one second. He knew I was fleeing because his remark had made me uncomfortable. He was right, of course. I was interested in Robert Crawford, the Scotland Yard Inspector. But I was also drawn to him as a man. Not that I'd ever admit it.

CHAPTER SIXTEEN

KITTY VISITS NED

I NEEDED TO KNOW what transpired between Ned and Inspector Crawford, so I decided to pay my brother a visit. To my surprise, I didn't encounter any opposition from Mother. Just the contrary. She encouraged me to talk to Ned and 'get the goods.' I blamed her use of slang on those lurid detective stories she'd been reading. But I was happy to see her on the mend.

With Betsy in tow, we made our way to Worthington & Son, Father's firm, situated in London's financial center close to the Royal Exchange. As I opened the door, a cacophony of sounds assaulted my ears. Royal typewriters, Burroughs adding machines, a teletype apparatus, all battled to see which created the greatest noise. At least a dozen desks dotted the left side of the space, with as many men behind them. On the right, six women were busily typing away. One was attached to some sort of dictation equipment.

The receptionist—a matronly figure in a dark business dress, her hair styled in Marcelled finger waves— snapped to attention as soon as we stepped in the door. "Miss Worthington."

"Hello, Dotty." She'd worked forever for Father. Nothing happened in the firm she didn't know about.

"Are you here to meet with your father?" She darted a glance toward the back. "I'm afraid he's meeting with a client."

"No." I smiled to put her at ease. "It's Ned I wanted to see. Is he available?"

"Yes. Would you like me to announce you?"

"No need. I'll show myself in." I didn't want Ned to dream up an excuse not to talk to me.

After directing Betsy to one of the seats in the reception area, I strolled past the myriad of busy bees to Ned's office in the back of the space. After knocking on his door, I entered without waiting for a response.

"Kitty!" He rose to greet me. Dark shadows haunted the skin beneath his eyes. Something I hated to see.

"Hello, Ned." I dropped a kiss on his cheek before availing myself of the fine art nouveau armchair in front of his desk.

His brow wrinkled. "Anything wrong? It's not Mother, is it?"

"She's fine," I assured him. "She's up and about, discussing menus with Cook."

He breathed a visible sigh of relief. "That's good. I was worried. Father said—"

I waved away his concern. "A minor ailment. Nothing to worry about." Actually, it had been more serious than that, but he had enough on his plate. No sense piling more trouble on it, especially since he'd probably blame himself for her upset.

"That's good to hear." Somewhat less tense, he leaned back into his seat. His oak desk was neat as a pin. Two wire baskets occupied opposite corners, each filled with folders. A telephone and an adding machine took up the rest of the surface. "What brings you here?"

"I wanted to discuss my settlement. We never finished our conversation on the train. Since my birthday's coming up soon, I thought this would be a good time to talk about the terms." My real reason for my visit was to find out what Inspector Crawford and Ned discussed the night before. But it was best to open with a discussion about my settlement, something he'd feel comfortable discussing.

"Let me fetch your folder." He walked toward a mahogany cabinet on the side of the room, unlocked it, and retrieved a file.

After popping it open on his desk, he rambled on about my inheritance and the investments he was making. But after several minutes of mind-numbing details, half of which I did not understand, I deemed enough was enough.

"It all sounds wonderful, Ned."

Appearing much more relaxed than when I'd arrived, he smiled. "Yes, it is, if I say so myself. Do you have any suggestions? I would be glad to take them into consideration."

"I don't now. Maybe later."

"Very well." He closed the file and glanced expectantly at me. "Anything else you'd like to discuss?"

Just the opening I needed. "Yes, actually there is." I cleared my throat. "What happened yesterday at Scotland Yard?"

His brow wrinkled, but he answered my question nonetheless. "I was . . . interrogated by Inspector Crawford."

I knew that much but not what was discussed. "What did he ask you? What did you tell him?"

"He knew about the blackmail, so there was no point in denying it. He also showed me a note he'd found in Rose's purse. The language was similar to the ones I received."

"But not the same."

"No. She demanded more money from me. A lot more."

"So it stands to reason she was blackmailing other people as well."

He templed his hands. "That's the only logical conclusion."

"I think it could be Mary Earnshaw," I suggested.

"Why?"

"She hired Rose right out of the orphanage. She worked there for three years. But then some silver pieces went missing. According to her, Rose was the culprit, so she terminated Rose's employment. Without a reference, of course."

"How did you find all this out?"

"From Mrs. Earnshaw herself. Mother and I visited her to find out how Col. Earnshaw was faring."

His head bowed while he pondered the ramifications. "But that was all in the past. The note mentioned something the blackmailed person was doing right now."

"Yes, 'a dirty little secret'," I said.

His head jerked up. "How do you know what was in that blackmail note?"

I hadn't told him I'd been making inquiries, mainly because I knew he wouldn't approve. The visit to Mary Earnshaw had been innocuous enough. But meeting with Inspector Crawford was another thing altogether. There was no purpose to the meeting other than I was investigating the murder. Even though Ned would be angry at me, I had to tell him the truth. "I visited Inspector Crawford yesterday. When he had cause to step out of his office, I read his file on Rose. Or part of it anyway."

"Kitty." He frowned. "That's outrageous behavior."

"Oh, please Ned, don't get on your high horse. I can't sit still while you're blamed for something you didn't do."

"It was just an interrogation. He hasn't charged me with anything."

"Not yet," I pointed out. "Tomorrow, who knows? Besides, that's not the only thing we have to worry about. Have you seen the newspapers?"

He dismissed my comment with a wave of his hand. "You know I only study *The Financial Times*."

"Well, you really need to read some of those gossip rags. Those vultures are circling around us. Why do you think Mother was so upset last night?"

"I thought you said she was fine."

"Today. Last night was a different story. She's worried about you. Those sordid papers she subscribes to have been particularly nasty."

His face grew pale. "What are they saying?"

"They know about Rose's blackmailing scheme. How long do you think it'll take them to point the finger at you? Did any reporters see you at Scotland Yard?"

"I don't think so. It was pouring when I arrived. I had my brolly with me."

"Well, thank heaven for that. There was nothing in the tabloids this morning about your interrogation. Maybe they won't find out." Unless some enterprising reporter bribed a low-level police officer.

"I'm not the only suspect, you know," Ned said in his defense. "Bertie Jackson, Jack Trevvyan. Even Ivy Burton. We were all hovering around Rose before she became deadly ill."

"Ivy didn't offer her anything to drink, did she?"

"No."

"So the only three viable suspects are Jackson, Trevvyan, and you. Right now, I don't see a motive for Mr. Jackson to kill her. Do you?"

He shrugged. "Not anything I can think of."

"Her husband said he regretted marrying her, but I don't know if he'd go so far as to kill her. Which leaves . . ."

"Me. It leaves me. I swear, Kitty, I didn't kill her."

I reached across the desk and covered his hand with my own. "Oh, Ned, of course you didn't."

"Why do you believe me?" His voice choked with emotion.

"Because I know you. You're my big brother, the one who always watched out for us when we were growing up. You don't have an evil bone in your body."

"You don't know what I'm capable of."

For a moment, I was thrown by his comment. But then it came to me. "Something you got up to with Rose, I suppose."

His face flushed, confirming my suspicion. Ned was a grown man. If Rose agreed to whatever happened between them, who was I to judge?

"Was it consensual? What you did with Rose?"

His head snapped up. "Of course, it was. I would never force—I could never—I'm not discussing this with you." His complexion turned from pink to a bright red.

I fought back a smile. Although I had no personal knowledge of intimate relations between men and women, I'd heard enough from the more adventuresome students at finishing school to guess. "Very well. Keep your secrets. It shouldn't pertain to the investigation anyway. She wasn't pregnant, you know."

"She wasn't? How do you know?"

"I managed to skim the medical examiner's report. It mentioned she wasn't expecting a child."

He collapsed back into his office chair. "Well, thank heaven for that at least."

"I hazard to guess she not only employed that lie to blackmail you but also to force Jack Trevvyan to marry her."

His gaze narrowed as he considered my statement. "I can see that. She wanted respectability and would have seen him as a way to gain it. All she needed to do was create the illusion of a pregnancy. Once she'd informed him he was the father, he would have had no choice but to marry her. To do otherwise would cause a scandal, and that's the last thing he would have wanted. His employer would have terminated his employment if such a thing occurred."

"It fits, Ned. Once he discovered her blackmailing schemes, the scales fell from his eyes. He saw her for what she truly was. A schemer. He regretted marrying her, but it was much too late for regrets. By that point, he was stuck with her."

A rueful smile rolled across his lips. "She demanded I marry her, you know. That was the reason I terminated our arrangement."

Arrangement. A polite word for a man of means who had a mistress. Ned would have provided for her during their liaison. The place she lived, the food she ate, the clothes on her back. And in return they would have had relations. Rose who'd been fired from a respectable position, whose tavern job had gone up in flames, who'd worked as a hostess at a gambling saloon would have seen her arrangement with Ned as a way to gain security. But she wanted more. She wanted to make it permanent. Which, of course, Ned would never agree to. Once he ended things, she'd come up with the blackmail scheme as a way to ensure a future for her and her new husband. What she'd done was wrong, but I understood what had driven her to do such a thing.

"She wanted more than you could give her."

"It's done all the time, Kitty. At least, while I was her . . . protector, she was safe."

"I'm not judging you, Ned."

"Yes, you are. I can see it in your eyes."

"Well, maybe the pedestal I'd put you on stands a tad lower, and it's a trifle wobblier. But you're still my brother, and I love you. I honestly believe you did not commit this crime."

"Thank you for that."

"You're welcome." I cleared my throat and stood. There was much work to be done to keep that noose from being slung about Ned's neck. "I better go. Mother will worry if I don't return soon. We have a dinner to attend this evening."

He rounded the desk and placed his hands on my shoulders. "Kitty, whoever this person is, he has killed before. He won't hesitate to do it again. Please be careful."

Guess I hadn't fooled him for a minute as to my intentions. "I will." After giving him a kiss on the cheek, I stepped out of his office. "Oh, and by the way," I said loud enough for anyone outside his office to hear. "I'd like a motorcar for my birthday, a roadster. Red, if you can manage it."

I left him shaking his head but in a lighter frame of mind than when I found him. Good. I was going to have to use all the ingenuity and skill I could muster to advance this investigation. Maybe I couldn't prove his innocence, but if I could throw reasonable doubt on his guilt or point Inspector Crawford in another direction, surely Ned would not be charged. Mother could not survive the loss of another child.

CHAPTER SEVENTEEN

A NEW TACT

I ARRIVED HOME to find Mother waiting for me, eager to hear about my discussion with Ned. After barely giving me enough time to hand my things to Carlton, she led me to the drawing room where we would not be disturbed. I'd missed elevenses, so she ordered a light repast of tea and small sandwiches. As was her way, she allowed me enough time to satisfy my hunger before delving into the topic that was uppermost in her mind.

"What did Ned say?"

"First and foremost, he was not arrested, only interrogated. No charges were leveled against him. Inspector Crawford only wished to ascertain facts."

"But Ned had already revealed what he'd seen."

"That's true. But additional information came to light that needed to be followed upon. Ned was called in to clarify them."

Her gaze narrowed. "What information?"

I'd never in my life lied to Mother. Well, not since I was eight and fibbed about stealing biscuits from the kitchen. But if there was ever a time to prevaricate, it was now. "I don't know."

The same brow she'd raised then hiked up now. "You're not speaking the truth."

Should have known she'd catch me out. I've never been able to fool her. "You're right. I'm not. It's not my tale to tell."

She eyed me askance. "I suppose you've been sworn to secrecy."

"I promised Ned, Mother," I said, biting into a watercress sandwich.

"Umm."

Her next logical step would be to demand answers from Ned. Something that would upset him for more than one reason. But she'd never do such a thing. After Oxford, Ned had set up a separate residence so he could lead a private life. Mother knew that better than anyone. She had to suspect he'd enjoyed a special relationship with Rose Trevvyan. After all, enough hints had been dropped in the tabloids.

Seemingly out of the blue, she veered to another topic. "Last night, you spent some time with Lord Rutledge."

She had to have learned that from Father.

"Yes. I asked him about Inspector Crawford."

"Why?"

"He's leading the investigation, and I wanted to learn the measure of the man. I felt Lord Rutledge could provide me with the knowledge I sought."

"Was that the only reason?"

The question was casually delivered, but I knew better. She, like Lord Rutledge, suspected I had a personal interest in the inspector. But that was something I was not ready to admit. "Yes. What else could it be?"

Surprisingly, she asked no more questions. I, on the other hand, had several of my own. Recent events had perked my curiosity about Lord Rutledge. Since Mother had known him for a long time, I figured there was no time like the present to satisfy it. "Why didn't Lord Rutledge ever marry?"

She faced me, lips pursed. "What a question, Kitty."

That expression would have put me off in the past, but I'd grown beyond its power to dissuade me. "To which there must be an answer."

"Of course, there is. He was engaged once. Mind you this was before we knew him, so I only have the information second hand."

"I understand."

"Mere weeks before their wedding, his fiancée died of typhoid fever. It's fair to say he never got over her death. Although he's had plenty of opportunities to marry, he never has." She folded her hands on her lap. "A shame, really."

"What do you mean?"

"His was not a fecund family. He's the only son of an only son which means he has no heirs. When he passes, there will be no one to inherit the viscountcy or the property that goes along with the title."

"What happens to it all?"

"The title, unfortunately, will go extinct, and the property will revert to the Crown."

"All of it?" Many years ago, when Father set out to make his mark on the world, Lord Rutledge had been one of the first to entrust him with his finances. Father had grown it to a tidy sum.

"No. Only the land and his estates. He's free to leave his fortune to whomever he wishes which he'll probably donate to some charity or another. Hopefully, the Ladies Benevolent Society would be one of them." Coming to her feet, she ran a discerning eye over me. "You'll want to have a light wash before luncheon. The city can be so filthy."

Which explained why Mother never visited Father's firm. She preferred the more rarefied air of Mayfair. "Yes, Mother."

"And wear your new midnight blue gown tonight. You'll look quite lovely in it."

It must have arrived while I was at Ned's office. "As you wish."

But before I could get away, she pinned her gaze on me. "How is Betsy doing, by the way?"

I grinned for all I was worth. "Splendid."

"Umm." She could embed so many meanings into that one utterance. In this case, I suspected doubt. "We'll need to revisit the issue when her trial period is over. Just so you know, Cummings is keeping a weather eye on her."

As if I didn't have enough to worry about. The last thing I wanted was to lose Betsy. She'd been invaluable in my investigation into Rose's murder. Her absence would be disastrous.

Rather than a light wash, I decided a soak in the tub was my better option. Mainly, because it would give me time to think about everything I'd learned and my discussion with Ned. While I luxuriated in gardenia-scented suds, it occurred to me there was one person who'd been on the train I had yet to talk to. The waiter. I had to figure out a way to contact him.

Fortune soon favored me in the form of Lord Newcastle, one of the guests at dinner. If anyone could arrange a meeting with the waiter, it would be him. After all, he'd done the same with Bertie Jackson.

When he was seated next to me at dinner, I felt the stars had aligned in my favor. Thankfully, the gentleman on my right was conversing about horses with the lady by his side. That conversation was bound to last a while unless the lady expired from boredom.

Taking advantage of the opportunity, I leaned closer to Newcastle. "Milord, how pleasant to see you once more."

His lips quirked. "Minx. You saw me last night and thoroughly ignored me."

"My apologies. The weight of playing hostess played havoc with me."

"And tonight, you have no such responsibilities."

"None whatsoever." I fluttered my eyes at him.

He laughed.

His action was not lost on Mother who smiled at the seeming rapport between him and me. At some point I would have to reveal we were nothing more than friends. But I couldn't do it now when there was so much happening.

"I gather you want some favor from me," Newcastle whispered.

I sipped from my wine glass. "Ned always said you were right sharp."

Just then the footman appeared with the meat course, a mouthwatering Beef Wellington. By necessity, Newcastle waited until the footman moved on before continuing our conversation. "Tell me what you need."

"The name and address of the waiter on the train."

His left brow hiked up. "That might not be easy to acquire."

"With your contacts?" I scoffed. "I doubt it would take more than two days."

Newcastle not only met my challenge but bettered it. I had the information I needed the very next day. Not only did he obtain an address but arranged a time the waiter—Dickie Collins—would be available to meet with me. However, the information came with a requirement—he insisted on accompanying me. Dickie Collins apparently lived in a less than desirable part of town and his lordship would not allow me to travel there without an escort. Since he'd failed to provide Mr. Collins's address—crafty devil that he was—I had no choice but to agree to his terms.

On the day of the arranged meeting, Newcastle promptly arrived in his roadster at the agreed upon time. Mother, believing he was taking his courtship to the next level, thoroughly approved. Of course, Betsy would need to chaperone, since I needed to avoid the slightest hint of scandal. Just as we were piling into his lordship's motorcar, Marlowe appeared, a bouquet of flowers in hand. He glared at Newcastle, whom he must have perceived as stealing a march on him. As I was eager to avoid a confrontation on my doorstep, I asked Newcastle if he could join us.

Once he agreed, Marlowe climbed into the backseat. An explanation was clearly due him, one I would have to provide. I switched seats with Betsy and joined Marlowe in the back. After swearing him to secrecy, I explained what was going on. To my utter surprise, he threw himself wholeheartedly into the plan, going so far as to offer suggestions as to how to proceed. Maybe he had a secret desire to play Sherlock Holmes.

On our way to our destination, Lord Newcastle provided a thorough explanation about the dwelling located at our destination. Located in London's East End, Dickie Collins's home was part of the newly erected, five story-block Riverside Mansions. Built for workers and their families, it contained baths and running hot water in each flat, communal laundry rooms, a doctor's surgery and even lifts. "They cleared out the slums to build it."

"All those people live together in one great, big building?" I asked.

"Yes," Newcastle answered.

To me, living cheek by jowl with neighbors seemed awfully crowded. But apparently its residents thought it a definite improvement over the previous structures where disease and crime had run rampant.

Upon our arrival, Marlowe opted to remain behind guarding the roadster. A good decision since some sketchy-looking men were loitering in front of the building. Newcastle, Betsy, and I rode the lift to the top floor where we were greeted by the waiter I remembered from the train. The flat was spotless, but sparsely furnished. Only a small sofa that had seen better days occupied the front room. We were introduced to his wife, Molly, and a fussy baby girl who appeared to be but a couple of months old, and then Molly and the infant disappeared into the flat, leaving us to discuss things.

Betsy and I took Dickie's offer to sit on the couch. He and Newcastle remained standing as there was no room for them.

"I can't offer tea and such. We're plumb out." Dickie's face flushed red.

I smiled to put him at ease. "There's no need, Mr. Collins."

"Dickie, please."

"Very well, Dickie." I edged closer to the edge of the sofa as I'd felt a spring against my back. "Do you know why we're here?"

"The note explained you wanted to talk about the murder on the Golden Arrow?"

"That's right."

"I already talked to the bloke from Scotland Yard."

"Inspector Crawford."

"That's the one. I tell him." He stopped. "I told him I didn't see nothing."

"I understand. But I'd like to hear it from you. Could you take me through it, please?"

"Like I told him. I come around and took the orders, friendly like."

"Yes, you were. And polite too."

"Ta. I started on one side, like I always do. Then I fetched the drinks and food. I brought you coffee, tea, sandwiches, and soup."

"You remembered."

He puffed up with pride. "I never forget an order."

"That's a wonderful skill to have." He seemed quite bright and a hard worker. Pleasant, as well. All useful qualities for a waiter to have.

"Done with that side of the train, I moved to the other passengers. That lady, the one who died. She didn't look too good."

"No, she didn't."

"The bloke who was with her told her she needed chamomile tea. Ladies sometimes order that after a choppy channel crossing. Helps calm a dicky tummy, you see."

Newcastle made some sort of sound which I roundly ignored. "How splendid of you to know that."

"Well, it helps the passengers. I'd rather give them tea than have them ride the white bus and me having to clean it up."

Though I'd never heard that expression, I got the gist of it. "That sounds most unpleasant."

"It is."

"So did you get the tea?"

"I couldn't. The older lady with the fox collar. Well, she wanted to be waited on next. So I took her order. But then the bloke, he got up and said he'd get it."

"What did you do then?"

"Well, Miss, that's my job. It's the whole point of me being there, innit?" Upset did not begin to describe him.

"Of course, it is."

"I chased him to the bar car. That's where the kitchen is. He ordered the tea with me all the while saying let me take care of it, sir. But he paid no attention to me."

"How rude."

Dickie softened a little. "He was worried about his lady friend, that's all. My Molly, she was awful sick while she was expecting our little one. The mornings were the worst."

"So I've heard. Did you get the tea right away?"

"The kitchen was crowded like and we had to wait for the order. But when it was ready, the cook put it on a tray. But the bloke didn't pay no mind. He grabbed the cup and plate and rushed right back with it. It sloshed all over the place."

"How very unfortunate. He chanced having no tea at all."

"That's what I thought, Miss, but he wouldn't let me do it. By the time we got back to his lady, tea had spilled all over the saucer. It was a right mess."

"What happened next?"

"A couple of blokes were at the table. They were trying to help the sick lady. When she wouldn't take her medicine, the woman with the fox collar asked her companion to help out. She came over and told the sick lady to take her medicine, that it would be over soon. But the sick lady refused to take the medicine from her husband. She wanted the young bloke to give it to her. Funny way of putting it if you ask me, Miss."

"Yes. So did she take the medicine from the young bloke?"

"She did. Right after, she made a face and said it was vile."

So far, he'd gotten everything right. "And then what?"

"Her husband told her to drink the tea, that it would wash the bad taste away."

"And did she?"

"Not right off. It needed sugar. But there was no bowl on the table because he didn't take the tray, like I told him to. That's where the sugar bowl was, Miss," he said in his defense.

"I understand. Did she get her sweetener?"

He nodded. "The older lady with the red hair offered a sugar bowl, and the sick lady's husband dropped two cubes in the tea."

"And then what?"

"She started to shake, and her face turned a weird color. And then she said "Oh, God. I'm going to be sick." She got up and stumbled. Her husband got her to the loo. And then—"

No need for him to finish the telling. I knew. "And then she died."

"Yes, Miss."

"Anything else you recall?"

He thought for a long time before he responded, "No. But the thing is Miss. She seemed familiar like. But I couldn't place her. It was after I came home I remembered. She was at the orphanage, Miss. That's where I grew up. I was a foundling, left at a church." His gaze darted down as if he was embarrassed by that admission.

"Were you really?" How very sad to be abandoned by your mother.

"Yes, Miss. I lived there until I turned sixteen. They kept the boys separate from the girls, even at the yard."

"The play yard?"

He nodded. "But we were only kept apart by a fence. So, we could see each other. The woman who died. She was there."

"Rose Trevvyan? I'd known she'd grown up in the orphanage, so it was not a revelation.

"Yes. She was Rose Miles back then. I know the other one too. The one who helped her. You see, I have a really good memory. I remember orders, and I remember faces."

"How very splendid." His recollection did not reveal anything new. Ivy herself had told me she'd been at the orphanage at the same time as Rose. I asked him several questions about Rose's background, but he had no knowledge of her origins. I would have to find out another way.

"Dickie, I need to know more information about what went on at the orphanage."

"Those records are probably sealed, Miss Worthington," Lord Newcastle said, a tinge of disapproval in his voice. One I would need to ignore. Faint hearts never won a battle. And this one I needed to win for Ned's sake.

"I can get them for you, Miss," Dickie said.

My ears perked up. "You can?"

"I know people who work there. They'll give me those records. It will cost you, though."

Of course, it would. "How much?"

He thought about it. "Five pounds? Maybe more?"

Unfortunately, I had no money on me. "I can get it for you tomorrow. Will ten pounds do?"

"Yes."

"And I'll add more for your troubles."

"Nah, Miss, you don't have to pay me nothing."

Mrs. Collins suddenly emerged from the depths of the flat, extremely agitated. "You ask for money, Dickie."

His face turned bright red. "Molly, don't."

"You have no job. No way to pay the rent. You ask for money."

Shocked to my very core, I asked, "What happened to your position at the Golden Arrow?"

"They let him go." Mrs. Collins turned to me. "That Scotland Yard blighter told him he couldn't leave town. How is Dickie supposed to do that when he works on a train?"

Obviously, their situation was dire, especially with a new baby. No way I would allow that child to suffer. I faced Newcastle. "How much do you have on you?"

"Enough." He may have disapproved about obtaining orphanage records, but he felt the need to help this family as keenly as I did.

"Give me twenty pounds."

"No. Miss. It's too much," Dickie protested.

After Newcastle handed me the money, I passed it to Dickie. "This is a down payment. I'll give you another twenty once you get me what I need. The files on Rose Miles and Ivy Burton." Might as well find out if Ivy was telling the truth about her relationship with Rose. "If you can manage it, I want to know about their friendship, too."

"Ta, Miss," he said pocketing the money. "I won't let you down. But Rose and Ivy weren't no friends."

That surprised me. "They weren't?"

"No, Miss. They were sisters."

CHAPTER EIGHTEEN

A REVELATION

*D*ICKIE'S REVELATION ASTOUNDED ME. Why would Ivy hide her relationship to Rose? Did she think Lady Ainsley would frown on her connection to a gambling saloon hostess? Would Ivy have feared dismissal if Lady Ainsley found out Rose was her sister? As much as Lady Ainsley prized her title, she certainly would not have wanted that taint on her. Or could it be her sister's betrayal had cut Ivy so deep she didn't want to acknowledge it? Whatever the reason, the fact remained. She'd lied to me. Or at least she hadn't told me the entire truth. It was something I needed to investigate.

Dickie was as good as his word. Barely two days passed before I received a note from him. He had the information I needed and could meet in Grosvenor Square across the street from where I lived. I dispatched Betsy with a response setting two o'clock the next day as the time.

His note was written in a beautiful cursive hand. That did not surprise me. The orphanage, after all, prided itself on teaching penmanship to its students. There had to be a position where his hardworking qualities and pleasant personality would be of benefit. Or maybe he could get his job back. After the matter of Rose's murder was settled, I would ask Father to intercede on his behalf. In the meantime, I vowed to help Dickie and his family in any way I could.

At the agreed upon time, Betsy and I set out, accompanied by Sir Winston, who was pleased as punch to be liberated from the house. With no set course in mind, we roamed around the park. When I spotted Dickie behind an oak tree, I handed Sir Winston's leash to Betsy and made my way to him.

Pleasantries exchanged, he handed me the files. "Begging your pardon, Miss, but I have to return them to my friend tonight. The coppers have been sniffing around, and he'll get into trouble if they're found missing."

"I understand." A quick peek told me the folders contained a myriad of papers of assorted sizes, many of which included notations. I needed time to review the contents. Unfortunately, that was something I did not have. I pointed to the nearest bench. "Here, let's take a seat."

His nervous gaze darted here and there. "Better not, Miss. Might look dodgy. I ain't quality." He was clean and neatly dressed, but his pants, shirt, and coat branded him as one from the lower class. To be seen together would call attention to him and me. Something neither of us wanted.

"Ah, I see. I'll be as quick as I can then."

"Yes, Miss."

After perching on the bench, I opened Rose's folder and skimmed through it. She'd entered the orphanage after her mother died from consumption and remained there until she'd gone to work for the Earnshaws. Although she'd performed adequately in her studies and had learned the skills to enter domestic service, she hadn't distinguished herself in any way.

One item in the file grabbed my sudden attention—Rose's birth certificate. It had been signed by both her mother, Martha Burton, and her father, Albert Jackson Miles. It didn't take a great leap of logic to determine Bertie Jackson was her father. Granted, Albert Jackson was a common enough name, but the coincidence was too great to ignore, especially when he'd mentioned Rose resembled a woman he'd once loved.

I was so absorbed by the contents of the file, I didn't notice the man in front of me until I heard the deep, sonorous tone of his voice.

"Miss Worthington."

My heart lurched, as I gazed up. Of all the places my nemesis could be, he had to be here. Tucking the folder against my side, I greeted him with a smile. "Inspector Crawford. How pleasant to see you."

His right brow quirked up at my lively greeting. Our previous encounter had not exactly ended on friendly terms. He frowned while his gaze searched my nearest surroundings. "You're not here by yourself?"

"Of course not. My maid Betsy accompanied me."

"Where is she? Shouldn't she be watching over you?" He was dressed in a herringbone pattern suit, a white shirt, and a tucked-in tie that showed him off very well indeed. Same as every proper Englishman who inhabited London, he carried a black umbrella.

"She's with Sir Winston. They're off in the park somewhere." I scanned the distance, but they were nowhere to be seen.

"Sir Winston? Do you mean to tell me your escort abandoned you to wander off with your maid?" His lip curled in disgust.

"Well"—I fought back a smile—"He's not exactly my escort."

"Well, what is he, pray tell?"

I thought to tell him the truth, but I was enjoying his outrage too much. "A dear companion."

"Whatever he is"—he huffed—"he shouldn't have left you unprotected."

Taking affront, I arched a brow of my own. "I can protect myself, you know."

He returned a storm-filled gaze to me. "Somehow, I doubt that. I grant you this is not the sort of neighborhood one is likely to find the criminal element, but you need to be watched over."

"Why?" I wasn't just asking; I truly wanted to know.

"I just explained it to you."

"No, you didn't. You provided your opinion but failed to include a reason."

"Very well. Aside from the fact a footpad could be near by—"

"In the middle of the day, in Grosvenor Square?" I scoffed.

"You think crime only occurs in the dodgier parts of the city?" If the expression on his face was anything to go by, he believed me incredibly naive.

"Of course not, but we enjoy a great deal of protection, Inspector. A whole cadre of police officers guard the square. Why, there is one now." I nodded to a young man wearing the blue uniform of the Metropolitan Police approaching us now. "See?"

"He can't be everywhere."

"Several patrol the area. So, you see, I'm perfectly safe." I offered him my sweetest smile.

"You still need a chaperone. If you were seen alone talking to a man, your reputation would suffer."

"Isn't that what you're doing now? Talking to me while I'm alone?"

"It's different." It's a wonder he could speak through his gritted teeth.

"How?"

"I am an officer of the law." He searched the surroundings. "In which direction did Sir Winston and your maid travel? I need to have a word with him."

Before he could hare off on a wild goose chase, Betsy's voice screeched out, "Sir Winston, come back here. Don't run away." A squirrel darted in front of us chased by my beloved hound, barking up a treat.

Inspector Crawford silently watched the merry pursuit before turning back to me. "Sir Winston is a dog?" he asked, outraged.

"There are no flies on you, Inspector," I said, fighting back a grin. It would not do to laugh at him.

Arriving with her hair windblown, Betsy curtsied and wheezed out, "Begging your pardon, Miss," before taking off after the miscreant.

Off in the distance, Sir Winston almost caught up to the squirrel.

But just as he was about to snap his jaw on the hapless creature, the squirrel ran up a tree. Sir Winston howled in triumph. After all, he'd cornered his quarry.

"That dog needs discipline," Inspector Crawford said.

"No, he doesn't," I said. "He's perfect the way he is." Aside from his occasional stomach troubles, that is.

"What do you have there?" Inspector Crawford pointed to the files, suddenly changing course.

I tossed the leather bag I brought with me over the folders. Anticipating the need to fit a couple of them into it, I'd chosen a roomy one I'd used to tote schoolbooks. "Nothing of interest to you."

His brow curled with doubt. "You wouldn't be doing a spot of investigation into the case?"

"Of course not. You've warned me off. I would never disobey a direct order from Scotland Yard." A drop of moisture suddenly fell on me. While we were bandying words, dark clouds had rolled in and were threatening to break loose. In no time at all, rain would pour down.

"Looks like the weather has turned," he said. "And here you are without an umbrella." He popped his open. Stepping closer, he held it over me and politely asked, "May I escort you home?"

I shivered. From the sound of his voice? From the nip in the air? We were suddenly enclosed in a world where it was just him and me. No one else existed. But a few moments ago, we'd been adversaries, playing a cat-and-mouse game if you will. But now it felt different, as if he wasn't asking merely to be polite. Maybe it wasn't real. Maybe it was wishful thinking on my part, but I couldn't deny my attraction to him. Whatever it was, it needed to end. "It's not necessary, Inspector. It's but a few steps."

"But who knows if Sir Winston should prove recalcitrant once more." His smile threatened to knock me down for the count.

But I couldn't have that. "Unlikely. He knows where his comforts lie."

As if to prove my point, Sir Winston gave up his pursuit of the squirrel and rushed toward us with my sprite of a maid gamely holding his leash.

"Betsy, this is Inspector Crawford." It might be bad form to introduce my maid to him, but right now I didn't give a toss.

She bobbed a curtsy. "Sir."

While they exchanged pleasantries, I tucked the files into the leather bag and surreptitiously glanced toward the tree where Dickie Collins had stood. He was no longer there. Not a surprise. He'd probably taken off as soon as he spotted the detective.

Inspector Crawford crooked his arm at me. "Shall we?"

I had no choice but to curl my hand around his elbow. To do otherwise would be churlish. This close I couldn't help but smell his after shave, a combination of lime and bergamot that tickled my senses.

In no time at all, we were in front of Worthington House. As if he'd sensed our arrival, Carlton had already opened the front door and stood ready to receive us. A bright light flashed above us, followed moments later by a crash of thunder. That's all it took for Sir Winston, with Betsy in tow, to scramble up the steps. A fan of storms, he was not.

I couldn't leave Inspector Crawford standing in the open with the imminent prospect of a lightning storm, never mind a deluge. The polite thing would be to invite him into the house. I hesitated. "I would invite you in, but—"

"It would toss the cat among the pigeons?" he said with a crooked smile.

"Something like that." Mother would be beyond herself if she spotted the Inspector inside our home. As far as she was concerned, he was the devil incarnate for interrogating her beloved son.

"Not to worry. I'll hail a cab."

I breathed a sigh of relief. Last thing I wanted was for him to get drenched. "Thank you for escorting me home."

"You're most welcome." His gaze was imbued with warmth and something else, an emotion I did not recognize.

I turned to climb the stairs, but before I took the first step, he stopped me. "Miss Worthington. A word of warning."

"Yes." I swiveled back to him.

He glanced upward toward Carlton who stood ready at his post. We were too far away for him to overhear our conversation, but Inspector Crawford took no chances. Leaning into me, he whispered. "I meant what I said. It would be a mistake to continue your investigation into Rose Trevvyan's murder."

"But I'm not—"

He held up a hand. "Please do not insult my intelligence. I know what you've been doing. You must stop. Any interference will land you in trouble."

In a show of rebellion, I hitched up my chin. "What kind of trouble?"

"It could land you in jail."

I offered him the sweetest smile I could produce. "Then it's a good thing I'm not."

His gaze narrowed, but he didn't say another word. The skies chose that moment to open up.

"Goodbye, Inspector Crawford," I snapped out. Resolutely climbing the steps to my sanctuary, I hoped he got drenched to the skin.

Under Carlton's watchful eye, I made my way to my room where Betsy soon joined me. She'd dropped off Sir Winston in the kitchen in his favorite warm spot close to the hearth. Windblown and disturbed as I was, all I wanted was a nice, hot soak. Thankfully we had no social engagements that evening. Just as well, for the storm did not let up for hours.

Worried about Dickie, I hoped he'd made it safely home. His family needed him. It would not do for him to fall ill. I was less concerned about Inspector Crawford. He would not have been caught in the rain for long. After all, he had the means to hire a taxi.

After a bath and a change of clothes, I settled down to read the files for there was much there to absorb. I stopped only long enough to join my family for dinner. But then, claiming I had a headache, I made my way back to my room. As I reviewed the files, I discovered not only the dates Rose and Ivy had been residents of The Children's Place, but their activities throughout their time. The orphanage believed in not only educating the students in their letters and numbers but teaching them a trade as well. Most of them were trained for domestic service, but there were a few who possessed other talents. Ivy had been one of them.

After developing an affinity for nursing, she'd been assigned to the orphanage's infirmary where she'd assisted the matron. Whenever another student became ill or suffered some other calamity, Ivy had been called upon to help. She'd been so good she'd been recommended for a nursing program after she graduated out of the orphanage. But somehow, she'd ended up in Lady Ainsley's employ, as a tweeny.

What had propelled that decision I could only imagine. Since Lady Ainsley was a patron of the Children's Place, she'd more than likely enjoyed preference over the students. For some reason, she'd chosen Ivy to come work for her. And poor Ivy had been delegated to menial work instead of the nursing program which would have meant a brighter future.

Just as I was finishing my study of the files, Betsy appeared. Dickie had shown up at the kitchen door eager to get them back.

"Don't tell me he remained outside in this deluge all this time?"

"No, Miss. He found shelter in a pub not far from here."

"Thank God. Ask Neville to drive him home." Mother had no plans for this evening, so our chauffeur was free.

"Oh, no, Miss. That won't do."

"Why not?"

"If he arrived in a motorcar driven by a chauffeur, it might cause him trouble."

"What kind of trouble?"

"The kind where he'd get hurt. They don't like people getting ideas above their stations in that part of London."

I was outraged for Dickie. "That's ridiculous."

"Yes, Miss."

"I suppose taking a cab would also be out of the question."

She nodded.

"Very well." I handed the files to her, along with the promised twenty pounds tucked into an envelope. The money, minus the five Dickie would have passed on to the orphanage employee, would go a long way toward supporting his family while he was unemployed. I had to satisfy myself with that.

Betsy returned in no time at all. She reported Dickie would take the underground to avoid the remnants of the storm. He'd also told her he knew someone who worked for the Earnshaws and would share information, if needed. For a fee, of course. Apparently, Mary Earnshaw did not pay her retainers well, and they were amenable to bribes. Somehow, that detail did not surprise me.

CHAPTER NINETEEN

FAMILY TIES

*T*HE SHOCKING DETAILS in the orphanage files required explanations. Both Bertie Jackson and Ivy Burton had hidden their relationship to Rose. Why? A desire for secrecy or something more nefarious? Whatever their reasons, I needed to find out, and the only way to do that was to meet with them again. The gambling saloon owner would be the more accessible, given Ivy Burton's time was not her own. So, I sent him a note asking for another appointment. His prompt reply set the meeting for the next day.

Although I'd been ready with an excuse for leaving the house, it hadn't been needed. That morning Cook had developed a culinary emergency. Apparently, the haddock had gone off. With another dinner party scheduled for that night, she and Mother had to put their heads together for a change of menu. So in the end, my escape had been managed quite easily.

At Jackson's, I was led once more to the private office where its owner waited for me. His ramrod-straight posture and thundercloud expression were not the least welcoming. But I was not about to be deterred.

Still, it wouldn't hurt to start things on a less hostile footing.

"Thank you for seeing me, Mr. Jackson."

"What could you possibly want to know now, Miss Worthington?" he barked out.

So much for my attempt to turn him up sweet. I pointed to the chair I'd previously used. "May I sit?" It'd be harder for him to toss me out on my ear if I were seated.

He grudgingly nodded.

I perched on the chair as unobtrusively as I could. "I've come across some information, sir, that I wish to verify."

He folded massive arms across his chest and glowered at me. "And what would that be?"

I took a deep breath. "That you're Rose's father."

In an instant, his bluster vanished, and he seemed to shrink in upon himself. Taking his time, he rounded his desk before heavily dropping into the leather chair. "How did you discover that bit of news?" My statement had taken the wind out of his sails.

"I have my sources, Mr. Jackson. Is it true?"

"Do you mind if I smoke?"

Although I liked the scent of cigars, I'd always hated smoke being blown on my face. But I was not about to deny him, now when it might make him more likely to answer my questions. "No, I don't."

He retrieved a cigar from a humidor, snipped the end, and lit it. Turning his head away from me, he blew out a cherry-scented cloud. After a couple of puffs, he rested the cigar on the round bronze ashtray on his desk. That noble object depicted a golden naked woman holding court. How very appropriate for a gambling saloon.

"'Tis a long story, lass." His voice held a touch of melancholy.

I folded my hands on my lap. "I have the time."

"I came to London many years ago"—a soft smile lit his features—"a ruddy, cocky beggar. I loved the ladies, and the ladies, well, they loved me."

If he thought he would shock me, he had another think coming. I was made of sterner stuff.

"And then one night, I saw her—a barmaid in a low tavern. Angel blond hair, eyes sky blue. I vowed to make her mine; no other man would touch her. Being the blackguard I was, I set about conquering her, but she would not have me. Turned out, she was innocent. In a tavern. In St. Giles. She was a good girl, she was."

"Was she?" That surprised me. St. Giles was the worst area in London, full of thugs and thieves.

"I finally convinced her to let me in, but she demanded one thing from me. I had to marry her. So, God help me, I did. In no time at all, she was with child, and then a girl was born."

"Rose."

"Yes. Beautiful, just like her mother. But the babe proved too much for her. She cried all the time. For months, I found no peace. So I stayed away while I made my mark on the world. An opportunity came up. One I couldn't turn down. But it required me to leave town. Seeing how it would take me away from the misery that was home, I jumped at the chance."

"Did you?"

"Yes, lass. I did." He sighed before taking another puff of the cigar.

He seemed to regret his actions from so many years ago, but it was much too late. The damage had been done.

"I promised to send money to her, that I would return in due time. For a few months, I kept my vow. But then after other opportunities came my way, Rose and her mother became a faint memory. One day I got word from someone I'd known. Rose's mother had moved on. She'd taken another man to her bed. A bed I'd paid for. So, I stopped sending money. A year passed and then many others. I forgot all about Rose and her mother. Until . . ."

He seemed lost in his thoughts. "Until?" I prompted.

"I saw a lass on the streets of St. Giles, the spitting image of the very woman I'd married."

"Rose."

He bowed his head. "Yes. You know the rest. I offered to house her, feed her, give her a job. She was so desperate, she agreed to everything."

"And so she came to work for you."

He nodded. "For three years, she did just that. And then a couple of months ago, she told me she was leaving to get married."

"Did she ask you for money, Mr. Jackson?" I had to know.

A sad smile twisted his mouth. "Figured that out, did you? What a clever puss you are."

I took that as a compliment.

He stubbed out the cigar. "Yes, she did. She needed some blunt to make her marriage a success."

Rose had bitten the very hand that had fed her.

"I offered her a bonus for all the years she worked for me, but it wasn't enough. She needed more." A hard gusty sigh issued from him as his mood turned somber. "If I didn't pay what she wanted, she would tell my wife we were having an affair."

Just like I thought. Rose had gotten a taste for blackmail. She'd demanded money from a person she knew could afford it—her employer.

"Did you pay?"

"Yes, I did." He stared right at me, almost as if he was making a confession. "It was hard seeing what she'd turned into, but I owed her for all the years I hadn't been there for her. I shouldn't have . . . abandoned her. Even if her mother had taken up with another man, Rose was still my daughter."

"Did you ever find out what happened to her mother?"

He nodded. "After Rose came to work for me, I hired a detective to look into it. He found out her mother died of consumption. And Rose had been placed in the orphanage. She lived there until she was old enough to go into service."

"With Mary Earnshaw."

"That's right. You know the rest." He leaned forward. "Miss Worthington, I'm not the young buck I once was. I've worked hard to achieve what I have now. A good and loving wife, a child on the way, a successful business. I would not jeopardize everything I have by murdering Rose. I would have continued to pay to make amends." Tears shimmered in his eyes. Honesty blazed on his face.

I believed him. With nothing more to learn from him, I came to my feet. "Thank you for your time, Mr. Jackson."

"What will you do with the information I gave you?"

"Nothing."

"You won't tell Scotland Yard?"

"No. I believe you loved Rose and would never have hurt her. All your actions from the moment you saw her point toward that conclusion."

"Thank you."

"Whatever for?"

"For believing me." He came to his feet. "If there's anything I can do for you, please let me know."

"I will." And with that parting statement, I sailed out of his office toward where Betsy waited for me. I'd effectively dismissed Bertie Jackson as a suspect, which left Ivy Burton, Jack Trevvyan, and Mary Earnshaw. One of them had killed Rose. Which one? I vowed to find out.

CHAPTER TWENTY

A SISTER'S LOVE

ASTING NO TIME, I called on Ivy the next morning. As before, Lady Ainsley was still in bed, leaving Ivy free to meet with me.

"Good morning, Miss Worthington. To what do I owe the pleasure?" The change in her demeanor was astounding. Where before she'd seemed downtrodden, this morning she was all smiles. Something that was bound to change once I revealed what I knew.

"I discovered some things about your past. Yours and Rose's."

"Whatever do you mean?" The smile disappeared, replaced by a wary expression.

"She was your sister."

Her skin paled. "However, did you discover that information?"

"I have my ways, Miss Burton."

"No doubt you paid off somebody at the orphanage," she snapped out.

Heavens. What a transformation! She'd turned into a shrew. I refused to confirm her statement, though. Last thing I wished was to get someone into trouble.

Stopping and starting in turns, she paced the room, until she suddenly halted in front of me. "Or that worm talked," she hissed.

"What are you talking about?" I said, as calmly as I could.

"Dickie Collins. The waiter on the train. I recognized him from that shock of red hair. He got that from his drunkard father who beat his mother to death," she spit out.

Dickie had told me he'd been a foundling. Poor lad probably was too embarrassed to tell me the truth. But if she thought her statement would make me look unfavorably on Dickie, she'd be wrong. On the contrary, it only served to make me feel kinder toward him. He'd made something of himself and wanted nothing more than to provide for his family. Ivy's father, on the other hand, was a mystery. "Speaking of fathers, you and Rose did not share one."

"No. Hers disappeared, left our mother to fend for herself. At least mine stuck by her until he was stabbed one night over a tankard of ale. With Ma sick as she was, she didn't last long. That's when social services stuck us in the orphanage."

"Where you were housed and fed and taught a trade." That much I knew from Mother's work with the Ladies Benevolent Society.

Her upper lip curled in disdain. "Among other things."

"What do you mean?"

"They birched us, Miss Worthington, when we didn't suit their notions of propriety."

I was shocked. I'd never heard of such a thing happening at the orphanage. "There is no excuse for hitting children. Didn't you complain?"

"To whom?" She scoffed. "Anyone who dared got beaten twice as hard."

"They're not still doing it, are they? Because Mother and Lady Ainsley can do something about it."

"God only knows. You'll never get the truth out of the children."

Maybe so. But there was a way to find out. An independent physical examination by a physician would confirm such abuse. I made a vow, then and there, I would discover if she was telling the truth. If she was, whoever was responsible would be let go.

She took a deep breath, let it out, before she finally came to rest on one of the dainty chairs in the drawing room. Looking sheepishly at me, she said, "I'm sorry I snapped at you."

I didn't believe she was sorry at all. But I needed information from her, so I decided to accept the extended olive leaf. "It's I who should apologize, Miss Burton. I shouldn't have sprung it on you."

Same as my previous visit, she took to worrying her hands on her lap. "No one knows that Rose was my sister. Not even Lady Ainsley. She would not look kindly upon it."

"I understand." Just as I'd thought. Her connection to Rose would prove detrimental to her employment. She'd want to hide that fact from Lady Ainsley.

"Rose was a rabble rouser. Got us into trouble more than once."

Funny. That was not mentioned in Rose's file. But if punishment had been doled out, the staff would not have included it on her record. They would want anyone examining the files to believe everything was above board.

"Things became easier once she left. I put my head down and buckled down to learn a trade. I wanted to work as a shop girl."

"I . . . see." Her file had revealed quite a different aspiration. She'd been assigned to the orphanage's infirmary where she proved proficient at handling the sick and injured. So much so, she would have been recommended to a nursing program when she left the orphanage.

"There would have been more freedom to come and go and would have paid better than a domestic position, too."

I decided to go along with her story to see where it led. "But that didn't happen?"

"One opportunity came open, but it was given to another girl. She wasn't as sharp as me, mind you." Her upper lip curled in disdain.

"How disappointing."

"Domestics is all the fine folks want. A slavey to fetch and carry and clean up after them." There was a bitter tone to her voice.

I could understand her disappointment. She'd been hired by Lady Ainsley as a tweeny when she'd dreamed of becoming a nurse. Still, domestic work was not bad. A person had a roof over one's head, and more than enough food. "But the orphanage always places their students in good homes."

She let out a bitter laugh. "People put up nice shiny fronts when they're out with their kind, but in the privacy of their homes, 'tis another story altogether."

I got the feeling she was no longer talking about herself, but her sister. "Is that what happened with Rose?"

Raising her gaze from her lap, she directed a wary smile at me. "You're a sharp one, Miss Worthington, aren't you?"

Deeming silence the best option, I said nothing.

"At first, everything went fine, but then the colonel got handsy with her. He'd corner her in the drawing room. Told her she needed to give in if she knew what was good for her."

How very disgusting. If it was true. Not only could Ivy be lying, but Rose could have as well.

"That's why she was let go. She didn't steal the silver. That's the excuse Mrs. Earnshaw used to get rid of Rose. She was jealous of her."

Dear God.

Her lip curled in a sneer. "I hope the old goat dies a painful death."

"Why didn't you tell me this before?"

"Would you have believed me?"

"I don't know."

"There is your answer. And that's not all. Mrs. Earnshaw and that attendant, the one who's waiting on Colonel Earnshaw. Well, they have something going on."

Another lie? Or the truth? "How do you know?"

"Servants talk, Miss Worthington. Rose remained friends with the Earnshaws' upstairs maid. The attendant has been slipping into Mrs. Earnshaw's bedroom late at night."

"Could be servants' gossip."

"Servants know a lot about the people they work for, Miss Worthington."

I had to agree with that statement. After all, Betsy knew plenty about my activities, and Cummings was most certainly familiar with Mother's foibles.

"And that's not all." A triumphant grin rode her lips.

I waited on tenterhooks to hear what she would say next.

"Last year, the colonel's older brother passed. He'd never married and left his entire fortune to the colonel. A substantial one, I've heard. Apparently, he owned a diamond mine in South Africa."

This was news to me, but then Mother would not have mentioned it, even if she'd known.

"Rather convenient that the colonel became ill right after he inherited all that money, don't you think?"

"What are you implying?"

"Mrs. Earnshaw worked as a nurse at St. Thomas Hospital. That's how she met the colonel after he was injured during the Boer War."

This much I already knew.

"She knows quite a bit about potions and nostrums. Maybe she's tired of the old goat and wants to hurry his death along. She'd be a rich widow, free to do whatever and whoever she wished."

Dear God. If that is true, it puts an entire new spin on things.

"Why are you telling me this now?"

"I didn't know what you were about before. But I've been hearing things. You're putting your beak in here and there. Scotland Yard, Mrs. Earnshaw, Bertie Jackson."

"How on earth do you know?"

"Like you, I have my sources. If I were you, I'd be looking at Mary Earnshaw. She had the opportunity and most certainly the means to kill Rose."

"What means?" I already suspected it, but I wanted to learn if her thinking aligned with mine.

"The sugar bowl, Miss Worthington. She handed it to Jack. She could have put poison in those cubes."

"Even if what you're saying is true, what motive could she possibly have?"

"Oh, didn't I tell you." A triumphant smile rolled over her lips. "Rose was blackmailing her."

CHAPTER TWENTY-ONE

A SCANDAL AT THE BALL

*A*FTER IVY DROPPED HER BOMBSHELL, it hadn't taken me long to learn how she knew Rose had blackmailed Mary Earnshaw. Jack Trevvyan had told her. Apparently, after Rose's funeral, he'd sent Ivy a note requesting a meeting on her next half day off. Since privacy was of supreme importance, he suggested they meet in the rooms he kept close to his place of business. She'd agreed but arrived heavily veiled so her identity could not be ascertained.

Apparently, he'd apologized for his caddish behavior, stating he should have never broken faith with her. He wouldn't blame her if she wanted nothing to do with him, but he asked her to forgive him. His most fervent wish was to repair their friendship and go on as before.

Ivy, who'd always been the plain sparrow to her sister's bird of paradise, had been unable to deny him. She'd said yes with one requirement—that he ask her to be his wife. After he'd duly proposed, she now envisioned a future as Jack's wife. Of course, they would have to keep their now reestablished relationship secret. No hint of their attachment could leak out while he was supposedly grieving for Rose. Otherwise, his career at the law firm would suffer.

The cheek of the man. To come running back to Ivy after he'd betrayed her with her very own sister. How could he be such a cad? And how could she be foolish enough to accept him?

She'd agreed to a year's mourning period. After all, that was what custom demanded. But she had to be worried about the delay. He'd left her high and dry before. What were the chances he wouldn't do so again? Jack Trevvyan was a handsome man with a bright future at the law firm. More than likely, he was in high demand with the ladies, especially now that his face had been splashed all over the gossip rags and labeled 'The Dashing Widower.' If I were her, I'd be quaking in my shoes.

And another thing. The proposal made no sense from his point of view, either. Why would he agree to marry her? He was already a strong suspect in Rose's murder. An engagement to Ivy would make him even more vulnerable. If Inspector Crawford were to find out, he could conclude Jack and Ivy planned the murder together. After all, Jack had deeply regretted his marriage after he discovered Rose's blackmailing scheme. He couldn't divorce Rose because of the scandal it would cause. So, he would have had to come up with another way out. What if he'd chosen Rose's death?

I had to hand it to him. He'd played his cards right so far. His portrayal of the grieving widower on the train, at the inquest, and, going by the photos in the papers, at the funeral, had been flawless. Which begged the question. Why would he jeopardize the public's sympathy by getting engaged to Ivy? The whole thing made no sense.

The only way to find out the truth was to talk to him. But how to go about it? I doubted he would agree to an interview. Ivy would more than likely caution him against talking to me. Somehow, I had to find a way.

Providence soon smiled upon me, however, the next evening at a ball when Lord Marlowe asked me to dance.

As we whirled around the room to the tune of a waltz, he leaned toward me. "Did you obtain the information you wanted from Mr. Collins?"

"I did. But that prompted more avenues of investigation." I told him what I'd discovered about Bertie Jackson's and Ivy Burton's relationships to Rose.

"Do you suspect them?"

"Not Bertie Jackson. I believe him sincere in his wish to help Rose. Guilt is a powerful motivator."

When the music came to an end, rather than returning to Mother's side, we headed toward the refreshment table where I quenched my thirst with some rather tasty punch before making our way to an alcove where a blue brocade settee invited one to rest. Although in plain sight, the nook provided sufficient semi-privacy to resume our conversation.

"What about Miss Burton?" he asked.

"She's a . . . puzzle."

His brow wrinkled. "How so?"

"I've known her, or rather observed her, for several years. In every instance, she was the perfect companion, fetching and carrying for Lady Ainsley, patiently attending to her every whim. But two days ago, she revealed an entirely different side to her. One who deeply resents her lot in life."

"Wouldn't that be the true Ivy?"

"I imagine. But resentment does not make her a killer. More than anything, she wants to marry Jack Trevvyan."

"How on earth would she accomplish that? He just buried his wife."

I stared him straight in the eye. "They're engaged."

He stiffened as outrage poured out of his every pore.

"Just so." I told him about his meeting with Ivy which had ended with a proposal. "For the life of me, I can't figure out why he would ask her to marry him. If Inspector Crawford were to find out, it would make Jack an even stronger suspect."

"Well"—Lord Marlowe glanced off in the distance—"I can think of one reason."

"What's that?"

His gaze bounced back to me. "A wife cannot be compelled to testify against her husband in a criminal proceeding."

I gasped. So there was a method to the madness. "And I suppose neither could a wife?"

"Exactly so."

"I need to talk to Jack Trevvyan. He is the key to this whole thing. But I don't know how to go about it."

"Leave it to me. I can arrange it for you."

"Are you sure you want to become this involved?" He'd only accompanied us to Dickie Collins's home, but if he arranged this meeting, he'd be even more immersed in the investigation.

"Yes, I'm sure. I'd do anything for you, Miss Worthington." Gazing in adoration, he brought my hand to his lips and dropped a kiss on my fingers.

Oh, heavens. I'd taken his behavior as a light flirtation, something to pass the season. But seemingly, he was dead serious about courting me.

I needed to let him know I had no intention to marry. "Lord Marlowe—"

But before I could continue, a commotion close to us garnered all our attention.

A red-faced Lord Newcastle, eyes blazing, fists clenched, up against Lord Wakefield, the husband of the woman he loved. Between them stood Lady Wakefield, flushed and trembling. The cause of the altercation was not difficult to determine. A purple bruise, no amount of maquillage could disguise, marred her right cheek. Not only that, but her hair was disheveled, and her gown was torn.

"How dare you hit her?" Newcastle bellowed.

A smug look rolled over Wakefield's face. "She's my wife, Marlowe, my property if you will. I can do whatever I wish with her."

This was not going to end well.

"You bastard." Newcastle swung a mean right hook at Lord Wakefield, knocking the older man to the ground.

"Simon, please don't." Lady Wakefield exclaimed, helpless to stop what was happening.

Lord Marlowe wasted no time running toward the melee. I

followed, as quickly as I could, intending to go to Lady Wakefield's aid. Just as I reached her, Mother met up with me.

The vast majority of the guests stood around the scene gawking. Only a few came forth to help. One of Lord Wakefield's cronies, going by his age, helped the lord to his feet. Marlowe was holding Newcastle back. "You don't want to do this, old man. Think of Lady Wakefield. You're doing her no favors."

I wasn't about to stick around to see what would happen next. Grabbing Lady Wakefield's arm, I said, "You must come with us now."

"That's right, dear," Mother said. "Let us take you home."

"But—"

We didn't allow her to object but bundled her out the ballroom door. After directing a footman for our things, we rushed her down the steps of the mansion where our Bentley and Neville waited for us.

After we'd settled in the motorcar, Mother tucked a rug around Lady Wakefield as she was shivering with shock.

"Where would you like to go, Lady Wakefield?" Mother asked. "I can offer you refuge, if you wish." One of Mother's charities was a sanctuary for abused women. I'd never been so proud of her as I was right now.

"Home. I'd like to go home."

Mother looked doubtful. "Are you sure, my dear?"

"Yes. I'll be safe enough. Lord Wakefield won't . . . discipline me again. At least not tonight."

Discipline? Is that what that dastard called it? She may be safe tonight but what about the next day and the day after that? "Why do you stay with him?"

"Kitty!" Mother chided.

A forlorn smile rolled over Lady Wakefield's lips. "Where would I go?"

"Family, friends . . . Lord Newcastle."

Her sad gaze found me. "Miss . . . Worthington, is it?"

"Yes." We'd never been introduced so it was a wonder she knew my name. "And this is my mother, Mrs. Worthington."

"How do you do?" Lady Wakefield said in the cultured tones of one who'd been raised with a silver spoon in her mouth.

"How could you marry such a man?" It wasn't mere curiosity. I truly wanted to know.

"Easily. My family was facing ruin, a result of generations of gamblers, spendthrifts, and ne'er do wells."

Now there was a word.

"Why should you pay the price for their sins?"

"Because I could. My marriage to Lord Wakefield ensured my family would not be turned out of our home and provided security for my younger sisters. I have three."

"But Lord Newcastle could provide—"

She frowned. "No. He could not. He's not my husband. And the scandal would be too great." She patted my hand. "It's not as bad as you think. He goes weeks without—"

"Hitting you."

"Kitty!" Mother again.

"Yes."

"What set him off?"

"I got my courses."

"I . . . don't understand."

"It means I'm not expecting."

"He hit you because you're not pregnant?"

Mother apparently had given up stopping me because she merely tsked her disapproval.

"I'm a disappointment to him. We've been married four years, and I have yet to quicken with child." She glanced down at her fingers. "I'm afraid I'm barren."

Since I had no knowledge of the subject, there was nothing I could say to that. Silence reigned the remainder of the drive. When we arrived at her home, a townhouse across from Belgrave Square, she hugged Mother and me before alighting from the motorcar. Mother had the last word. "If you have need of anything, Lady Wakefield, I'll be glad to be of help. Here's my card."

Taking it, Lady Wakefield stashed it in her purse. Hopefully, she would put it to good use when her situation became too much to bear.

"Thank you, Mrs. Worthington, Miss Worthington." And with that, she gathered whatever dignity she had left and walked up the steps to her house.

"Mother."

"I know, dear." She patted my clenched hands. "But there's nothing we can do. She must take that first step."

I glanced back, but Lady Wakefield was no longer there. She'd made it safely inside. "What will happen to her?"

"Parliament is in session, and Lord Wakefield's presence is required. If she's wise, she'll retire to their country estate while he remains in town."

A separation would certainly prevent any further 'discipline,' at least on a temporary basis. She'd mentioned they'd been married four years. Had she dealt with his abuse all that time? Or was it a more recent occurrence? However long, it was horrible what she had to endure. And all because she could not provide him with the heir he needed to ensure continuity of his title. But was it really her fault? "May I ask a question?"

"Of course, dear." Mother seemed to brace herself. She probably sensed what was coming for I'd been an inquisitive child and grown more so as the years passed.

"Lady Wakefield said she was barren, that she could not have a child. Is that a woman's fault? Or could it be the man's?" My only education about sexual congress came from the discussions at the finishing school and Margaret's 'Yoke of Womanhood' pamphlet. But the latter had focused on the burdens of having too many children, not the actual process.

Mother pinched her lips. The subject was distasteful to her. But she'd never been one to shy away from an answer. "No one really knows, Kitty. But Lord Wakefield was married before and that union did not produce children, either."

"So it could as easily be his deficiency, if you will."

"I would think so."

"And yet, he's holding Lady Wakefield responsible."

"I can't imagine he would ever hold himself accountable. Men like Lord Wakefield rarely do." She allowed some time to pass as she stared out into the night. "Lord Newcastle?"

"Yes."

"He's not a likely candidate for your hand." A statement. Not a question.

"No, Mother. He's not."

"A shame. What about Lord Marlowe? You spent a long time with him in that alcove."

"Umm," was all I allowed myself to say. After all, I didn't want to shatter *all* her hopes in one night.

CHAPTER TWENTY-TWO

A REGRETFUL HUSBAND

*L*ORD MARLOWE WAS AS GOOD AS HIS WORD. Two days after the ball I received a note from him. Jack Trevvyan would be at his house that afternoon at two. The problem now became how to make my escape. As I was running out of reasons to leave the house, I told Mother I'd spotted the most darling tennis headbands at the milliner's, and I just had to have one for Wimbledon.

"Tennis headbands?" She frowned. "Never heard of such things."

"They're made from terry cloth."

"Like towels?"

"Yes. To absorb, er, perspiration. It gets so hot on the stands, you know. Practical and fashionable at the same time."

"Sounds extremely silly to me, but if that's the fashion?"

"It is," I said with as much excitement as I could muster. With Wimbledon around the corner, everyone who was anyone was scrambling for fashionable designs to wear at the tennis match. I had nothing to worry about for my outfit was already hanging in my closet. Angelique had created a darling square bodiced, flower print, dropped waist gown which suited me to a T. All I needed to complement it was a wide-brimmed summer hat to keep out the sun. The tennis headbands had become the latest rage, one I thought would not last. They weren't the least bit flattering.

"Very well, but don't be late," Mother said. "We've been invited to dinner at Lord Rutledge's this evening."

"I won't."

Since Mother had no appointments that day which required the motorcar, I commandeered Neville and the Bentley. Soon, Betsy and I were being whisked down the streets of Mayfair to Lord Marlowe's home at Berkeley Square. As it wasn't far, we arrived in no time.

I'd looked forward to my discussion with Jack Trevvyan, but now I found myself anxious about the meeting. After all, we were not acquaintances. He could refuse to talk to me. Somehow, I sensed he wouldn't, though, if for no other reason than Lord Marlowe would not look favorably on his refusal.

Since I had no wish to be recognized, I'd come heavily veiled. As expected, I found Lord Marlowe waiting for me in the drawing room. "Miss Worthington, what a delightful pleasure to see you."

"Lord Marlowe," I curtsied. Needless to say, my visiting him, even with a chaperone in tow, was not cricket. But since only he and the butler would know my identity, my reputation should remain intact. Rather than being asked to wait in the hallway, Betsy was tucked away in a small room where a feast of tea and scones had been laid out. Her beaming smile told me how pleased she was by his gesture, a delicacy I did not expect.

"Ready?" Lord Marlowe asked.

"As I'll ever be."

"He's in my office. Shall I lead the way?"

"Please."

As we entered, Jack Trevvyan came to his feet. When he turned around, surprise rolled over his face.

"You've met Miss Worthington?"

"Er, yes." Mr. Trevvyan appeared confused by my presence. I couldn't blame him. I'd be as well.

Marlowe took on his loftiest tone. "She has a few questions for you. I would appreciate it if you answered them."

A gentle caution, but a caution, nonetheless.

Mr. Trevvyan's mouth twisted in distaste before he gave in. "Very well."

"I'll leave you to it then." Lord Marlowe said.

"Thank you."

"If you need anything?"

"I'll ring."

Mr. Trevvyan was seated on a tufted leather seat across from a comfortable looking settee. Making my way there, I settled into it. "First of all, let me offer you my sincerest condolences."

He nodded his acceptance.

"No matter what Lord Marlowe said, you don't have to talk to me. You are free to leave, if you wish." If he proved recalcitrant, the interview would not go well, so I needed to provide him with a way out.

"Really?"

"Yes. But I hope you will remain. I'm only trying to discover the truth."

"About Rose?"

"And the manner of her death." I had to be honest so he couldn't claim later on he'd been tricked.

The mantel clock ticked away the minutes while he pondered what I'd said.

"I'll talk to you, Miss Worthington. I want to get to the truth as well."

"Thank you." I took a deep breath and dug right in. "Rose was a rather complicated person, wasn't she?"

"Yes, she was."

"A wife to you."

"And a sister to Ivy," he volunteered.

"She told you?"

"Ivy and I have no secrets from each other. She shared with me the details of your discussion."

"I see. You're aware Bertie Jackson was Rose's father?"

"Yes, Rose informed me before she"—he cleared his throat—"asked him for money."

A rather rosy manner to look upon the blackmail.

"She'd also been my brother's *chère amie*."

He stiffened. "You know that, do you?"

"I do." I allowed a tight smile to shape my lips. "I'm also cognizant of the fact she was blackmailing him."

He took a deep breath, let it out. "I did not approve of her doing that. But she wanted money, lots of it. She thought she could keep it up forever. She didn't realize it was not only immoral but illegal. Or if she did, she didn't care." He fixed his gaze on me. "I tried to get her to stop."

"I know you did."

He startled. "How?"

"I overhead you talking in the hallway at the Paris Ritz," I explained. "You said you regretted marrying her."

He tossed his head. "I didn't mean it. I was angry."

And I knew the reason for his anger. "She could become a liability to your career."

"Yes. If it ever got out, I would be dismissed. And there would be no hope of my obtaining another position. But I was also afraid for her."

"How so?"

"Blackmailers often pay a price. Her death proved me right. Someone killed her."

We'd finally reached the crux of the matter. "You think she was killed by someone she was blackmailing?"

"I do."

"Who?"

His lips curled up in a snarl. "Your brother comes to mind."

"But he wasn't the only one she blackmailed, was he? She demanded money from Mr. Jackson as well."

"Yes."

"Who else? Who else did she blackmail?"

"Mrs. Earnshaw. Rose believed she was poisoning her husband."

"Did she pay?"

"Yes. Although there is no way to prove it. You see, she paid in cash."

Wise woman. "How much?"

He glanced down. In shame? In embarrassment? Who knew? "Two hundred pounds. Twice. Once before we met. A second time after I proposed. I didn't know about any of her schemes until after we'd married. And then it was too late."

"Did you poison her, Mr. Trevvyan?"

His head jerked up at that. "No! I could never—she was carrying my child, for heaven's sakes." He bowed his head. "Or at least I thought she was."

Even though I already knew the answer, I had to ask, "It wasn't your child?"

"It was nobody's child. She wasn't pregnant at all."

"How do you know?"

"The Scotland Yard inspector told me." He took in a big breath. Slowly let it out. "She lied about that and . . . so many other things."

Yes, she did. But she was not the only liar. Ivy had lied as well. And there was one thing I was curious about that concerned her. "Why did you ask Ivy to marry you?"

"What?"

"You're engaged to her, aren't you?" Or did Ivy lie about that too?

"I didn't know she'd told you. But, yes, we are. I shouldn't have broken things off with her. She'll make me a much more suitable wife than Rose ever would have."

"Will she?"

"Of course, she will. She'll be an asset, not a hindrance. And she'll never, ever do me wrong." A boastful smile rode his lips. "She loves me, you see."

Ahh, but did he love her? I certainly saw no such emotion in him. His thoughts were only of himself and his career. Would that be enough to keep him true to his promise? I doubted it. If someone came along who offered a better opportunity for advancement, he would jump at the chance. And Ivy would be doomed to remain a lady's companion forever.

Having discovered as much as I could, I dismissed him. Once he'd gone, Lord Marlowe returned. "How did it go?"

"He gave me much to think about." Mr. Trevvyan had appeared honest in his responses. Much of what he'd said confirmed other things I had learned. But where did that leave me? Ned hadn't killed Rose, and I had my doubts Bertie Jackson would have done such a thing. He honestly regretted abandoning Rose's mother and looked upon the blackmail as a way to make amends. Jack Trevvyan wouldn't have killed her, since he believed she was carrying his child. Which left Mary Earnshaw who could have laced the sugar cubes with poison. But how to prove that would be tricky indeed.

"If I can be of any further help, I'm at your service," Lord Marlowe said with a small bow.

"Thank you, Milord. That's a comforting thing to know." I started to stand, but before I could do so, he cleared his throat.

"Miss Worthington."

Oh, heavens. I knew what was coming. A proposal of marriage. As much as I wanted to avoid his declaration, I had to allow him his say. It was the least I could do after he'd arranged the meeting with Jack Trevvyan.

Sitting once more, I waited for the ax to fall.

"Miss Worthington," he repeated.

"Yes," I prompted wanting to get it over with.

"I was wondering—"

Suddenly, I couldn't do it. I could not allow him to make a cake of himself.

"About our friendship?" I asked, hoping to communicate that's all he was to me.

Encircling my hands with his own, he raised me to my feet. "Our friendship?"

"Lord Marlowe, you are the finest of men. Your family is one of the oldest in England and, if I may be indulged, you are one of the handsomest men of my acquaintance."

He quirked a brow. And did I detect a note of amusement on his lips?

Ignoring it all, I continued, "I know you have a fine fortune and extensive property."

"You leave me speechless, Miss Worthington."

"I cannot marry you," I ended in a rush.

He burst out laughing.

"What?" Did I get it wrong?

"I was not going to propose marriage but invite you to the theatre."

"The theatre?" Where was a hole to sink into when one needed it?

"You mentioned you enjoyed Gilbert & Sullivan. *The Mikado* is playing at the Prince's Theatre for the foreseeable future."

I squinted. "Forgive me, but I'm confused."

He let go of my hands and folded his own behind him. "How so?"

"You make a point of dancing with me at every ball. Two sets if you can arrange it."

"I do."

"You arrive at my home laden with flowers."

He nodded.

"You sought a secluded spot at the latest ball."

"I did."

"But you are not interested in marrying me?"

He tilted his head. "Did you want me to propose?"

"No! I do not, sir." I rushed to disavow him of that notion.

"Miss Worthington, you are a lovely young woman, with a great deal of intelligence, and a member of a fine family. Any man would be fortunate to call you his."

"But not you."

"No. You see, my wife needs to need me. Desperately. Love me, if it can be arranged."

I was outraged on his behalf. "Of course, she'll love you. You're an extremely lovable person."

"Thank you. If I may continue?"

I nodded my assent.

"You are much too independent for my needs. I'd never know where you were. You'd be as likely to be at the modiste's as gallivanting around London in pursuit of a criminal."

"And you can't have that?"

"No. A man likes surety in his wife. Able to put his hands on her, as it were, whenever he wished."

"Oh, my." I could only imagine the manner in which his hands would be laid on Lady Marlowe. I fought back a laugh, but in the end it burst out of me in a most unseemly way. I snorted.

He smiled in return. "Just so."

In total charity with one another, we started for the door, but then a thought occurred to me. "Wait, if you're not interested in me, why are you asking me to the theatre?"

He raised a very aristocratic vow. "You're this season's incomparable, Miss Worthington. One must be seen with you. It raises my social capital, you see."

"You are a rogue, sir. A rogue in sheep's clothing." And here I'd thought him bland and uninteresting. I hoped whomever he married led him a merry chase.

He bowed. "Your servant, ma'am."

Without further ado, we strolled into the room where Betsy waited for me.

"You'll let me know what dates work best for you for the theatre?" he asked.

"I will. Thank you, Lord Marlowe. You're a man amongst men."

He bowed. "Was there ever any doubt?"

CHAPTER TWENTY-THREE

KITTY INVESTIGATES

*A*T DINNER THAT NIGHT, Lord Rutledge apologized for the lack of symmetry in numbers. One guest had sent his regrets. He'd been unavoidably detained and unable to attend. More than likely, it was Inspector Crawford. As his mentor, Lord Rutledge had been diligent about introducing him to high society. An uphill climb in my opinion as the upper class was reluctant to associate with Scotland Yard. Narrow minded, if you asked me. You never knew when you'd need a friend in that place.

The topic around the dinner table was of the row at the ball. Not only had several of the dinner guests witnessed the altercation between Lords Wakefield and Newcastle, but that lurid rag, the *Tel-All* had splashed the details all over its front page. After declaring themselves suitably shocked, the guests proceeded to share the latest on-dits. Lady Wakefield apparently had fled to the country while her dastardly husband remained in town. While no one had spotted Lord Newcastle at any of his usual haunts, it was roundly believed he was still in London, and he was merely playing least in sight. A disappointment to many of the guests who would have enjoyed another round of fisticuffs.

Thoroughly disgusted with the character assassination, I turned to

Lady Emma Carlyle, who was seated next to me. The debutante I'd met at an earlier ball turned out to be a wonderful dinner companion. She was erudite about topics that had nothing to do with the cut of a gown or the latest gossip and was particularly interested in the plight of the poor.

"How's your season going?" I asked when there was a lull in our conversation.

She pursed her lips. "It isn't. Mama's afraid I won't 'take.'" A fate worse than death for most debutantes, the exception being myself and my sister, Margaret. Neither of us wished for marriage proposals.

The correct reaction to her statement would be a show of sympathy, but I sensed she would not welcome such a response. Instead, I asked, "How do you feel about it?"

"I'm disappointed for Mama. She has such high hopes for me."

Don't they all? Even now, Mother was engaged in conversation with a marquis who'd shown an interest in me. The loss of Lord Newcastle as a possible suitor had been a disappointment to her, and she was working hard to replace him in my marriage stakes. Even if I were inclined to marry, the marquis would be an unlikely choice. Not only was he long in the tooth but suffered from a slight paunch. When his smile revealed a set of yellowed teeth, I shuddered and turned my attention back to Lady Emma. "But you don't?"

She shook her head and her very old-fashioned curls bounced on her brow. "I haven't found anyone who's anything more than a fribble. All men talk about are their estates, their motorcars, and themselves." She sighed. "I know I must marry. I just wish some had more weight to them."

We were definitely of like minds. "I agree."

She smiled. "You, however, are a success. Your dance card is always full."

I grinned. "I do love to dance." It was one of the few things that made balls bearable.

"Lords Newcastle and Marlowe seem to be especially interested. Well"—she caught her bottom lip— "maybe not Lord Newcastle."

I laughed. "We're just friends."

177

"Really?"

I nodded. "You might want to take a second look at Lord Marlowe. He's definitely not a fribble." Although I had to agree with her, in public he could come across that way.

She blushed. Could there be some interest there? Worth encouraging if she were.

"I'll consider your advice."

Once dinner was finished, we moved to the drawing room for tea. Wanting to avoid the gossip, I sat next to Lady Emma on a gold settee. "I hope I'm not stepping out of line."

She gazed expectantly at me.

"If I may, and believe me I don't mean it as an insult, but your coiffure seems somewhat old-fashioned."

She laughed. "Seems, Miss Worthington? It's downright ancient."

"Why don't you change it?"

"My maid doesn't have the foggiest idea as to the current fashion. I wouldn't let her near me with a pair of shearing scissors."

I smiled. "Well, goodness, I can help with that."

"Can you?"

"I know the most marvelous place, Antoine's on the West End. He knows what style suits a lady's features best. I can inquire about an appointment if you wish."

Her grin was one of pure excitement. "Oh, please do."

"Capital. I'll send a note around when it's set. I'm due for a trim myself, so I'll probably join you."

We arrived home to the sad news that Colonel Earnshaw had passed away. Mother immediately made plans to pay a mourning call on Mary Earnshaw who, she insisted, would appreciate the support of her friends.

But as it turned out, something else upended her plans.

With nothing on our schedule the following morning, I planned to join her for a coze. Among other things, I wanted to make it emphatically clear the marquis would not do.

As was her usual habit, she searched for the *Tell-All* on the entryway table, as she liked to peruse it over her morning tea. "Where is the paper, Carlton?"

"It was not delivered, ma'am. I do apologize." The tops of his ears pinked up. He was the worst liar.

Mother, however, did not let on. "Did you send for another copy?"

"Begging your pardon. But none can be found."

Mother was a master of the eyebrow. While a hike of her right one expressed surprise. The left one denoted doubt. This morning, it was the latter she employed. "In all of London?"

"Yes, ma'am." A line of perspiration popped up across Carlton's upper lip. I truly felt sorry for the man.

"Carlton, I'm heading to the morning room. Please have someone bring me hot tea and toast. And a copy of the morning paper. If it's not there in the next thirty minutes, heads will roll. Do you understand?"

"Yes, Mrs. Worthington." He bowed.

Fearing the worst, I followed Mother into the morning room where she busied herself with the post. That apparently had no trouble finding its way to our home. Fifteen minutes later, the downstairs maid arrived with a pot of tea, toast, cups. And the morning paper.

After being duly thanked, the hapless maid dashed out the door. Given the servants' behavior, I strongly suspected the newspaper was the bearer of bad news.

"Shall I pour, Mother?" I offered, hoping to delay the dismay that was sure to come.

"Please do." She grabbed the morning paper, wrangled it into submission, and started reading. The longer she read, the stormier her expression became. Whatever news graced the front page was bad.

I considered drawing the bell pull and asking for Cummings to bring her smelling salts, but Mother appeared more angry than ill.

"How dare they?" she snarled.

I extended my hand. "May I?"

She shoved it at me.

179

Financier Dandy Questioned by Scotland Yard. Is an arrest imminent? The headline screamed.

I don't know how the newspaper got all the information, but everything had been laid out in black and white. Ned's relationship with Rose. Her supposed pregnancy. Her claim that Ned was the father. And the *coup d'état*, the blackmailing scheme.

"Was Ned having an affair with that woman?" Mother snapped out.

"How would I know?"

"Because you have been investigating her murder since you arrived home."

What? "How—how did you know?"

"Please, Kitty. We're beyond that now. All those visits to the modiste when I practically had to drag you there for your presentation gown fitting. Now, suddenly, you're eager for an outfit and a headband for a tennis match? Never mind the trips to the library and God knows where else. I wasn't born yesteryear. I know what you've been doing."

And here I thought I'd been so clever. "And you allowed me to do it?" I was astonished, to say the least. Should have known she'd figure it out. I never could get anything past her.

"I was fine with it. As long as you were properly chaperoned, of course. Now tell me what you've discovered."

"Wouldn't you rather talk to Ned?" I said, hoping to postpone the inevitable.

"I can head to his office and ask him questions certain to embarrass him. Do you want me to do that? Because I will." She had thrown off her gloves and was ready to duke it out barefisted.

But she was right. If she asked Ned if he'd engaged in a liaison with Rose Trevvyan, their relationship would never be the same. He wouldn't ever be able to look Mother in the eye again. The details would be better coming from me. Heaving a deep sigh, I asked, "What do you want to know?"

"Everything."

Not holding anything back, I told her about Ned's connection to

Rose, the conversation I overheard at the Ritz, my discussions with Bertie Jackson, Mary Earnshaw, Jack Trevvyan, and Ivy Burton. All the blackmailing details. I also shared my conclusions. That I believed neither Bertie Jackson nor Jack Trevvyan killed Rose. Bertie Jackson because he was Rose's father and Jack because he believed he was the father of the baby she'd supposedly carried.

"They could be lying."

"I don't think so. Bertie Jackson truly appears to regret abandoning his wife and daughter. And Jack Trevvyan's story rings true."

"Wait. What do you mean by 'the baby she supposedly carried'?"

I took a deep breath. "The medical coroner's report confirmed Rose wasn't expecting a child."

She stiffened. "And how do you know this?"

"I met with Inspector Crawford at Scotland Yard. While I was in his office, he had to step out of the room. Rose Trevvyan's file lay on his desk, so I looked at it."

"Without his permission?" Her voice rose in outrage.

"He's a stickler for procedure, Mother. He would have never granted it to me."

"Ummmph." Her mouth puckered up. Clearly, she didn't approve. But then she shrugged. "So where do you stand with the investigation?" Seemingly, she'd come to terms with what I'd done.

However, she would doubt what I was about to say. So, I took a deep breath and marched on. "I think Mary Earnshaw killed Rose."

"Mary?" she choked out.

"I have very good reasons for believing that, Mother. Rose was blackmailing her for supposedly poisoning the Colonel."

"But he's been ill for a year. Every doctor, as well as that Paris specialist, has confirmed he had cancer."

"But what if she was giving him something that made him worse or rushed his death? Remember, Mary Earnshaw was a nurse. Over time, she would have become familiar not only with illnesses and cures, but also medications. Those can be used not only to relieve suffering but to cause it."

"Why would she kill the colonel now. She'd been married to him for over twenty years."

"A year ago, the colonel inherited quite a sizable fortune from his brother. Maybe she wanted to get her hands on it."

"But why? She could enjoy the newly acquired wealth just as well married to him."

"Not really. Her activities have been curtailed because of his illness. Maybe she got tired of waiting for him to die. Besides, I also learned she's enjoying a liaison with his attendant."

"Kitty! You shouldn't know such things."

"Mother, I know what happens between men and women." I busied myself with my fingers. "Well, at least some of it."

She huffed. "And where did you learn that?"

I bit back a smile. "At finishing school."

She glared at me, looked away, glared at me again. "I'll need to write a strongly-worded letter to that school."

"Please don't. They weren't the ones doing the instructing."

"Then who?"

"The other girls. Some of them were quite knowledgeable." I bit down on my lip.

"Well, I'll be—" For a few seconds, she remained speechless. And then a thought occurred to her. "You didn't . . .?"

I understood what she wanted to know. At least in this I could reassure her. "I remain untouched."

"Well, thank heavens. I wouldn't know how to explain *that* to your father." She cleared her throat. "Getting back to the Earnshaws."

"Yes," I breathed a sigh of relief as we returned to the subject of Colonel Earnshaw.

"It seems awfully far-fetched, Kitty. How could it even be proved? The colonel has died."

"Same as Rose Trevvyan. With a post-mortem."

"But his physician would by now have signed a death certificate as to the cause of death. Who would gainsay him?"

"There's only one way. I'll have to search their house for evidence."

She stood and stamped her foot. "No. I forbid you to do such a thing."

"Would you rather see Ned swing for a crime he did not commit? The paper is sure hinting at it."

"Of course not."

"Then I must do it."

She sat back down. For a long minute, she didn't say a thing. I knew the best course was to let her think it through. "How would you go about it?" she finally asked.

"Someone I know is familiar with one of the Earnshaws' domestics. He'll find out about Mrs. Earnshaw's schedule. When she's out of the house, I'll sneak in."

"That's too dangerous."

"What's the alternative, Mother?"

"What if you get caught?"

"I won't. I'll make sure."

"What do you hope to find?"

"Evidence of poison and the blackmailing letters."

"And then what?"

"I'll take the evidence to Inspector Crawford."

"He won't like it."

She was right about that. "I dare say he won't. But once I present him with proof, he'll have no choice but to investigate." I just prayed I was not too late.

"You must take someone with you. Betsy. She can raise the alarm if you don't emerge in a timely manner. And Neville. So you can make a quick getaway."

Mother's love for American crime novels was showing. Again. "Very well."

"And you must let me know when you plan to do this."

"Yes, Mother." Who knew she'd get on board so fast?

Not wasting time, I sent a note to Dickie explaining I needed him to find out when Mrs. Earnshaw would be stepping out of the house. It didn't take long. Two days later, he came through.

Betsy rushed to tell me. "Begging your pardon, Miss. But Dickie Collins is at the back door."

"Show him here."

Her eyes grew big. Someone like Dickie would never be invited into drawing room, a place we used to greet our upper-class guests.

"It's all right. Mother approves."

"Very well, Miss."

A few minutes later, she reappeared with Dickie trailing her.

"Coo," he said, staring all around the space.

"I know. It's a bit much, isn't it?"

"Naw." He shrugged. "It's plush."

"It is that. Do you have news?"

"Mrs. Earnshaw is meeting with her law man tomorrow at two. Right after the funeral. Her lady's maid and the colonel's man are going with her. My mate, Ellie, and the cook are the only staff left. Mrs. Earnshaw let go of everyone else."

That was strange. "Why would Mrs. Earnshaw dismiss everyone. Do you know?"

"Ellie says she's taking a bunk."

"She's leaving? But where would she go?"

"Ellie overheard Mrs. Earnshaw and the colonel's man. They're taking a boat to South America."

"But they'll need money." You can't finance a long trip without funds.

"Mrs. Earnshaw is bringing some kind of animal bonds."

Animal bonds. Animal bonds. "Bearer bonds, you mean?"

He snapped his fingers. "Dat's it!" His face scrunched. "Wot are those?"

"They're as good as cash." I'd heard Father talking about them. "That's probably why she's meeting with the solicitor. He must have arranged to get them from the bank." But why was she in such a hurry to leave England? It would only call attention to her guilt. Maybe, just maybe, the jig was up. Inspector Crawford suspected her of murder, and she wanted to get ahead of the law. Which made it even more important for me find evidence.

"Thank you, Dickie. You've done well." I handed him an envelope with another forty pounds. "Please thank your friend, Ellie, as well. If she could leave the back door open for me, I would appreciate it."

"I'll tell her. And you don't have to worry about the cook, none. She likes her tipple." He winked.

"I understand." So, the cook liked to drink. More than likely, she'd be passed out or so bosky she wouldn't know which end was up.

He touched his cap. "Thank you, Miss. If you need other errands run, I'm your man."

"Good to know." I rang for Carlton. "Please show Mr. Collins out. The front door, if you please."

"Naw, Miss," Dickie said. "The back one is good enough for the likes of me. I thank you, just the same."

"As you wish." I nodded.

Without batting an eye, Carlton said, "This way, sir."

CHAPTER TWENTY-FOUR

BREAKING AND ENTERING

*T*HE NEXT DAY PROVED THE MAXIM the best laid plans of man—or in my case, woman—often go awry. With Mother's blessing, I'd planned for Neville to drive me to the Earnshaws'. But then she'd received a missive from Lady Ainsley. An emergency meeting of the Ladies Benevolent Society had been called for that afternoon, and her presence was required. All was not lost, however, since the timing did not directly conflict with my mission. So we decided Neville would drive her to Lady Ainsley's and return to take me to the Earnshaws'. It really should not have been a problem. But fate had other plans.

When the time came for me to leave, Neville was nowhere to be found. I waited far longer than I should have; but, since a delay would be fatal, I decided to hail a taxi. The original scheme had called for Betsy to accompany me, but someone had to remain behind to inform Neville. A change of plans was clearly called for. As soon as he made an appearance, the two of them were to travel to the Earnshaws'. With any luck, I would be in and out within the hour and rendezvous with them.

Rather than have the taxi drive me right up to the house, I alighted two streets away. I then walked down the mews that serviced the grand houses from the rear, rather than the road that fronted the homes. Upon my arrival at the Earnshaws', I discovered Ellie had come through. She'd left the back door open for me.

Tiptoeing into a house that was silent as a tomb, I discovered she was nowhere to be found and neither was the cook. Even so, I climbed the stairs as quietly as I could to the second floor where I knew, from something Mrs. Earnshaw had mentioned, the family's bedrooms were located. If there was any evidence to be discovered, that was as good a place as any to look.

To my disappointment, Mrs. Earnshaw's bedroom had been scrubbed clean, the armoire emptied, and the bed stripped. There wasn't so much as a pair of shoes in the room. Neither was there any luggage. She must have planned to go straight from the solicitor's office to the ship and had her trunks delivered there.

The colonel's room did not give up any secrets, either. His bed was neatly made, and his clothes tucked in the wardrobe. Although the bottles on the dresser raised my hopes, they were not medications, but toiletries and such. Next came the room adjacent to the colonel's, the attendant's as it turned out. It made sense he would have been placed next to the colonel's bedchamber so he could easily take care of him. Of course, another purpose to this location came to mind. As he'd be only two rooms away from Mrs. Earnshaw, they could engage in as much naughtiness as they wished with none the wiser. Except, someone had. Ellie. Not much you can hide from domestic staff.

Hoping to find something, I searched the wardrobe and the chest of drawers with no luck. The desk was locked, so no evidence to be discovered there. I'd just gotten down on the floor to search underneath the bed when someone walked into the room. Someone wearing men's boots. Barely taking a breath, I kept silent as steps crept closer and closer. And then they stopped altogether, and I ceased to breathe.

"Well, lookee here." The colonel's attendant loomed over me, a sneer on his face.

I rushed to my feet. Whatever he planned to do to me, I would take standing up.

"Wot you doing?"

I decided to brazen it out. "Looking for evidence."

"Of wot?"

"Blackmail." Best not mention the poison in case he was in on it.

"U'se come to the right ploice then." He strutted to a sideboard I had yet to search, retrieved some documents, and handed them to me. "The witch tol' me to burn them, but oi kept them. In case she turned nasty." An oily grin rolled over his lips.

Flipping open one of the papers, I skimmed its contents.

"I know what you're doing. You want me to keep your dirty little secret, bring two hundred quid to Clapham Court, or I'll go to the coppers. Send the colonel's man. He'll know me when he sees me."

It matched almost word for word the note in Rose Trevvyan's file.

"Did Mrs. Earnshaw pay?"

"Oi. She sent me with the blunt."

"Who sent the note?"

He let out a nasty laugh. "Loike you don't know."

I remained silent and stared at him.

"The mort on the train. The one who croaked."

"Rose Trevvyan?" He had to confirm the identity of the blackmailer.

"Oi. She was Rose Miles before. Wouldna give me the toime of day when she worked 'ere. 'er nose always up in the air. See where that landed her. Toes up."

His words proved Mary Earnshaw had not only paid the blackmail but had known who the blackmailer was.

"What was the 'dirty little secret'?"

"The witch was doing the colonel in with her potions and such."

"Why?" If he was willing to talk, I had to get as much information as I could. I would need it to present to Inspector Crawford.

"'Is bleedin' fortune. 'E got a bloody good amount when 'is brother dropped off the twig." He gazed off into the distance. "'E wasn't 'alf bad, you know. Shared his tipple 'e did. Generous on Boxing Day, too."

His soft reminisce turned into a frown. "It were the witch 'oo was a skinflint."

"Is that why you performed these extra services for 'er?"

"Know about that, do you? Well, ain't you clever? Yeah, I gave it to 'er." He puffed out his chest. "She loiked it too."

Frankly, I wouldn't go anywhere near the man.

"Oi know where she keeps her potions too." He leaned closer, and I almost recoiled from the stench of him. He smelled of rotten eggs and rotten fish. "Wanna see?"

Forcing down my gag reflex, I said, "Yes, please."

Not trusting him for a second, I remained wary as he led the way to the top floor and a door beneath the eaves. After turning to make sure I was watching him, he grabbed a key from a hook on the wall and turned the lock. A chemical odor drifted to where I stood, not pleasant, but not entirely disagreeable.

"This is where she keeps her witches' brews." He tossed over his shoulder.

Rather than join him, I stayed outside the room. In case I had to run, I'd have a lead on him. Unfortunately, that meant I couldn't see clearly into the space as it lay in shadows. "Why are you telling me all this?"

"Oi'm getting out. Taking plenty of loot wit me. Oi figure if Oi told ye what the 'ag did, you'd tell the coppers. They'll be so rushed off their feet looking for 'er, they won't come ofter me."

Not likely to happen. The Metropolitan Police had all manners of modern communications and could easily telephone or send a telegram to all police stations throughout England and beyond. But who was I to disavow him of that notion? One thing he said caught my attention, though. "What loot?"

"Silver and such. Plenty around the 'ouse."

"Have you been stealing the silver all this time?"

He sniffed. "Me and the butler. He turned a bloind eye. Oi gave 'im a cut."

"Was that happening when Rose Miles worked here?"

"That's when Oi started. Put the blame on 'er, Oi did. The auld 'ag never knew."

"Did Mrs. Earnshaw poison Rose?"

He shook his head. "Don know nuthink 'bout dat. Only the colonel."

"Did you help her?"

"Naw. But Oi didn't stop 'er. More than my loife was worth. She would 'ave turned on me, she would 'ave. That's why Oi'm getting out. Don't want no poison in mah tea one day."

"I understand." He was probably right. If she'd killed her husband, and more than likely Rose as well, there was nothing to stop her from murdering him.

He showed me a bottle. "This roight here is what she used. There's more too. Wanna see?"

Heaven help me, I threw every caution out the window and stepped into the room. In a wink, he pushed me out of the way and locked me in. How very, very stupid of me.

I pounded on the door. "Let me out."

"Naw. You'll go stroight to the coppers. And I need toime to get away. Oi'll call them when Oi'm clear. Mind ye, if'n she gets back before they get 'ere, don't let 'er near you. She can kill you without 'alfway trying."

As the clatter of his steps faded away, my mind whirled. *Heavens!* What was I going to do?

Since something had detained Neville, I couldn't depend on his and Betsy's help. Mrs. Earnshaw might return or maybe she'd head right to the ship. If the former, she might stop by her potions room to pick something up. Would she arrive before the police did? Could I even count on the word of the attendant to call them? Of course not. The man would just take whatever valuables he found and get out of town as quickly as he could. I was definitely in a pickle.

I turned around to find something to pry open the lock. That's when I realized the room had been emptied out as much as the bedrooms had. There were no bottles, no stoppers, no liquids or powders. Hoping to find something in the drawers nestled below the working table, I jerked them open. They were all empty. The only item that had been left was a lone broom in the corner. Clearly, the place had been wiped clean. Of course, it had. Mrs. Earnshaw would have removed any evidence of her crimes. And I'd been played for a fool.

Despondent, I leaned back against the door and slid to the floor. My only hope was that, at some point, Neville and Betsy would come to the rescue. I tortured myself with the thoughts of what my disappearance would do to Mother. She would worry when she arrived home, and I was nowhere to be found. I had to get out, not only for my sake but hers. Throwing caution to the wind, I pounded on the door, shouting until my throat was raw. Finally, after what seemed like forever, a key turned on the lock.

Grabbing the broom I'd spotted earlier, I hid behind the door. Whoever stepped in, I would knock out and make my getaway. When the door burst open, I closed my eyes and struck hard.

A whole string of curses rang out in a voice I recognized. "What the blazes are you doing?" Inspector Crawford glared at me, rubbing the back of his head.

"Hitting you?" I couldn't hold back my grin. I'd never been so glad to see anyone in my life.

"Why?"

"I thought you were Mrs. Earnshaw."

He started to toss his head, but then thought better of it. He'd probably develop a lump where I'd beaned him. "She won't be back. We arrested her."

"For murdering Rose?"

"For murdering her husband. What are you doing here?"

"Looking for evidence." I hung my head in disappointment. "Unfortunately, the room has been wiped clean."

"I know. We confiscated everything in it."

I jerked up my gaze. "When did you do that?"

"This morning."

"How? Why?" I didn't even know what questions to ask.

"The day Colonel Earnshaw died his physician reported his death to Scotland Yard as suspicious. Of course, we couldn't just take his word for it. We had to investigate. We didn't want to alarm Mary Earnshaw. After all, her husband could have died of natural causes. But we also could not allow the burial to proceed as usual. So we allowed the undertakers to claim the remains, but we cautioned them not to prepare the body for interment."

"You can do that?"

He fixed his gaze on me. "Of course, we can. We're the law."

"What happened then?"

"We requested an inquest."

"Like Rose's?"

"Yes and no. It had to be done double quick since we didn't want to give the game away. After the coroner heard the physician's testimony, he ordered a post-mortem. The results came in this morning. Turned out, the colonel's doctor was correct. Colonel Earnshaw had been poisoned."

"I knew it!" All my suspicions had been confirmed.

"We moved in and arrested Mary Earnshaw. A servant told us about this room, so we collected everything in here. And transported all the evidence and everyone to Scotland Yard."

"Who's everyone?"

"Mary Earnshaw, a maid, and the cook. The colonel's attendant was nowhere to be found."

"He came back."

"We know."

"How?"

"We kept a lookout across the street. Spotted him loading a dray cart."

"Is that how you found out I was here?"

"Eventually. The police officers who nabbed him brought him in for questioning, but I was busy with Mary Earnshaw and the other servants. It took me about two hours to get to him. It was the first thing he blurted out."

"Did he?"

"Yes. He hoped by telling me your whereabouts I would go easy on him."

"Will you?"

"No. He locked you in, remember. That's a charge of false imprisonment."

"Oh."

He appeared dumbfounded by my show of sympathy. "Don't tell me you feel sorry for him. He's a thief, a kidnapper. Maybe even a murderer."

I shook my head. "I don't think he killed the colonel."

"Well, if he didn't, he certainly aided and abetted." Widening the door, he pointed toward the opening. "Now, let's go. I have a lot to do."

"That's all right, Inspector. I can find my own way home." If Neville and Betsy weren't waiting outside, I would hail a cab.

He glared at me from his very imposing height. "You're not going home, Miss Worthington."

"I'm not? Where am I going?"

"To jail. I'm arresting you for breaking and entering."

CHAPTER TWENTY-FIVE

CRIME AND PUNISHMENT

*T*HE CHEEK OF THE MAN! No matter how vehemently I protested his abuse of justice, Inspector Crawford carted me off to the clink. At least he hadn't put handcuffs on me. If he had, I would have screeched like a wild woman.

As soon as we arrived at the Scotland Yard Police Station, he escorted me to what I could only assume was the charge room. There, he ordered a fresh-faced officer to take my fingerprints.

"Really, Inspector!" I huffed out. "There's no need to treat me like a common criminal."

"You are a criminal, Miss Worthington, common or otherwise."

The lone policeman in the room glanced from Inspector Crawford to me and back again. "You sure, Guv? She's quality."

Inspector Crawford turned a thundercloud glare toward the officer. "Do your job, Constable Peters."

"Yes, Sir." With an apologetic look at me, the officer said, "Sorry, Miss."

"Don't apologize. You're only doing your job."

"Yes, Miss." The constable wrote my name on a sheet of paper, opened a pot of ink, and extended his palm. "If you would."

Glaring at the inspector, I stuck out my right hand. The constable was as gentle as he could while he smeared the disgusting liquid over my hands and pressed my fingers into the paper. When done, he passed me a cloth so I could clean up.

"We'll need her photographed as well," Inspector Crawford commanded.

I ached to stick out my tongue at him, but I didn't. I was a lady, after all.

The constable led me to a wall marked with height measurements. He set up the camera and snapped two photographs, one of me facing forward, the other of my profile. Finished, he asked, "What now, Sir?"

"Put her in a cell."

"Not the detention room?"

"The detention room is for those detained for misdemeanors, as you very well know, Constable. Criminals who've committed more serious offenses are held in jail cells."

Unable to contain my anger any longer, I spit out, "I hate you." So much for my good intentions.

He quirked a brow. "I warned you about interfering, Miss Worthington. You break the law; you pay the price." His gaze darted to the Constable. "Go on."

The police officer escorted me to the bowels of the police station and a corridor lined with doors on one side. He pulled one open to reveal a cell within. As soon as I stepped in, he locked the door behind me. My new accommodations held a cot, a lav, and a very small, barred window. Now I knew how those suffragettes who'd fought for the women's vote had felt.

Sitting on the cot, which appeared neat and clean, I didn't despair. Someone was bound to come looking for me. I only prayed it wouldn't be Mother. While I waited, I planned my revenge against the high and mighty Inspector Crawford. I'd just gotten to the tar and feathering portion when the door opened again.

The same officer who'd locked me in stood on the other side. "Bail has been set for you, Miss."

"Thank you, Constable. You are to be commended for your service." Head held high, I sailed out of the cell.

"Yes, Miss."

After he escorted me the way I'd come, I found Ned waiting for me.

"Kitty." His face was a deathly shade of pale, his lips a slash of white. I'd never seen him this upset.

It took a while to be processed out, as they called it. I was given an official-looking note about the charges being leveled against me, with breaking and entering and burglary being the most onerous sounding ones. By the time we emerged, it was full-on dark. Thankfully, there were no reporters to witness my walk of shame.

I'd half expected the Bentley with Neville at the wheel, but Ned hailed a cab. Made sense. He wouldn't want anyone to recognize his motorcar, or ours, parked in front of a police station.

Once we were safely away, I turned to him and whispered, "Thank you for coming." Last thing I wanted was for the taxi driver to over-hear our conversation.

"What were you thinking, Kitty?" He responded in like manner. "Breaking and entering. Burglary. Those are extremely serious charges. You could go to jail. Permanently."

"I got proof Rose was blackmailing Mary Earnshaw."

"What?"

I delved into a deep pocket I'd asked Angelique to sew into the side of my new utilitarian gown and retrieved the blackmailing notes. "See for yourself."

There was enough ambient light in the cab for him to read.

After a few minutes, he glanced up. "Two letters, each demanding two hundred pounds."

"She must have known Mary Earnshaw could afford it."

He allowed the letters to drop to his lap. "But how did Rose find out Mary Earnshaw was poisoning her husband?"

"She probably stayed in touch with someone from the staff, just as she did with Ivy. That person may have noticed something odd and told Rose."

"That's a lot of ifs and maybes, Kitty. What would a few letters prove anyway?"

"Maybe Mary Earnshaw got tired of paying off Rose and killed her."

"How? She never went near Rose."

"I think the poison was in the sugar bowl Mary Earnshaw handed to Jack Trevvyan. He was in such a hurry to bring the tea to Rose, he forgot it."

"You think Mrs. Earnshaw poisoned the sugar cubes?"

"Yes."

"But that's insane. She would have had to carry the poison with her."

"Not so crazy, Ned. She could have placed it in a tin. And then when the opportunity presented itself, she took it."

"But—"

"She paid, Ned. She paid the blackmail. She wouldn't have done it unless she was guilty."

"How do you know this?"

"The Colonel's attendant. He caught me searching his room. He gave me those." I pointed to the letters. "He told me she paid."

"Kitty." He chided.

"And then he locked me in her dispensary room, Ned.

"Dispensary room?"

"That's where she brewed her potions. Scotland Yard has all that evidence now. They confiscated it this morning after the medical examiner reported Colonel Earnshaw had been poisoned. Inspector Crawford arrested her today."

"What?"

"It will probably be all over the news tomorrow. She's very familiar with potions and such. Before she married Colonel Earnshaw, she worked as a nurse at a hospital. According to the attendant, she prepared many of the concoctions she gave him."

"He could be lying as well."

"He gave me the letters, Ned. He wouldn't have done such a thing if he was guilty."

"He had them? Why?"

"She asked him to burn them, but he held on to them. In case things went south, he wanted proof that he was not the one who killed the Colonel."

"But why would she trust him with that task? Why wouldn't she do it herself?"

"They were lovers."

"Good lord. And he told you all that?"

"He wanted someone to know. And then he locked me up while he stole the silver and whatever money was still in the house." It was all well and good that Mary Earnshaw had been arrested for her husband's murder, but it had nothing to do with Rose's death. That still needed to be proved.

He got a hold of my hands, "Kitty, you do understand how much danger you put yourself in. You could have been hurt. If Inspector Crawford hadn't found you—"

A thought occurred to me, one I'd been too preoccupied with other things to worry about. "How did you know I'd been arrested?"

"He called me."

"Who?"

"Inspector Crawford. He telephoned the office. Thank goodness he caught me. I was on my way out."

"Wait! Do you mean to tell me that dastard telephoned you after he arrested me?" The nerve of that man.

"I'm grateful he did. Otherwise, you'd have spent all night in that hellish place."

"It wasn't that bad." It was clean and neat. They probably would have fed me.

His eyes practically bugged out. "Kitty, you were in jail. We were lucky there weren't any newspaper reporters around, probably because it's so late. But in the morning, there very well could have been."

I shuddered. It would kill Mother to see my photo splashed across the front page of one of those gossip rags. I could only imagine the headline—*Wealthy debutante a jailbird*. "Yes. You're right." Tucking my hands on my lap, I asked, "Does Mother know where I was?"

"No. I telephoned to tell her I was bringing you home, that's all. She didn't ask where you were."

"She knew where I'd gone, Ned."

"She . . . knew? Don't tell me she approved."

"Not approved exactly. Let's just say she agreed to let me do it."

"Why?"

I remained silent, but he figured it out any way.

"Kitty, this is my problem."

"You're wrong. It's the family's as well. Do you honestly believe Mother isn't suffering because of what's happening to you? Father too, I suspect. He just manages to hide it better. He doesn't know, does he? About what I did?"

Ned shook his head. "He'd already left the office by the time Inspector Crawford telephoned."

Any hope that Father was ignorant of what I'd done ended the second I walked into Worthington House. Even from the front door, I heard his outrage. "How could you let her do such a thing, Mildred?"

All right, he knew where I'd gone, but not where I'd been. With any luck, he wouldn't find out.

"We thought it was a good plan, Edward." Mother's voice.

With Ned staunchly by my side, I entered the drawing room.

In the next instant, Father marched up to me. "And just where have you been, young lady? Your mother's been worried sick about you."

A glance at Mother told me the past few hours had taken a toll on her. Not only was she trembling, but her usually faultlessly pinned hair was coming undone.

"I went to the Earnshaws'."

"You've been there all this time?"

I bit my lip. "Not exactly."

"Kitty."

Any hope of lying to him vanished. I had to speak the truth.

"I was in jail, Father."

"Ohhhhh." Mother collapsed on the couch, holding a handkerchief to her mouth.

Flying to Mother's side, Ned put his arm around her shoulders. "It's all right, dearest. Everything's going to be all right."

Father apparently couldn't even get a moan out as he seemed to have lost his power of speech.

"I'm so sorry," I said.

"Jail?" Father finally croaked out. "How? Why?"

I revealed the whole sorry tale from the moment I entered the Earnshaws' house to the moment I was put into a cell and the door slammed shut. "And then Ned came to fetch me."

Father waggled a finger at me. "You will not go anywhere. You will remain in the house."

Mother had kept silent throughout my entire recitation. But his edict woke something in her. She came to her feet and walked to his side. "Now, Edward, be reasonable, she can't become a hermit. It's her season. She's been invited to balls, soirees, afternoon teas. If she suddenly disappears, people will talk. Right now, the only people who know something's amiss are some of our staff."

"And half of Scotland Yard!" Father yelled, waving his arms.

"Actually, Father, Inspector Crawford did not take me to Scotland Yard proper, but a small police station. Only one constable was there. He took my fingerprints and photographed me."

His eyes bugged out. "You were fingerprinted and photographed?"

I really should have quit while I was ahead.

"That man is never to set foot inside this house. You hear me, Mildred?"

That man being presumably Inspector Crawford.

"Of course, dear. Now, Kitty, I think we've had enough excitement for today. Why don't you retire to your room and have a nice, long soak in your tub? We'll talk more tomorrow."

"Yes, Mother. Goodnight." I kissed her on the cheek. "Thank you."

"You're welcome, sweetheart."

"Ned."

"Goodnight, Kitty."

"Father."

He glared at me.

Feeling all the weight of the world on my shoulders, I dragged my feet up the stairs to my room where I found Betsy and Sir Winston waiting for me.

"Oh, Miss." Betsy threw herself weeping into my arms. "I failed you."

"Nonsense." I put my arms around her, and we clung to each other as we sank to the floor. Sir Winston offered his own doggy comfort by laying his head on my feet.

After the storm of her grief had passed, I asked, "What happened to Neville?" There had to be a reason he hadn't returned to pick me up.

Wiping tears from her face, she said, "A lorry backed into him. He was taken to hospital. That's why he never made it back."

"He's injured?" A lorry against a Bentley was an uneven match, to say the least.

"Cuts and bruises, that's all. He's in his room, resting." She sniffed. "He's so sorry, Miss."

"There's no need for him to apologize. What's important is he's not seriously hurt." I sat on my bed and allowed her to stand on her own. "Now tell me what happened after I left the house."

Before she could speak, there was a knock on the door, and Betsy rushed to open it. Nellie, Cook's assistant, stood in the hallway holding a tray laden with food and drink. "Begging your pardon, Miss, but Cook thought you might like something to eat."

It was after ten. I was more than hungry. I was starving. "Splendid, Nellie."

She placed the tray on the table, bobbed a curtsy, and left.

"Would you like some?" I asked Betsy, pulling a chair up to the table. "There's more than enough here for me." Along with generous portions of ham, there was a slew of asparagus spears, a mountain of potatoes, half a loaf of bread, and three servings of pudding. Cook had exceeded herself.

"Oh, no, Miss. Thank ye kindly, but I already ate."

"Very well," I waved a fork at her. "Go on, please." While Betsy related her tale, I tucked in.

"Well, Miss. About an hour after you left, Mrs. Worthington arrived in a taxi. That was something. Apparently, she's never taken one before."

I gave myself permission to employ a small smile. "No, I don't expect she would have."

"Well, as soon as Mrs. Worthington arrived, she discovered I was still here, and Neville hadn't returned. She became terribly worried seeing how you'd gone off by yourself. Never you mind, Neville's whereabouts were a mystery. She didn't know what to do or who to call. Then everything happened at once. Someone from hospital contacted the house, explained what had happened to Neville. And then Master Ned telephoned as well. He told Mrs. Worthington he was bringing you home. And she was not to worry."

"That wouldn't have stopped her."

Betsy bit back a smile. "No, Miss. If anything, she fretted even more."

"Mr. Worthington arrived home to find the house at sixes and sevens. With no dinner on the table. And you know what a stickler he is for that."

"Yes, I do," I said, chewing down on a bite of ham, and chasing it with a gulp of coffee. Maybe food tasted better after a stint in the clink.

"Soon, the to-do started. I have never heard the master yell like that."

Me neither.

"I decided to play least in sight then, Miss, and come here to wait for you."

"Wise move, Betsy." Sooner or later, she would have been dragged into that contretemps.

"And now here we are."

Yes, here we were.

"If I may be so bold to ask, Miss. Where were you?"

"Well—" For the next hour, I told her about my adventures, including my being hauled off to jail. By the end of it, I honestly thought her opinion of me rose a little.

CHAPTER TWENTY-SIX

CUT TO THE QUICK

THE FOLLOWING WEEK RATTLED EVERYONE'S NERVES. For a couple of days after my arrest, Mother thought it would be best to keep me housebound. But when no scandal surfaced about my stint in the clink, she decided it was safe to rejoin society.

Personally, I thought I'd been saved by the news about Mary Earnshaw's arrest since it gave the tabloids something else to talk about. But that turned out to be a two-day wonder for soon they moved on to the public's outrage over Rose Trevvyan's death. Where swift justice had been brought to bear on the murder of a prominent figure, the killing of a working girl had been left unsolved. The papers claimed Scotland Yard only served the prominent Whigs in power, without a thought for the common man.

As the days went by, the gossip rags sank their sharpest talons into Ned, who was seen by many as Rose's murderer. Mother pretended everything was normal, but our invitations soon started to dry up. At those events we attended, we were cut dead by members of the upper crust who saw an association with us to be avoided at all costs. Lords Newcastle and Marlowe remained our stalwart champions, however.

They visited our box at the theatre and conversed with us throughout the entire performance. So much so, we were often shushed.

But it was no use. My debut season was dead as a dodo. I didn't care for myself. After all I'd never wished for an advantageous marriage, or any marriage at all. But I was disappointed for Mother.

She refused to give up, however. She figured Lord Marlowe would come through with a proposal. He had no close relatives who would frown upon his connection to us, and obviously, he didn't give a hoot about our persona non grata status for he hadn't abandoned us in our hour of need. Maybe I should have disavowed her of that notion, but I could not dash all her hopes. Not now when things appeared so bleak.

The only way out of this disaster was to identify Rose's murderer. But I was no closer to doing that than before. I had lots of theories but no proof. Blackmail certainly provided a motive, but the letters she'd sent to Mrs. Earnshaw would not be enough. She'd also extorted money from Bertie Jackson and Ned. Looking at it from Scotland Yard's point of view, any of the three could have done it.

Jack Trevvyan could have also murdered her. He'd disapproved of her blackmailing schemes and wanted out of the marriage. He swore he wouldn't have killed the woman who carried his child, but what if he'd known she wasn't pregnant? No, he had to remain a suspect as well.

And then there was Ivy. She had to harbor some resentment toward Rose after she'd stolen Jack from her. But would she have hated Rose enough to kill her? And how would she have even gone about it when she hadn't provided Rose with food or drink?

Searching for enlightenment, I reviewed the sketches I'd done on that fateful trip with as much of an open mind as I could muster. I recalled everyone's positions when Rose had become ill. Bertie Jackson had approached her with his flask and offered her whiskey. He knew Rose suffered from headaches, and a bit of whiskey had apparently helped. So it was natural he would offer the liquor to her. Ned had chosen a different way to assist her. Familiar with her megrims, he knew about the medicine and suggested she take it. Her husband had offered chamomile tea as a solution for her upset stomach. It had been Ivy that finally got across to her, urging Rose to take her medicine. Rose had done so, but finding the draught bitter, she'd drank the tea, but only after the sugar provided by Mary Earnshaw had been added to the brew.

And then she'd begun to convulse. She'd put a hand to her mouth and claimed she was going to be sick. When Rose jumped to her feet, clutching her stomach, Bertie Jackson, Ned, and Ivy had stepped away. Jack Trevvyan had put his arm around her and rushed her to the bathroom. And that's the last time we'd seen Rose alive.

We'd heard her awful retching sounds and the soothing noises from her husband. And then a deathly stillness settled in, which was worse than anything that happened before. Jack had stepped out of the bathroom, a look of horror in his face, and provided the death knell. "She's dead. Oh, God. She's dead."

No matter how much I wracked my brains, I could find nothing to identify the murderer. Mainly because I didn't know how the poison had been administered. It could have been in the tea, the medicine bottle, the flask, or the sugar cubes. But Scotland Yard knew, as they would have analyzed everything in that train car. All of which meant I needed to talk to Inspector Crawford. Again.

The next day, I approached Mother in the morning room where she was planning my birthday celebration as if nothing untoward had occurred. Until and unless Rose's murder was solved, few people would attend which only added more urgency to my course of action. "Mother, I want to visit Scotland Yard."

She glanced up from addressing an invitation. "What?"

"I need to talk to Inspector Crawford."

"Dearest, your father—"

"What he doesn't know won't hurt him." I was not to be denied. Ned's wellbeing, and indeed our entire family's reputation, depended on it.

She laid down her pen and peered at me. "What do you hope to gain, Kitty?"

"The truth."

She sighed softly. "You will be careful, dear. I really would prefer not to see you land in jail again."

I fought back a smile. "Of course, Mother."

Without a second to waste, I wrote a note to Inspector Crawford and dispatched it through our footman, asking him to wait for a response. Once more, I expected him to deny me, but as before he agreed to a time and date the following day at two. The time seemed auspicious. Was I doomed to fail?

That night I went over everything once more. While I was going through my sketchbook, I recalled doodling some impressions in the bar car while I'd waited for my interview. They'd been rudimentary, to say the least, as I'd done them in a lackadaisical manner without much care to them. But at this point, I was desperate. Not expecting to gain much knowledge, I spread everything on my bed and studied everything carefully. Almost immediately, something stood out. There was one thing in the earlier sketches that was missing from the doodles.

In my mind, I retraced the steps of that person, and little by little a narrative emerged. I knew who had poisoned Rose and how it had been carried out.

The following day, I set out for Scotland Yard with Betsy at my side and Neville at the wheel of the brand spanking new Rolls Royce Phantom Father had bought. To avoid recognition, I wore the same dark clothing and mourning veil as before. Rather than have Betsy accompany me inside the building, I asked her to remain with Neville. I'd be safe enough within those hallowed halls, and she could enjoy time with her sweetheart away from prying eyes. They deserved it after everything they'd been through.

Once more I rode the lift where Inspector Crawford's office was located. Upon my arrival, polite as ever, he came to his feet.

Even though, I was practically jumping out of my skin with excitement, I forced myself to do the polite thing. "Inspector Crawford, thank you for taking time out of your busy schedule to see me."

He nodded. "Would you like some tea?" He pointed to a tray which held a teapot, cups, a pitcher of milk, and a sugar bowl.

Needless to say, I was surprised by the warm welcome. At our previous meeting, we hadn't parted on the best of terms. But who was I to turn down his olive branch? "Please."

After asking for my preference as to how I'd like my tea served, he took his time filling my cup, pouring the milk, dropping a single sugar cube into the brew. Only after he offered me the cup did he ask, "Now, what can I do for you, Miss Worthington?"

Knowing it was more than likely he would deny my request, I took a deep breath. "I need to know where the poison that killed Rose Trevvyan was found."

"We only found remnants of the cyanide in the spoon."

His answer surprised me, not only because of where the substance was found but that he'd answered my inquiry at all. But since he was in a sharing mood, I pressed on. "What about the tea, the medicine bottle, the flask of whiskey. The sugar cubes."

He shook his head. "No."

"Just as I thought." I bit down on my lip as I pondered how to phrase my next request. "If you could indulge me in one more thing, Inspector."

His gaze narrowed as he considered my request. But then he seemed to reach a decision. "If it's within my power, I will."

"Scotland Yard made a list of everyone's belongings. Is that correct?"

"It is."

"And everything in their possession?"

He nodded.

"I need to see the itemized list of the contents in one person's bag."

He tilted his head to the side and peered at me. "And what do you hope to gain, Miss Worthington?"

Almost word for word the same question Mother had asked. But one which deserved a different answer. "Enlightenment."

He leaned back in his chair and templed his long fingers above his very narrow waist. "You know I can't do that."

Disappointment filled me. To come this close only to be denied was not to be borne.

When he came to his feet, I thought it would lead to my dismissal. Instead, he walked to the cabinet that had seen better days and opened one of the drawers. Rifling through it, he fetched a thick folder, and then, leaning over my shoulder, he dropped it on his desk.

Perplexed, I gazed up at him. He was close enough for me to breathe in the light citrus scent of his aftershave. He'd shaved close this time.

"Ten minutes, Miss Worthington. Not a second more," he said, recalling me to my surroundings. And my purpose.

"Thank you."

I waited only long enough for him to step out of the office and close the door behind him before flipping open the folder. A few maddening minutes passed before I located the one thing I sought. I read it over once, twice, three times. And then I smiled. I had found what I needed.

The doorknob rattled, alerting me to his return. By the time he walked back in the room, the file folder was exactly where he'd left it.

After taking his seat behind his desk, he gazed at me. "Well, Miss Worthington."

"I know who killed Rose Trevvyan."

"So do I."

"But you can't prove it."

A rueful expression rolled across his face. "No."

"Is the culprit going to get away with it?"

His lips tightened. "Not if I have anything to say about it."

"But the evidence vanished into the night. How will you get the proof you need?"

"Through a confession."

"Ahhh." It would be difficult, for the murderer was too clever by half. But it was something that must be obtained. Unless Rose's murderer was caught, a cloud of suspicion would forever hang over Ned. And that was unacceptable.

Putting that thorny issue momentarily to the side, I asked, "What will happen to Mary Earnshaw?"

"She's been charged with the murder of her husband. If she's found guilty, which I fully expect, she'll hang."

"What about the colonel's attendant?"

"He'll stand trial for aiding and abetting in the murder. He should get a long sentence. Juries don't look favorably on the murder of a military man."

"He didn't kill the colonel. Mary Earnshaw did."

"He knew what she was doing and didn't stop her."

I glanced down at the dark gloves I'd worn, worried my fingers a little. "Mrs. Earnshaw treated Rose Trevvyan very shabbily, you know."

"How so?"

"She fired her for allegedly stealing the silver, but the attendant told me it'd been him."

"That tracks. We caught him hauling much of it out of the house. He'll be charged with that as well."

I turned my gaze upward, toward him. "You know, even after all she did, I feel sorry for Rose Trevvyan."

His brow wrinkled. "Why?"

"She had such a rough start in life. Losing her mother at such a young age. Placed in an orphanage. Yes, she was well fed and educated, but nothing takes the place of a mother." As I have good cause to know. "When she tried to make the best of it, she was fired for a trumped-up crime and abandoned to the mean streets of the city. If such a thing hadn't happened, she might not have turned out the way she did."

"You're a rare young woman, Miss Worthington. Most people don't possess that kind of awareness." For the first time in my presence, he smiled, and something within me trembled.

Which meant it was time for me to go. I came to my feet. "Thank you for seeing me."

"I'll walk you out."

He opened the door. On a whim, I shut it again.

"Inspector Crawford." Why was my voice shaking?

"Miss Worthington." He bowed his head.

I gazed directly at him. "My birthday is coming up, and my family is holding a ball to celebrate it. I would like you to come."

He was taken aback. Probably the last thing he expected was an invitation from me. "I can't imagine being welcomed at your home. Not after—"

"You threw me in the clink."

"Yes."

"How's that going, by the way? Am I going to be put on trial?"

"About that." He touched the back of his head where I'd struck him. "The paperwork seems to have disappeared."

I grinned. "Has it, really?"

"Yes. I had strong words with Constable Peters." His smile took the sting out of his statement. "Such a dereliction of duty cannot stand."

"Oh, you shouldn't be too hard on the lad. He seems bright enough." I nodded toward the way out. "I should go."

"It's been a pleasure, Miss Worthington," he said, holding open the door.

"You'll need a formal suit for the ball. You do have one?"

He choked out a laugh. "I haven't said I would come."

"Oh, you will." And with that parting shot, I sailed out of his office, lighter than I'd felt in a long time.

CHAPTER TWENTY-SEVEN

RESOLUTION

"*H*OW DID IT GO, DEAR?" Mother asked when I walked into the drawing room. Although she was casually perusing a fashion magazine, she didn't fool me for a second. She was aching to know how my discussion had gone.

"As well as could be desired. I expect significant progress will be made in the next few days."

"That's wonderful!" Mother clapped. It was so good to see her face filled with joy.

"By the way, I invited Inspector Crawford to my birthday ball."

Her smile vanished. "You did what? But your father."

Sitting next to her on the couch, I said, "I want him there, Mother."

For a few seconds, she scrutinized me with that piercing gaze of hers. "But what about Lord Marlowe?"

She must have read much more into my statement than I meant to convey. "A dear friend, no more."

"But, darling, an inspector from Scotland Yard? You could do so much better."

"We're not. He's not," I rushed to say. There was no understanding between Robert Crawford and me. None. We were just . . . terribly attracted to one another.

"As if that would stop you. You've always gotten your way. If you're set on the inspector, you'll get him."

I pressed her hands. "Have I been so impossible?"

"You've given me a merry chase, and that's the truth of it." She cupped my cheek. "But you are so very dear to me." She sighed. "I suppose I'll have to give up my dream of one of my children marrying into the nobility."

"There's always Margaret." I grinned.

"Oh, please." She dismissed my comment with a wave. "All that young lady thinks about are her books."

"You never know. She might surprise you."

"I certainly won't hold my breath." She came to her feet. "Well, I better see about dinner. Your father will be home soon. By the way, I'm off tomorrow to Lady Ainsley's. She wants to discuss the future of the Ladies Benevolent Society."

"What is that supposed to mean?"

She worried her fingers. "I think she wants me to resign."

One more casualty to our loss of status. "After all the work you've put into it? If it weren't for you, the donations would have dried up long ago."

"They've dried up now, Kitty. Between Mary Earnshaw being charged with murder, and the gossip in the newspapers, the society's reputation has suffered. Lady Ainsley feels it needs new blood. I can't blame her. Not really."

"Well, I can. I'm coming with you."

Her brow scrunched. "Why ever so?"

"To fight for you. Honestly, I didn't think Lady Ainsley would give in to public opinion."

"That's very sweet of you, but—"

"I'm coming, Mother, and that's final."

"Yes, dear."

The next morning while we headed toward Lady Ainsley's, Mother appeared quite resigned. I, on the other hand, was fighting mad. It was so unbearably unfair to her. She didn't need this piled on her plate with everything else she had to worry about. Somehow, I would convince Lady Ainsley to keep Mother on.

As I settled into the back seat, I noticed a small package in Mother's lap. "What is that?"

"A remedy for Lady Ainsley. She's been feeling rather poorly." That was Mother all over. Even when she was going to be sacked, she was offering a remedy for Lady Ainsley's wellbeing. I would have brought a purgative myself.

"What's wrong with her?"

"She's suffering from stomach pains. I think it's from all the stress. Some peppermint should help with her stomach troubles. Funny thing, though, her hair is falling out, too."

Well, that was odd. "What has her doctor prescribed?" Maybe her medication was causing the hair loss.

"Oh, she's taking something that Miss Burton gave her. She has quite a talent with nostrums and such, learned it at the orphanage. Apparently, she's been doing that for quite a long time. As well she should after what Lady Ainsley is doing for her."

Alarms went off in my head. "What is Lady Ainsley doing?"

She turned to me. "Oh, didn't I tell you? She revised her will. Made Ivy the main beneficiary. For all her years of service, she said. When Lady Ainsley passes, of course, which hopefully won't be for a long time."

Heavens!

Upon our arrival, we were shown into the drawing room. A sumptuous spread of tea and biscuits was proudly displayed on a table in the center of the room. Lady Ainsley was perched in one of the dainty chairs that abutted the table.

To say I was shocked by her appearance was an understatement. The vigorous woman I'd always known was no more. She'd lost a great deal of weight. Her complexion had grown quite pale. Not only that, but, as Mother had mentioned, her hair had thinned out on top.

"Thank you for coming, Mildred," Lady Ainsley spoke in a garrulous whisper. "Oh, and you brought Kitty? How wonderful." She didn't appear pleased. If anything, she seemed downright exhausted.

But before I could inquire about her health, her face twisted in pain, and she held a trembling hand to her stomach. "Ivy, dear, I think I need another dose of my medicine."

"Yes, Lady Ainsley." Ivy, who'd been tucked away at her usual spot in the back of the room, curtsied and left.

As soon as she did, I picked up one of the dainty chairs and placed it against the corner farthest from Lady Ainsley.

Mother reacted immediately. "Kitty, what are you doing?"

I took Mother's hands and walked her to the chair. "I want you to sit right here."

"Why ever so?"

"It would be for the best." I pressed a finger against my lips, signaling silence. The same gesture she used with my siblings and me when we'd been too rambunctious as children.

Her eyes widened, but then seemingly understanding my message, she nodded.

With a sigh of relief, I turned to the other occupant in the room. "Now, Lady Ainsley."

"Yes?" Confusion reigned on her face.

"How are you feeling?"

"Not well."

I believed her. She wasn't faking it this time. "What are your symptoms?"

"Stomach pains."

"Are they constant or do they come and go?"

"They are sharp. They're coming more often now."

"I see. And your hair. Mother says it's coming down."

"Yes. Clumps of it. I'm sorry to say."

"What did your physician say?"

Tears shimmered in her eyes. "He belittled my complaints. I dismissed him."

He probably thought it was more of the same as before. Only this time, her illness was quite real. "But you're taking medicine?"

"Yes. Ivy's recipe." She struggled to smile but failed. "She has an excellent way about her with potions and such."

"Mother says you've signed a new will."

Her mouth curled in disapproval as she darted a glance at Mother. "Mildred shouldn't have told you."

"Please, Lady Ainsley, it's important."

"Yes, I have."

"Who did you name as your beneficiary?"

"That should be of no interest to you, young lady," she said, in anger, as flashes of her old self shone through. "Honestly."

"Is it Ivy?" I prodded.

Her chin came up. "Yes, it is."

That's as much time as I had to question her as Ivy returned, a brown bottle in her hand.

"Here it is, Lady Ainsley. You'll feel better in no time." She started to unstopper the bottle, but before she could do so, I grabbed it from her.

"What are you doing?" Lady Ainsley asked.

"She's poisoning you."

"What?" Lady Ainsley's eyes grew wide with shock.

"Just like she poisoned her sister, Rose." I walked back to Mother and handed her the bottle. "Put it in your bag."

This time she didn't question me. She simply obeyed. "Yes, dear."

A wary look rolled over Ivy's face. And then she grabbed a chair and placed it against the door jam, effectively blocking anyone from entering the room.

"Ivy, what are you doing?" Lady Ainsley asked.

"Locking us in," I said, before turning to Ivy. "You don't honestly think you're going to get away with this."

An arrogant smile rolled across her lips. "Oh, I think I can. There'll be nobody to tell, you see, after you went berserk and killed Lady Ainsley and Mrs. Worthington."

Mother gasped. Lady Ainsley went silent.

One thing was clear, I had to keep Ivy away from them which meant I had to keep her talking. "Why exactly did I go berserk?"

"You snapped after being shunned by the nobs and your brother being suspected of murder."

"No one will believe you."

"No one to speak against me, since you all will be dead." Spittle flew from her mouth.

Heavens! She'd gone insane.

"I need that bottle, Mrs. Worthington." She circled around me trying to get to Mother.

But I wasn't about to let her get anywhere near her. Keeping my distance from Ivy, I blocked her path. "The medicine bottle on the train. That's how you poisoned Rose."

Ivy shook her head. "No idea what you're talking about. There was no poison in it."

"That's because you switched Rose's medicine with Lady Ainsley's."

"But my medicine wasn't poisoned." Lady Ainsley said. "I took it on the French train."

"It wasn't then. But when you boarded the Golden Arrow, Ivy made a trip to the lav. That's when she laced the medicine bottle with cyanide."

"And just where did I carry the poison?" Ivy asked.

"In that dragonfly brooch you'd pinned to your coat. I imagine it was hollowed out. Once you'd done the deed, you tossed the brooch down the lav. It would have been released with the refuse unto the railroad tracks."

Ivy's eyes widened, but then a look of smug superiority crawled across her face. "You can't prove I did no such thing."

Ignoring her statement, I continued showing the proof. "Your opportunity to poison your sister came up when Lady Ainsley asked you to intercede. While everyone was busy tending to Rose, you switched the bottles. You told her to take her medicine. You told her everything would be over soon. And it was, because you poisoned her."

"Your brother gave her the medicine."

"Which you'd laced with cyanide. Once he'd administered it to her, you switched bottles again."

"They would have found it on me then, wouldn't they?"

"They didn't because you got rid of it."

"How? I didn't leave the train."

"You pitched it out the window. Lady Ainsley complained about the stench coming from the lavatory, and she demanded you open the window. You must have thanked your lucky star such an opportunity had been handed to you. You grabbed the bottle laced with poison from your bag, wrestled with the window, and pitched it to the tracks. Brilliant, if I may say so."

She smirked. That's when I knew I had her.

"But, you see, Ivy, you made one fatal mistake."

"What's that?"

"You didn't have another bottle of Lady Ainsley's medicine."

"How do you know that?"

"Scotland Yard inventoried the contents of everyone's belongings. And that medicine bottle, the one you'd handed to Lady Ainsley on the French train, the one which should have been in your purse, was not listed in the inventory because it wasn't there. It was missing because you pitched it out the window."

Ivy bared her teeth. "You can't prove it. You can't prove any of it."

"Maybe so, but Scotland Yard can prove there's poison in the medicine you've been giving Lady Ainsley."

"Ivy! Is that true?" Lady Ainsley's tremulous voice was a far cry from her tone of old.

"Oh, shut up, you old cow."

"Ivy. Why?"

She turned on Lady Ainsley. "All this time waiting and fetching for you. You think I want to do that the rest of my life?"

"Oh, Ivy." Tears shimmered in Lady Ainsley's eyes.

She advanced on the matron, a snarl on her lips. "I hated every day, every minute of it."

I had to get her attention away from her employer. Otherwise, God only knew what she'd do to her.

"You hated Rose, didn't you?' I asked.

She spun toward me. "Of course, I did. She took Jack away from me. The slut."

"And you couldn't have that."

"No. He's mine. Mine." She pounded her chest.

"Somehow you discovered Rose and Jack were going to France for their honeymoon."

"The trollop told me. She bragged about it, she did."

"That's when you talked Lady Ainsley into going as well."

"I did. I knew my chance would come on the train after the channel crossing. Rose always had a dicey stomach."

"And then after you killed Rose, you were home free. Nobody would ever suspect the mild-mannered lady companion who barely spoke above a whisper, would they?"

"That's right."

"You would have gotten away with it, too." I took a deep breath, let it out. "But then things changed. Jack proposed, just as you hoped he would do. But he's a very ambitious man. If a better opportunity came along, he would more than likely jump at it. And there you'd be, jilted twice."

Her nostrils flared. "He wouldn't do such a thing. Jack loves me."

"But he loves ambition more. You know he does, Ivy. And you couldn't take the chance of losing him again. You saw your opportunity with Lady Ainsley. After all, she has no heirs to leave all that lovely money to. It might as well be you, right? Once she dies, you'll get her money. And then Jack will marry you for sure. But first you had to get rid of Rose." I went in for the *coup de grâce*. "I wonder who planned Rose's murder. Jack . . . or you?"

Her eyes blazed with unholy fire. "You leave him alone."

"You both did it, didn't you? He'll hang for sure, Ivy."

"He didn't. He didn't. I did it all. I killed Rose. It was only me."

I stood up straight and faced her down.

That's when she realized what she'd done. "You bitch." She came after me, but I was more than ready for her. I put up my dukes, leaned back on my right leg, pivoted, and in a perfectly executed roundhouse kick swung my leg right into her chest. She dropped to the ground and did not rise again.

I rushed to open the door to find a wide-eyed butler on the other side. "Anything amiss?"

"Plenty." I asked him to fetch Lady Ainsley's maid and call her physician. Then I asked for something to tie up Ivy.

"Tie her up, Miss?"

"Yes."

From behind me came Lady Ainsley's faint whisper, "Do as she says, Simms."

"Yes, ma'am."

Within minutes, Lady Ainsley's maid arrived to help her up.

As they walked past me, I said, "I sincerely hope Mother will remain a member of the society, Lady Ainsley."

"Not a member, Miss Worthington. A co-chair. That's why I asked her here."

"I see." More than likely, Mother would be the sole leader, at least for some time, for Lady Ainsley would need time to recuperate.

Leaning heavily on her maid, Lady Ainsley slowly made her way out.

The butler returned with a bit of rope and a message, "The physician is on his way, Miss. Do you need any help with Miss Burton? I was in his majesty's navy."

Well, then he would certainly know how to tie a knot. "Splendid. If you would, Simms."

It took him no time at all to truss up Ivy.

"Anything else I can do?"

"Call Scotland Yard and ask for Inspector Robert Crawford. Tell him Miss Kitty Worthington requires his presence and then give him this address." He started to step away, but I stopped him. "One more thing." I fetched the medicine bottle from Mother who was still sitting right where I left her. "Give him this. Tell him to examine the contents."

"Wouldn't you rather tell him yourself, Miss?"

"No." I couldn't allow anyone to learn about my part in this. It was bad enough Lady Ainsley's staff knew. I would have to depend on their discretion to keep my participation in Ivy's apprehension secret. "Don't worry, Simms. He'll understand."

"Very well, Miss."

Having accomplished as much as I could, I turned around. "Ready, Mother?"

"Yes, dear." It was only when we were in the Rolls Royce that Mother asked the question that had to be foremost in her mind.

"Wherever did you learn how to do that?" She mimicked the roundhouse kick with her fingers.

"Finishing school, Mother."

"Well, then"—she relaxed into the supple leather seat— "I'd say it was money well spent."

CHAPTER TWENTY-EIGHT

A BIRTHDAY CELEBRATION

"*I*NSPECTOR CRAWFORD." Although I'd invited him to my birthday ball, I honestly believed he would not come. Clearly, I'd been wrong, as I'd been so many times about him.

"We're not at Scotland Yard, Miss Worthington. A plain mister would do."

He was not dressed as a mere mister, or a detective inspector for that matter. His black tailcoat, white vest, white wing tip collar shirt, cuff links, satin stripe front pants, and oxford black shoes were in the highest fashion and made from the finest materials. How he could afford such attire on his detective inspector salary was beyond me. But then he'd been a puzzle since we'd first met. "I am surprised to see you, I must confess."

"Did you not invite me?"

"I did."

He glanced around a ballroom replete with captains of industry and guests born with silver spoons in their mouths. Tilting his head, he whispered, "Should I leave then?"

"Don't be si—"

"Silly?"

I laughed. A lesser man would quake at attending such an event.

After all, he had arrested me. Not only that, but his scrutiny of Ned had drawn the lurid interest of the gossip rags who'd spread the scurrilous gossip far and wide. As a result, not only had Ned suffered, but so had Father's business and my own debut season.

A minor hiccup, as it turned out. Once the true murderer had been revealed, acceptances to my birthday ball flooded in. So many, Mother had to increase the food order twice over. But I would neither forget nor forgive the fickleness of high society. As far as I was concerned, everyone, but the few true friends who'd stuck by us, could go straight to hell. "Silly is one thing you certainly are not, Inspector."

He pointed toward the side of the room where a mountain of presents awaited me. "I did bring a gift."

"*A Lady's Guide to Etiquette and Deportment*, perhaps?"

"Ah, no. Sorry to disappoint."

"No worries. I already have a copy. It sits on my night table where I can refer to it any time."

"Does it have a chapter on how to stay out of jail?" he inquired all politeness. Anyone observing would have thought we were discussing the weather, rather than one of the most painful experiences of my life.

"If it does, I haven't gotten around to it."

"That would explain your lapse of judgment then." That charming smile of his took away the sting.

But, as much as I was enjoying our repartee, I could not remain talking to him much longer. It would cause gossip, and that was the last thing I wished. Mother had worked too hard to make my birthday celebration a triumph for me to ruin it. But neither could I walk away. Tongues were bound to wag if I did. So, there was only one way out of this dilemma. "Do you dance, Inspector?"

His eyes widened in surprise. "Wouldn't you rather honor one of the fine lords dotted around the room?"

Not caring for that suggestion, I shrugged. "I've danced with most of them. It's your turn now."

"I thought it was a gentleman's prerogative to ask a lady to dance?"

"Is it? I haven't gotten to that particular chapter in the *Lady's Guide*."

"Ah. So you haven't studied it through?"

"I'm afraid I haven't studied it at all."

"Ahh. That explains a fair amount."

Why had he come if all he wanted was to bandy words with me? He was neither a member of high society nor a friend of the family. Just the opposite in fact. It had taken a fair amount of convincing to talk Father around. If it'd been up to him, he would have withdrawn the invitation. But after Mother argued Lord Rutledge would deem it an insult if Father treated his mentee as shabbily as all that, he'd finally agreed not to bar Inspector Crawford's entrance.

Deciding to take the higher road—he was an invited guest after all —I turned the subject toward him. "I hear congratulations are in order."

"Did you?"

"Your stock has risen, as it were, in Scotland Yard. Two murderers caught within a few days of each other."

"I can only take credit for the one. We both know who was responsible for the other. Your contribution should have been noted."

"It's nice of you to acknowledge it, Inspector, but Mother has no stomach for the notoriety that would have accompanied such recognition. She thought it would harm my reputation."

"A shame. Truly. You should have been awarded the laurels."

"Maybe another time, I will."

"Another time?" His brow took a hike. "My dear Miss Worthington, you don't mean to make a habit of investigating crimes?"

"Well. No. But if one happened to come along, and it involved someone close to me, I just might."

He mock shuddered. "Heaven help us."

The band struck up once more as they adjusted their instruments. "They're starting to play."

He glanced toward the bandstand. "Yes, they are."

"Well?" I hated standing here, begging him to dance when I'd turned down others. But suddenly a thought occurred to me. Maybe he didn't know how to waltz. "I'm sorry. You don't have to, of course. If you're not comfortable with the notion, we can converse instead." Much as I hated to do so. Too many eyes were on us, speculating what we were talking about.

"I would hate to disappoint a lady. I'll just have to charge into the fray and do my humble best."

"I won't let you stumble, if you're worried. I'm very proficient at the waltz."

"Shall we then?" He led me to the dance floor as the band struck up the first notes of one of my favorite waltzes—"The Blue Danube."

"It's not hard." I thought to reassure him. "Only three steps—one, two, three, one two three."

"Hush, Catherine," he said in a tone I'd never heard before. It strummed through every part of me, setting my senses on fire.

The music started in earnest and soon we were dancing—no, not dancing—flying. All I could do was hang on while he swirled us around the room. More than anything, I wanted to call him a fake. But he wasn't. He was as real and true and honorable as they came. It was me that assumed he couldn't dance. As we swayed around the room, the dance floor became a magical place where only he and I existed. Everyone and everything faded away.

But magic by its very nature is an ephemeral thing which eventually dissipates. As the last notes died out, he twirled me one last time and presented me to the crowd. Only then did I realize we were the sole dancers. Everyone else had taken to the sidelines to watch in wonder at the sight we'd made. While applause rained down on us, I stood trembling, clutching his hand. And then he stepped back and joined in the accolades, leaving me to stand alone. He meant it as a tribute, but all I felt was the absence of his warmth. I smiled and curtsied. What else could I do?

The band struck up another tune, and a crooked smile rolled across his lips. "Would you like some lemonade, Miss Worthington? You appear to be winded."

"Yes, please. It is rather warm." I was not about to admit it was he, not the dancing, who'd stolen my breath away.

At the refreshments table, I didn't wait for him to hand me a cup but helped myself. Only after I'd drained it, did I dare speak. "You're a fake, Inspector."

An arch of his brow told me in no uncertain terms what he thought of my statement. "I never said I couldn't dance, Miss Worthington. Lesson 1 in detection, don't ever underestimate your opponent."

"Are you my opponent?"

"In a manner of speaking."

Before I could ask him to explain that cryptic remark, a commotion at the entrance to the ballroom drew my eye. A woman and a man, not dressed in formal wear. The man I didn't know, but the woman?

"Margaret!" I flew toward my sister and embraced her.

"Kitty." She returned my effusive greeting before stepping back to look upon me. "You are too lovely for words."

In appearance she was the same as several months ago and yet there was something different about her. Or maybe it was I who'd changed. "Oh, I'm so glad you're home."

"I couldn't miss your birthday. It's not every day my sister turns one and twenty."

"No." I squeezed her hand.

She turned to the man standing alongside her. "May I introduce Sebastian Dalrymple. He's a Junior Research Fellow at Oxford. A brilliant botanist. I convinced him to join your celebration. Hope you don't mind that I brought him along."

"Of course not." I curtsied. "Very pleased to meet you, Mr. Dalrymple."

He bowed. "Sebastian, please." He was gorgeously tanned and of an athletic build with a full head of blond curls. Goodness, he was a sight to behold.

I wracked my brain for his name sounded familiar. But before I could divine his identity, the rest of our family converged on the three of us.

After embraces and introductions all around, it suddenly became clear. Mother hadn't made me memorize *Debrett's* for nothing. But I didn't dare mention what he was, or rather who he was. It would raise expectations in Mother and afford Margaret and her friend little peace.

"Would you like some refreshments or something to eat?" I offered. "We have enough food for an entire battalion, I believe."

"We are rather famished," Sebastian said.

Margaret laughed. "Sebastian has never been one to turn down sustenance."

Interesting. She knew him well enough to know his habits.

The supper dance had already been held, but Mother would never allow a guest to go hungry. As we headed toward where the food had been served, it occurred to me that all of us couldn't desert our guests. Someone had to remain behind. Ned and Father volunteered for that task, leaving Mother and I to join Margaret and Sebastian in the dining room where they enjoyed watercress salad, cream of mushroom soup, cold fillet of sole, beef tenderloin, and roasted spring vegetables. While Margaret was modest in her choices, Sebastian consumed a prodigious amount of the offerings in a short amount of time. Although I had to say, he had excellent manners. He never once confused the salad fork with the fish one.

Having had his fill, Sebastian addressed Mother. "Thank you, Mrs. Worthington. That was simply splendid."

Mother smiled. She loved to see her efforts appreciated. "Glad you enjoyed it."

I could tell she was dying to find out more about him. But this was neither the time nor the place. Her curiosity would have to wait to be satisfied.

We wandered back to the ballroom for we had abandoned our guests long enough. I was claimed for two more dances, but my heart was no longer in it. Not that I let on. I carried on as if I was thoroughly enjoying myself.

Margaret, as had been her wont during her season, was playing least in sight. This time, however, she was not hiding among the wallflowers, but next to Sebastian who dutifully remained by her side. Who was he to her? And she to him? I vowed to find out.

With the band taking another break, I headed over to Margaret and Sebastian. The rest of our family seemed of like mind, since Mother, Father, and Ned congregated around them as well.

But before I could start my inquiries, Sebastian said, "There's a marvelous motorcar out front. A Rolls Royce Silver Ghost, if I'm not mistaken."

"Maybe it belongs to one of our guests," I suggested.

"No, Kitty," Ned said. "It doesn't. Come, let me show you," he said, taking my hand.

As our family headed out of the ballroom, half the guests followed us through the house and down the front steps. Just as Sebastian mentioned, a gleaming motorcar sat in the driveway. Confused, I glanced up at Ned.

"It's your birthday present, Kitty. From all of us. Father, Mother, me."

For the first time in my life, I didn't know what to say other than, "It's beautiful."

"Mr. Dalrymple is correct. It's a Rolls Royce Silver Ghost."

I clapped. "So shiny."

"Yes, it is." He cleared his throat. "You will need to learn how to drive it and take appropriate care on the road. Neville will teach you." Ned nodded toward our chauffeur who stood to the side.

He doffed his cap. "Be glad to, Miss. It will be a pleasure to drive this beauty."

"If Neville needs a relief now and then, I can help," Lord Newcastle exclaimed, making his way through the throng.

No doubt he wanted an opportunity to drive the motorcar.

"Me as well," piped up Lord Marlowe as he joined us.

"With so many offers of assistance, I should be driving in no time."

"London citizens are sure to quake," Ned said. But then he smiled. First time I'd seen it in a long while.

Standing on my tip toes, I kissed him on the cheek. "Thank you, dear brother. You are the best."

"You deserve it, Kitty. If it weren't for you—"

I tapped his chest. "Don't. What are sisters for?"

"Sebastian Dalrymple?" Mother exclaimed.

Heavens! The penny had dropped.

"Is your grandfather the Duke of Wynchcombe?"

Sebastian bowed. "Guilty as charged, ma'am."

"Which makes you the heir." To a dukedom, no less. One which, if rumors were right, possessed quite extensive property.

"For my sins, Mrs. Worthington."

Curling my arm around Margaret's waist, I leaned close and whispered, "I can almost hear them."

Her brow knitted. "Hear what?"

"Wedding bells being rung for you."

"What? With Sebastian? But he's not. I'm not." She shot a panicked look toward him who returned her gaze with a humorous expression on his.

Smiling inwardly, for I did not wish to offend, I opened the motorcar's door and slid in. A myriad of choices faced me. Gears, knobs, thingamajigs. "How do you start it?"

Many of the men who stood within hearing distance laughed while others chortled. Some rudely scoffed.

Ned opened the door and handed me out of the car before turning to Neville. "Would you please show my sister how to 'start' the motorcar?"

"With pleasure, Mr. Worthington."

"Now, Miss, first thing you need to do is switch on the petrol line." He bent and turned a knob on the side of the Rolls Royce. "Then you open the door, remove the driver's seat, and turn on the battery."

"Goodness."

"Then you"— He continued showing me step by step.

By the time he got to the last one while sitting in the driver's seat, my head was swimming. But I was not about to let Ned, or any man present, get the better of me. "Seems pretty simple. One just has to learn the procedure. That's all." I slid once more into the car, this time the passenger's seat. "Anyone care for a ride?"

"Not with you at the wheel, Kitty," Ned said.

"I wouldn't dream of it." I gazed at Lord Newcastle, "Milord, would you do the honors?"

"With pleasure." Changing places with Neville, he climbed in, adjusted something on the wheel, fiddled with another gear, and then finally said, "Ready?"

"Not yet. Anyone else care to join us?"

Lord Marlowe leaped over the side of the Rolls Royce, landing on the back seat.

Sebastian, taking a more measured approach, turned to my sister, "What do you say, Megs?"

Megs? I mouthed soundlessly while glancing at Ned. He was valiantly fighting back a smile. And not succeeding. She never allowed us to address her as anything but Margaret. Clearly, 'Megs' and Sebastian were more than friends.

"Sebastian, I don't know." Margaret had a look of panic about her.

"Live a little, woman." And with that, he picked her up, deposited her next to Lord Marlowe in the back seat and climbed aboard himself.

"Ready?" Lord Newcastle asked.

"Ready!" We all yelled.

As the motorcar roared down the driveway, Marlowe exclaimed, "Pip pip and all that" to the crowd we left behind. Some day he would need to explain exactly what he meant by that.

EPILOGUE

ALL'S WELL THAT ENDS WELL

*O*UR EXCURSION into London proper had not lasted long. Not only did I have guests to attend to, but we'd failed to secure rugs for our jaunt. The gentlemen had offered their jackets to Margaret and me, which helped to keep us warm. Still, it was too cold to remain exposed to the elements for long.

Upon our return, it took us no time at all to thaw out, as we tripped the light fantastic well into the night. Near dawn, after bidding adieu to the last of our guests, I climbed the stairs to my bedroom, exhausted, but extremely grateful for my birthday celebration.

Betsy had fallen asleep in my sitting room but woke when I stepped into the room.

"Did you enjoy yourself, Miss?" she asked, stifling a yawn.

"Yes, thank you. It was lovely." Mother had outdone herself. I was glad more for her sake than mine the ball had gone as well as it had. She would need the goodwill of British high society to repair the reputation, and the fortunes, of the Ladies Benevolent Society. She couldn't count on Lady Ainsley to help since that unfortunate lady had had to repair to a Swiss Sanatorium to recuperate after her near brush with death. So, it would be up to Mother to lead the Society back to its former glory. I had no doubt she was more than up to the task.

While Betsy helped me out of my gown, she mumbled, "Dickie Collins came by, Miss. He wanted to thank you for your efforts on getting him another position. He's ever so pleased."

"Oh, I'm so glad." After explaining to Father the role Dickie Collins had played in my investigation into Rose Trevvyan's murder, I'd asked for his help in obtaining employment for the young man. Subsequently, Father had talked to the owner of one of the finer restaurants he visited in the City of London who'd agreed to take on Dickie on a trial basis. I had no doubt it would soon prove permanent. Dickie was not only a skilled server but had the pleasant personality to go along with that job.

After slipping into my nightclothes, I turned to climb into bed. That's when I noticed a box tied with a pretty blue ribbon sitting squarely on my bed. "What's this?"

It's the present from Inspector Crawford, Miss. I thought you might like to see what he brought you."

She knew me so well. "How lovely. Thank you, Betsy. Now get yourself to bed. And don't rise until noon."

She giggled softly. "Oh, Miss, as if I would. I'll be up with the birds to take Sir Winston for a walk."

"The birds are already up, Betsy," I said, pointing toward the window from where a flurry of tweets could be heard. "Leave word for someone else to deal with Sir Winston. That's an order, by the way."

"Yes, Miss," she said smiling. After bobbing a curtsy, she departed, hopefully to get a good night's sleep which she clearly deserved.

Once alone, I treaded toward the gift, almost afraid to open it. If it were something pedestrian, like perfume or a book, I'd be bound to be disappointed. But then I chastised myself. Inspector Crawford surely would have more imagination than that.

Sitting on the bed, I placed the box on my lap and untied the ribbon. I then took a deep breath and removed the lid. Inside were . . . loose papers. At first, I didn't realize what they were and then understanding dawned. My arrest documents. The ones that had been supposedly lost. There was the one with my fingerprints, another with the details of my arrest. The third was the photograph of my profile. The snap of my face was missing, though. Where had it gone? I thoroughly combed through the papers, but it was nowhere to be found. Did it get lost, misplaced? Or . . . did he hang on to it?

There was no way of knowing, of course. Still, I wondered. For some time, I sat staring off into the distance. But then exhaustion set in. I needed to take the advice I'd given to Betsy and get some sleep. After carefully putting everything back in the box, I locked it inside my writing desk. Tomorrow would be soon enough to discover where the photograph had gone.

~

Murder at Westminster

AMATEUR SLEUTH KITTY **Worthington once more jumps into the fray to catch the wily murderer of a high-ranking member of the nobility.**

London. 1923. Much to her consternation, Kitty Worthington's debut is a resounding success, prompting marriage proposals from lords, scoundrels, and ne'er do wells. Even as she dodges them, a new intrigue arises, and at Westminster, no less. A high-ranking member of the nobility is murdered, and her sister's beau is framed to take the fall.

With her beloved sister's happiness at stake, Kitty sets out to investigate, ably aided by her faithful maid, two noble lords, a titled lady, and Sir Winston, her still flatulent Basset Hound. As they dash about London from pillar to post, from the stews of St. Giles to the glittering mansions of Mayfair in search of the wily killer, can she convince the maddening Inspector Crawford to join the hunt? For if she fails to discover the murderer, her sister's beau may very well hang from the wrong end of a rope.

Murder at Westminster, the second book in **The Kitty Worthington Mysteries**, is another frolicking, historical cozy mystery filled with dodgy suspects, a wily villain, and an intrepid heroine sure to win your heart.

You may order it from Amazon.

CAST OF CHARACTERS

Kitty Worthington - Our amateur sleuth, about to make her debut into London Society

The Family
    Mildred Worthington - Kitty's mother
    Edward Worthington - Kitty's father
    Ned Worthington - Kitty's oldest brother
    Richard Worthington - Kitty's next older brother, in Egypt
    Margaret Worthington - Kitty's older sister, at Oxford

The Worthington Household
    Betsy - Kitty's Maid
    Carlton - the family butler
    Cummings - Mrs. Worthington's lady's maid
    Mrs. Simpson - the family housekeeper
    Neville - family chauffeur and Betsy's beau
    Sir Winston - a Bassett Hound with an, err, digestive problem

Golden Arrow Passengers and Staff

Rose and Jack Trevvyan - Newlyweds returning from their honeymoon in Nice

Lady Ainsley - Rich and titled Countess

Ivy Burton - Companion to Lady Ainsley

Mrs. Mary Earnshaw - Col. Earnshaw's wife

Col. Earnshaw - Husband to Mrs. Earnshaw

Cedric - Attendant to Col. Earnshaw

Bertie Jackson - Gambling saloon owner

Letty Jackson - Bertie's wife

Dickie Collins - Golden Arrow waiter

Detective Inspector Robert Crawford

Aristocrats

Lady Kingsley – Kitty's Court Presentation Sponsor

Lord Marlowe - An Earl in search of a wife. Maybe.

Lord Newcastle - Another Earl and Ned's friend. Definitely not in search of a wife

Lady Emma Carlyle - Debutante in search of a husband

ISBN-13: 978-1-943321-13-1 (Print)

Hearts Afire Publishing

First Edition: September 2021

ALSO BY MAGDA ALEXANDER

THE STORM DAMAGES SERIES
Contemporary Romance

Storm Damages

Storm Ravaged

Storm Redemption

Storm Conquered

ITALIAN STALLIONS SERIES
Contemporary Romance Novellas

A Christmas Kiss to Remember

My Smokin' Hot Valentine

CHICAGO OUTLAWS SERIES
Sports Romance

Dirty Filthy Boy

Roughing the Player

Made in United States
North Haven, CT
08 July 2022

21103045R00150